To Ai

# HERITAGE HOUSE

*Renny deGroot*

## RENNY DEGROOT

Toadhollow Publishing 7509 Cavan Rd Bewdley, Ontario K0L 1E0

Contact Renny at: http://www.rennydegroot.com

# ALSO BY RENNY DEGROOT

FICTION:
**Cape Breton Mystery Series**
Garden Girl (Book One)
Sea Child (Book Two)

**Historical Fiction:**
Family Business
After Paris
Torn Asunder

NON-FICTION:
32 Signal Regiment: Royal Canadian Signal Corps – A History

*Dedicated to my sister Anne-Marie*
*And my brother Max*
*You were there to hold my hands when I took the first steps*
*of my journey in Nova Scotia, and several decades later,*
*you are still supporting me.*
*Love you both.*

I invite readers to sign up for my monthly newsletter to get my latest news and read interviews with my various characters. Sign up here: http://rennydegroot.com/newsletter-sign-up/

# PROLOGUE

**March 2021**

GRETHA BRAUN BOLTED UPRIGHT in bed to the sound of shrieking coyotes. They wailed and yipped with excitement as the pack followed their prey, ghostly howls echoing through the forest surrounding her small, rented cabin in an isolated spot in Nova Scotia, Canada. The hair on her arms stood up, and she shivered in this lonely place. She had considered renting a cottage on Cape Breton Island itself to be closer to the as-yet, strangers, but decided against it, not knowing how it would all go. She needed to study the people before getting too friendly.

The keening of the coyotes faded, and Gretha lay back down. Her racing heart slowed, and she lay thinking about the house on Isle Madame she had just purchased, making plans for the renovations to make it her own. Naturally, she thought in German since she had only been in Canada for a week, but she reminded herself that she must practice thinking in English to ensure her communication with the locals would be seamless.

Gretha loved the house and the land already, even though she'd only seen it once. She felt a part of it. In her heart, she didn't feel like a foreigner but believed she belonged here. She was delighted with the new home and couldn't wait to start the adventure of her new life.

As she drifted off to sleep and with her defenses down, she wondered if she were stepping into a future life, or simply running away from her past one.

# CHAPTER ONE

GORDIE MACLEAN TURNED TO look, frowning at the rare sound of raised voices in his local building supply store on Isle Madame, a small island linked to Cape Breton Island by a bridge. He left the paper bag containing a pound of number 8, three-inch green deck screws sitting on the cashier's counter and walked over to have a quiet word with the man busily wagging his finger and shouting at the foreign-looking woman. She was elegant for these parts, with her blond hair swept up in a complicated bun and held in place with a fancy brown and yellow tortoiseshell comb. She stood rigidly erect, and looked down wordlessly at the man berating her, from her height of about five feet and eleven inches.

Gordie laid a hand on the arm of the scruffy-looking man. "Jack Fraser, what's going on here?"

The man turned his attention to Gordie, his voice lowered, but his appearance still angry and threatening. His dark hair was unkempt and wild, looking like a dark-haired Boris Johnson, the former British Prime Minister. Several days of beard growth showed streaks of grey, although Gordie knew that this man was only in his mid-forties.

Jack glared from hooded dark eyes. "*She*" Fraser pointed to the woman "bought my house. It's *my* house, and she had no right to buy it and now she's changing everything. She has no right." He repeated.

Gordie, who stood five feet and eight inches tall, was about the same height as Jack Fraser, so had to look up to the woman. "Don't pay any attention. I'll have a word with him."

Her shoulders dropped a fraction and her face seemed to relax. When she spoke, it was with a thick German accent. "We've met before. As I already explained to him, I didn't know the house was in dispute, but since I was able to buy it, it's now mine."

Jack puffed up to shout again, but Gordie spoke first. "Of course, it's yours." He turned back to Jack and gripped him by the upper arm. "Jack, come with me and leave this poor woman alone. You know very well that the house has been empty for over a year, and if you wanted it, you should have done something about paying the taxes and arranging some payment scheme with the bank. You had plenty of chances."

Fraser glowered. "I was working on it."

Gordie shook his head. "You know that's not true." He pulled out his wallet, handed Jack a twenty-dollar bill and gave him a shove towards the door. "Go down to the Bridge Bakery and I'll meet you there in a few minutes. Order a coffee for me."

Jack cursed but left, and the store's quiet rumble of conversation resumed.

MacLean held out his hand to the woman. "I'm Detective Gordie MacLean. I'm sorry you went through that. If you want to put in a report about Jack harassing you, I can have one of my colleagues from The Cape Breton Police Services call you."

"Gretha Braun." Her handshake was firm, the slim hand belying her strength. When she smiled, her face was quite beautiful. Her high cheekbones gave her face a strong, sculpted appearance, and her intense blue eyes seemed to drill into Gordie.

She shook her head. "Mr. Fraser has come to the house a few times, and he always leaves again. This is the first time he has approached me in public. It startled me, that's all. I don't want to make a fuss."

Gordie smiled. "We aren't all so grumpy. I know most of us are glad to see that fine old house taken on by someone who will care about it and bring it back to what it once was. I drove by the other day, and it looks like you've got the outside almost finished."

When she smiled, her eyes sparkled. "If you are going past again, please stop. I will give you the tour."

"I'll take you up on that. In fact, my partner, Vanessa, is coming over this afternoon. If you think you'll be home, I know she's dying to see what you've done with the house."

Gretha nodded. "I'll be home. Perhaps come around four o'clock and we can enjoy a drink out on the deck. The trees are becoming so beautiful with their autumn colours."

Gordie pulled out a card. "Here's my cell number. If something changes and it isn't convenient, just give me a call. Otherwise, we'll see you around four."

MacLean went down the road and had a quick cup of coffee with Jack Fraser before leaving the other man chatting amiably with the waitress and consuming breakfast on Gordie's twenty-dollar bill.

\*\*\*

As he expected, Vanessa Hunt loved the idea of visiting the renovated house. She clapped her hands together and Gordie smiled. The laugh creases around her eyes and at the corners of her smile just enhanced her beauty, in Gordie's opinion. Her shoulder-length blond hair had a few threads of grey streaked through it, but despite that, she didn't look her age of fifty-four. She wore a calf-length loose skirt in a pumpkin colour, with a white t-shirt and red cardigan. She liked to dress in the colours of fall.

Gordie's hair was snow white, and while it was still thick around the sides and back, if Gordie were honest with himself, he knew it was a little thinner on top, but neither he nor Vanessa ever mentioned that.

Vanessa grinned. "I've wanted to go inside for the past three months. I've even considered stopping to peek in the windows before."

He shook his head. "I'm glad you don't have to resort to that. Someone may call the police on you."

She laughed. "You'd bail me out if I was arrested for trespassing, wouldn't you?"

He pulled her towards him in a gentle hug. "Definitely."

Gordie's great Pyrenees dog, Taz, nosed in, pushing her way between Vanessa and Gordie and Vanessa pulled away. "Oh, Taz. Don't drool on me. It's very unsightly for a girl to walk around with a big slimy streak on her skirt."

"Let's go for a short walk together and then Taz can stay home while we go and socialize with Ms. Braun."

They turned right when they left Gordie MacLean's house, walking towards the coast. The wind was coming off the water and the September air was crisp with the scent of decaying leaves and a hint of the sea. Taz trotted along the edge of the road, stopping to sniff here and there. There were few houses along this stretch of road and even less traffic. It was a road that ended in a private property on the waterfront, but that was a good couple of kilometers away. They walked for ten minutes, chatting about this and that. It always amazed Gordie at how much they found to talk about. He had gone for most of his adult life keeping his thoughts to himself, but now, with Vanessa, it seemed that he was making up for lost time.

They turned back, Gordie calling for his dog. "Time to go home, Taz."

Vanessa continued her thought. "Seriously, we need to take

something. We can't visit a complete stranger and not take some sort of house-warming gift."

Gordie shook his head. "I don't think the rules are the same when it's a spontaneous visit."

She laughed out loud. "Is that right? Thank you, Miss Manners, for that insight."

He smiled. "Well, what do you suggest? We're not heading into Port Mulroy to go shopping. There isn't time."

"I'm thinking of that Blue Mountain vase you have. Remember when we were doing up your house last summer? I asked you if you ever used it, and you told me you don't even remember where it came from, let alone use it."

Gordie raised his eyebrows. "You want to give a used vase as a housewarming gift?"

"Why not? The pottery is closed now, so it's a piece of art. Are you willing to sacrifice a couple of your gorgeous sunflowers to go in the vase?"

He shrugged. "Let's face it. They're more your flowers than mine. You planted them. They just happen to be in my backyard."

She nodded. "That's settled, then. If you don't mind giving up the vase, it'll make a lovely gift, paired with the flowers."

They arrived home and Vanessa cleaned up the vase and then cut two huge sunflowers to go into it. Gordie had to admit that it looked pretty.

Vanessa held the vase and flowers clamped between her feet on the floor of the car while he drove. Gordie pulled into the driveway, and they sat for a moment admiring the house. Scaffolding covered the side where it was obvious that someone was in the middle of scraping off old paint, although the worker was nowhere to be seen now. The house had a traditional barrel-shaped roof for the main part of the structure, with two upper windows. Below that was a roofed veranda, front door, and bay window. The house-front faced north towards the water. To the left a wing came out, forming a second perpendicular barrel-shaped roof, facing east, with a large dormer window, also overlooking the water.

The land around the house was wild and overgrown. Bushes that had taken over the front steps and walkway had been rough-cut to make the way passable, but the grass was tall with weeds of every type.

Vanessa sighed. "Isn't it magnificent?"

"It will be one day, but there's a lot to be done before it's that."

"Oh, Gordie. How can you say that? The roof has been done, and I love how she's scraping the shingle siding down instead of just slapping vinyl on it. You can already see what it will look like when it's done. Oh, and look at the sign. She's named the house."

He looked to the simple wooden engraved sign tacked above the front door. It was clearly new and read *Heritage House* in script letters. "Nice."

Gretha must have seen them and came from around the back of the house. She gave a small, restrained wave; more of a gesture to come, than a wave.

Gordie got out and went to the passenger side to take the vase from Vanessa while she climbed out, and once on her feet, she reclaimed the flowers.

Gretha reached them and nodded. "Hello. Welcome."

Vanessa took the lead. "I'm Vanessa. Thank you so much for allowing us to intrude on your afternoon like this. I'm so glad to meet you and, of course, I've been dying to see what you are making of this gorgeous old house."

Gretha smiled. "It's my pleasure." She took the proffered flowers from Vanessa. "Thank you. They are lovely."

The tall German woman strode ahead, leading them around to a back door, expertly cradling the towering flowers in one hand and opening the door with the other. They stepped directly into a kitchen, sparkling with new cabinetry and appliances. Splashes of bright greens and blues in the towels and placemats offset the white cupboards.

Vanessa oohed and aahed over the new kitchen as she gazed around at all the fine details.

Gretha set the vase down on a table and turned to welcome them again. "Please come in. Would you like to see the house first or sit with a glass of wine instead?"

Before Gordie said anything, Vanessa spoke for both of them. "Oh, a tour please! We were admiring your house name sign. How did you come to call it Heritage House?"

She tilted her head as if considering her answer. "It seems like such a symbol of a past way of life. I know it's far too much for me, but I love the idea that it housed a big family, so it feels more than just a house. It is a place with a past, a heritage."

Vanessa smiled. "I love it."

Gretha nodded and led them through the house, pointing out the original elements, and those she had changed, like the kitchen. It was a large family home and even those areas that still needed repair were grand. Hardwood floors, high ceilings with crown moulding and large odd-sized windows gave the house a unique character and beauty.

"The new and repaired carpentry work is well done." Gordie stopped to admire the new trim around the large front window.

"Henry Davis." Gretha's voice lifted as she spoke of her contractor. "He's very talented, isn't he? He understands exactly what I like and want."

"Yes. He does nice work. I've heard of him. I didn't know he did fine carpentry. I'll have to remember that."

Vanessa sighed over many little corners and features, comparing them to her own old home, and Gordie drifted along behind the two women. He wanted to slide away, to sit outside.

As Gretha led the way into a third bedroom on the top floor, pointing out the chevron pattern of the hardwood for Vanessa, Gordie called out: "I'll meet you outside, if you don't mind?"

Vanessa waved him away. "Go on. We'll be along shortly."

Gordie went out to the back deck. Fire engine red cushions, the colour shocking against the grey, weather-beaten boards of the deck topped four black rattan cube chairs.

He couldn't see the water from here, but yellow, blue and white wildflowers dotted the expanse of the green backfield. The wild roses flourished and added splashes of glossy green and pink. Usually, Gordie didn't notice these common sights, but then, he didn't often just sit looking out at someone's yard.

The women joined him, Gretha carrying a bottle of white wine and Vanessa with two wine glasses and a can of Schooner beer.

Gretha set the bottle of wine down on the black glass and rattan coffee table. "Vanessa suggested a beer for you?"

He nodded. "I don't drink much alcohol, but once in a while, a cold beer is nice, thank you."

The German woman poured out a glass of wine for Vanessa and for herself while Gordie popped open the can of beer. She leaned forward to clink her glass against Vanessa's and Gordie's beer can. "Prost!"

Gordie smiled. "Cheers and welcome to the neighbourhood."

Vanessa settled back in her chair. "Now. Tell us about how you came to be here. I'm from away too, so I know it isn't easy to integrate with the locals. You have to really want it."

Gretha took her time. She sipped her wine for a moment and seemed to ponder the question carefully before responding.

# CHAPTER TWO

GORDIE WONDERED IF GRETHA was about to tell them it was none of their business when she finally took a breath and began.

"I travel quite a lot for my work, so I have been to Canada several times. Vancouver, Toronto, Ottawa. It wasn't until I saw Halifax that I thought perhaps I should buy a house. I was pre-disposed to like Canada. I had a Canadian school friend, and she spoke so highly of her home country."

Vanessa smiled. "How interesting. Do you keep in touch?"

Gretha nodded. "Social media makes these things simple. She lives in Alberta."

Gordie raised an eyebrow. "I'm surprised you didn't fall in love with the mountains in Alberta."

"No. I did visit once but no. It didn't speak to me like this place."

He laughed. "I can't argue with that. Are you retired now?" He saw her brow crease and added, "Not that you look old enough to retire, but some people retire very young."

"No. Not retired, but I have great flexibility with my work. I am an art historian."

Vanessa widened her eyes. "That's fascinating. That's probably why this old house appealed to you. It's like a piece of history and art all rolled into one."

Gretha smiled. "Exactly. I hope to be friends with Mr. Fraser one day so that he can tell me stories about the house. I want to preserve as much of the original structure as possible and what I can't preserve, perhaps I can replicate without it looking like a poor copy."

Gordie took another sip of beer and then set the can down. "I'm still curious why here, though. There must be beautiful places in Germany or Italy or wherever."

Gretha shrugged. "Sometimes a place just draws one in. There may be no explanation more than that."

He saw the piercing look Vanessa shot him, and he swallowed his curiosity. "Well, we are very glad to have you. As I said at the hardware store, this house was neglected for so long, it's good to see someone take it in hand."

Vanessa nodded. "It's been empty for quite some time, hasn't it, Gordie?"

"Yes. When Jack's father died, he left the house to Jack's sister and Jack got some money. At the time, he was living out in Alberta, working on the oil sands. He had no interest at all in the place, and he and his sister Margo weren't close. I remember years went by without him even coming home to visit. Then Margo died quite young with no heirs, so the house went to Jack. He came home long enough to bury his sister and sell off what he could of the furniture and gave the rest away. The house was up for sale for a long time, but there were no takers and then I guess eventually the government took it over for unpaid taxes."

"It's so sad to see those lovely old homes fall into ruin," Vanessa interjected.

Gretha pursed her lips as though holding back the questions before saying, "But he came back."

Gordie nodded. "We all know what happened when the

pandemic hit. The job out west suddenly wasn't there anymore. It wasn't until Jack came home with only a pickup truck towing his trailer that the rumours started. He got used to living the high life out west and squandered his money with nothing to show for it. His inheritance, his wages. All of it is gone, other than the truck and trailer. He put the trailer on his property for a while, but as you know, Gretha, the house wasn't livable anymore. Leaking roof, no electricity, dry rot and whatever else. He didn't even try to make a go of it. He just lived in his trailer until the government notified him that the property was going up for auction unless he paid up the taxes. That's when he moved the trailer to Floyd Sanders' place."

Vanessa asked the questions that it seemed Gretha didn't like to ask. "Who is that?"

"He has the dairy farm out on St. Mary's Road. He lets Jack put his trailer there in exchange for handyman work."

Gretha shook her head. "I understand why he is angry. To go from such a nice house to a small trailer in a farmyard. It must be terrible."

Gordie snorted. "Don't let him make you feel guilty. He told me often enough that he likes his trailer. It suits him, he told me. It's only now when he sees someone else making something of what he didn't want that he's jealous."

"My agent warned me against buying this house. Perhaps I should have listened."

Vanessa frowned. "Why did he warn you?"

"She. She would have liked me to buy a different house. Very beautiful but completely done inside already."

Vanessa nodded. "And no doubt much more expensive. Sounds like she was hoping to get a better commission."

Gretha shrugged. "She said that houses bought by auction are usually a problem, but in Germany, it is a common practice, so I wasn't worried. She was rather upset with me though, when I insisted." With an elegant gesture, she spread her hands. "Now perhaps she proves her point."

Gordie shook his head. "At heart, Jack's not a bad guy. He'll come around once he gets used to seeing his former house come to life again."

The German woman smiled. "Yes. The house and I together begin a new life."

Vanessa helped herself to more wine. "Does that mean you are moving here permanently?"

"I will see how things go. Right now, I'm just happy to work on the renovations with the carpenter and when winter comes, then I'll decide. My home is in Germany, of course, and all my things are there."

Vanessa nodded. "What about family? They must miss having you at home?"

"No. No real family to miss me. My mother died last year."

"Oh, I'm sorry. We are very much alike. When my mother died in Ontario, I moved here too. It's a place that promotes healing." Vanessa smiled. "I have a feeling you and I will be good friends, Gretha."

Gordie thought the answering smile the woman gave Vanessa was less than enthusiastic. "We should be going. We've taken up enough of your time, and my dog, Taz, will be looking for her supper."

They all rose and while Vanessa leaned in to give Gretha an impulsive hug, Gordie just nodded.

Gretha walked them to their car. "There was no need to bring anything, but thank you for the vase and flowers. I'm glad to make new friends here."

\*\*\*

Gordie mused about their visit on the 15-minute drive home. "I feel like I don't know much more about her than before we visited."

Vanessa laughed. "She's probably thinking the same about you right now. You're used to people telling you everything about themselves without you saying anything. You've met your match now."

He grinned sheepishly. "You're probably right."

"I like her. And what she's doing with that house! It's going to be spectacular when it's done, won't it?"

"It will. She does have a fine eye, no question there."

"Do you think that Jack Fraser guy will make her life miserable?"

"No, I'm sure he'll come around, eventually. I'll have a word with him."

"I hope so. I know from experience that it's hard enough to become accepted in a place where most people count back the generations they've been in the area. Not like me. I count by the years, and although I can't believe it's already been five years since I moved here from Ontario, that's just a drop in the bucket compared to everyone else."

Gordie laughed. "Now you have seniority over another newcomer."

Vanessa smiled contentedly and enjoyed the view for the rest of the drive home.

# CHAPTER THREE

MONDAY. GORDIE WAS HALFWAY to his office in Sydney, taking his time on the drive. It was the kind of day when the intense blue sky served as a surreal backdrop to the multitude of autumn trees clad in crimson, orange, gold, and copper. The phone rang and fractured his reverie. A glance at the call display on his dashboard showed the caller was his boss, Sergeant Arsenault.

He pushed the button on his steering wheel. "MacLean."

Arsenault's voice was even more brusque than usual. "MacLean, where are you?"

"I'm on my way in."

"I *know* that. Where exactly are you right now?"

"Just past Irish Cove. Why?"

"There's been a murder. You'll have to turn around."

"Where? Who?"

"On Isle Madame. Some tourist."

Gordie pulled into a small side road and executed a gravel-spitting U-turn. "Good God."

"I've already dispatched Albright so she'll meet you there. Texting you the address now. I talked to the woman who found the body and told her to stay there and not let anyone go inside. Keep me informed. John Allan and his forensics team are gathering their equipment and will be on the way shortly."

A moment later, Gordie heard the beep of an incoming text. He pulled into a look-off parking area and stopped to check the address. 21 Roscarberry Road. "What? No. It can't be." He called Sergeant Arsenault.

"Arsenault."

"Sarge, are you sure about this address?"

"Of course. Why?"

"And you said it was a tourist. Was it the owner of the house or someone else?"

He heard the clicking of his sergeant's keyboard as he pulled up the file. "Ms. Gretha Braun."

"Oh, my God. I was just there. I met her this past weekend. Vanessa and I went to visit her and got a tour of the house. I can't believe this."

After a short pause, Sergeant Arsenault spoke. "This sounds like a conflict of interest, MacLean. I might have to assign someone else to it."

"No!" With effort, Gordie lowered his voice. "I know this place and these people better than anyone else. I'll be objective. No worries there."

MacLean heard his boss sigh. "Carry on for now. Get the preliminaries done and tomorrow we'll meet and discuss what comes next." The phone disengaged before any further protest from Gordie.

The detective made the journey back considerably faster than the trip out. He motored past the turnoff to his own home without a glance, hastening to the house where he had been visiting only two days earlier. He parked on the edge of the road well away from the house itself, cautious in his desire to avoid destroying evidence. There were two cars parked in the driveway, Gretha's red leased Ford Escape he had seen when he visited, and behind that, a grey Lexus SUV.

As he approached the grey car, a woman jumped out. "Are you the police?"

"Yes. Please get back in your car and back out. Pull over beyond the property. Park in front of the neighbour's house, please."

The woman did as he instructed, and he followed on foot to her car. She climbed out again, and he noticed the dark stain on the jacket of her tailored grey pin-striped pantsuit. *A lawyer?*

He handed his card to her. "Detective Gordie MacLean. Who are you?"

"Linda Hickson."

"OK, Linda. Please, just stay here for a few moments while I take a quick look inside."

She nodded and Gordie went back to his Santa Fe, pulling out white forensics booties, which he put over his shoes and latex gloves that he pulled on as he walked. He followed the cracked walkway to the front door, studying the ground as he went for any sign of blood or other evidence. He tried the front door but found it locked and then he moved around to the back door. The door was ajar. He pushed it open and stepped inside.

Aside from some creaking and the lazy bang of a window shutter on an upstairs window, the house was silent, but he called out anyway. "Cape Breton Police Services. Is anyone home?" He walked through the kitchen and into the large living room, where he saw her. Gretha Braun lay on her back with a large gash in her chest; blood stained her shirt and pooled on the floor where she lay. Gordie knelt and touched her neck. Gretha was cold to the touch. She had been dead for some time. He shook his head, rose, and took several detailed notes of the scene. He used one page to make a rough sketch showing the location of the victim, noticing that there were no significant signs of a struggle. No overturned furniture or seat cushions on the floor. It appeared to him that the attacker had surprised her. The person stood in front of her, perhaps talking, perhaps arguing prior to suddenly producing a weapon. She had no time to turn and run or put up a fight. These were just his own thoughts, but he was careful not to come to any conclusions before the forensics team did its work. After he made several pages of notes, he retraced his steps exactly back into the kitchen and outside. For a moment, he saw himself sitting there on the deck with the cold can of beer, enjoying the company of this woman. Gordie went back the way he had come, stopping at his car to remove the booties and gloves before he reached the woman who had called in the crime.

He pulled out his black pen and notebook, wrote down the date and time and then began. "For the record, may I have your full name and date of birth please?"

The woman tossed her head and her dark red shoulder-length hair flipped back from her face. "Linda Alice Hickson. Twenty-third of May, 1978,"

"What brought you here today, Linda?"

"I'm Gretha's realtor."

Gordie frowned. "I'm confused. I understood that the sale of this house closed months ago. Why would she need her real estate agent visiting, unless the two of you had become friends?"

Hickson scowled. "First of all, I'm a realtor, not a real estate agent. Secondly, although the house indeed closed some time ago, we had some outstanding business still."

"My apologies. I wasn't aware there was a difference. We'll have to talk to you in more detail later about the outstanding business. For now, please take me through what happened this morning."

She sighed. "I arrived here at eight o'clock because I know Gretha generally gets going very early in the day and I wanted to catch her in."

Gordie glanced at her before writing the time.

She flushed and continued. "I knocked, and when there was no answer, I pushed open the door."

"Was that the front or back door?"

"Back. The front needs to be replaced, like so many other things in this house, and doesn't open easily."

He nodded. "Why did you go inside when she didn't answer? Perhaps she was sleeping or in the shower?"

Hickson snapped. "I told you. I know her and knew she'd be up and about." Her voice lowered. "I thought she might be ignoring me, and I wasn't leaving without talking to her."

"So, you pushed open the door. Did you have to press down on the latch or was the door ajar?"

Her bottom teeth nibbled her top lip as she thought. "The door was ajar just a little. Not wide open, but not tight on the latch."

He wrote it down and then looked at her again to continue.

Now her voice lost its bravado and became shaky. "I didn't smell coffee or hear the radio. She always puts the radio on when she gets up so she can get the weather forecast and local news." Linda shook her head. "She took delight in listening to the local news." She took a deep breath. "I knew something wasn't right then, but I kept calling her name. Maybe part of me thought the same as you. That she had a late start and was in the shower or something. I almost went back out because I felt uncomfortable, but I took a couple more steps and then I saw her lying there." Linda gulped. "It was awful."

"Did you go to her? See if you could help her?"

"I did. It was like I couldn't help it. I knew, but I went and knelt anyway. I touched her and then I realized what I was doing and jumped back up."

"Did you touch anything other than her body?"

"No. Definitely not. I put my hand on her for a second. I thought I should stop the blood like they teach you in first aid classes, but it was sticky and awful. Christ. She didn't even feel like a real person."

Gordie used his pen to point to Hickson's suit. "Can you tell me about the stain, please?"

She looked down and her eyes widened. "Oh, God. I don't know. I must have wiped my hand on my suit."

A metallic-blue Jeep Renegade approached, and Gordie lifted his hand to wave to Detective Roxanne Albright who slowed down beside where he and Linda Hickson stood. "Park down beyond this car and then can you start laying out the crime scene tape? It's going to get busy here."

Albright nodded and drove on.

Gordie made a note of the time when his partner arrived and then he focused on Linda Hickson again. "Ms. Hickson, I'm going to call for one of my colleagues to come and get you. You'll be taken to the West Arichat RCMP Station, where you'll need to give us your clothing and then you'll go through what you've just told me again for a formal statement."

"My clothes? Can't I just go home and change and give you these?"

"I'm afraid not. After your statement, someone will take you home."

"What about my car? I need my car."

"When the forensics team arrives, someone will search your car and then we will get it back home for you. Are you willing to give us your keys to search it and deliver it to your house?"

She pulled the keys out of her jacket pocket. "I haven't done anything wrong."

"It's just standard procedure. Nothing to worry about."

Gordie took the keys and locked the car with the remote before stepping away to call for more personnel. A couple of uniforms were already en route, and Gordie nodded when told that one of them knew what to do as a crime scene control. He had a logbook with him for that very purpose.

This little corner of Isle Madame was soon going to look like a circus had arrived in town.

# CHAPTER FOUR

JOHN ALLAN AND HIS two forensics specialists arrived, and as the team suited up in white jumpsuits and booties, Gordie briefed them on the scene. The specialists each began working the scene while John stayed on for a moment longer.

John zipped up his coveralls and snugged the hood over his head. "Did the woman who found her touch anything other than the body?"

"It's hard to know. I'm not sure she even knows herself. She had blood on her jacket, which she claims came to be there after she touched the victim and then wiped her hands on herself. I've had her taken to the Mountie shop down the road where they will take the clothes and get her statement and fingerprints."

Allan nodded and looked up at the house. "They don't build them like this anymore." He sighed. "We'll be here a while, so I better get at it."

Gordie watched him for a moment as Allan carefully followed the yellow marked path that his assistants had laid out. He turned away when Roxanne Albright approached. The slim but muscular young woman only stood five feet and five inches, but her regime of running and weights gave her a solid build. She wore her below-the-shoulder length dark hair parted in the middle and snugged back in a bun. The style emphasized her high cheekbones and slightly exotic-looking almond-shaped brown eyes.

"OK, boss. Where do we start?"

They went to Gordie's car, and he popped open the back so they could sit for a moment perched on the back to make notes and create a plan.

Gordie turned to a fresh page in his flip notebook. "We need to go door-to-door checking to see what people know. It's usually a quiet road here since it dead ends at a small stony harbour. No sandy beach or dock or anything."

"OK. Do you want to pull one of the constables to help with that? Or shall we?"

"Let's do it ourselves. There are too many onlookers cruising past now. The word's out that something is going on, and sure as hell, the minute we pull the constable, someone will cross the line to try and get some photographs." He pointed to one of the uniforms. "In fact, I'm going to position her so she can keep an eye on the back because it won't be long before someone comes across that field."

Roxanne nodded. "Sounds good. I'll work this side of the road from here down to the end by the water, and then I'll come back the other side. Do you want to start here and work back towards the turnoff from the main road?"

He gave her a thumbs up and she stood, pulled out her identification to have it in hand and walked to the first neighbour's house. Gordie smiled to himself when he saw an elderly woman pull open the door while Roxanne was still only halfway up the walk.

*\*\*\**

Roxanne absent-mindedly stroked Taz's head. She and MacLean sat at his kitchen table with their notebooks open in front of them.

Gordie tipped the teapot to warm up his cup of tea but found the pot empty. He stood and filled the kettle to set it to boil again.

Roxanne set the black mug with a faded photo of the great Pyrenees dog she was currently fondling on her empty plate and slid it away from her. "No more for me. I'm floating as it is. Thanks for the sandwich, though. That hit the spot."

He sat down again after clicking on the kettle. "I've got some oatcakes. You'll need a cup of tea to go with that."

She shook her head. "I won't have any. Nana will expect me to eat when I get home. You know her. She's made a fish chowder, so I better keep room for it."

Gordie nodded. "OK, then. Let's go over what we have learned so far. I'll go first. The neighbour directly to the left of Braun's house, Ms. Anne Murphy, had a glass of wine with the victim yesterday evening."

"So that's the evening of Sunday, September 26."

"Right. The contractor, Henry Davis, had been there earlier. Anne had seen him and said something about that to the victim like 'It's not usual to find a contractor to work on a Sunday', but Gretha just responded by saying he wasn't there to work and then changed the subject. The other person who had been earlier in the day was a friend of Gretha's called Mia White. She owns the bakery in town, and she dropped by with some plum dumplings for Gretha. They've become good friends and see each other a lot, according to Anne."

"Plum dumpling. That sounds good."

Gordie smiled. "Anne said they were. They each had one with a glass of wine when Anne went to visit."

"That's the substance of what Anne had to say. Both those visitors were long gone, and Anne didn't think that there had been any problems."

"Why do you suppose the contractor was there on a Sunday?"

"Hard to say. Maybe to get paid? Maybe to confirm some project so he could order materials."

"Anything from anyone else?"

He shook his head. "Nothing. Everyone is on at least an acre, most even more, so the houses are too far apart to hear much or even see anything unless you happen to be going by when someone else is pulling out of the driveway. What about you?"

"A whole lot of not much. The neighbours to the immediate right, Gloria and Frank Bagnell, remember the motion sensor light located on the back of the victim's house lighting up after they went to bed. Gloria had already been asleep, and it woke her for a moment, but she didn't look at the clock. It felt very late to her, but Frank figures it was somewhere after eleven. They go to bed at ten and he was still just dozing, not yet sound asleep. Gloria gave it a glancing thought and assumed it was a raccoon or porcupine that triggered the light. Neither heard any noises. No raised voices or screams or anything."

"Anyone else remember anything?"

"No. The ones right across from the victim's house are away for a few days so no one was there. Along the rest of the few houses between the crime scene and the shore, people were more interested in asking *me* questions rather than answering them. They all said that she was a friendly, gracious lady and they all loved that she was fixing up the house. One man down near the end said we should talk to the previous owner, who seemed unhappy that Braun had bought the house and was fixing it up."

"Jack Fraser."

Roxanne raised her eyebrows, so Gordie explained the exchange he had witnessed in the hardware store, followed by the visit that he and Vanessa had made to Gretha.

Roxanne crossed her arms. "You're just telling me this now? You knew the victim? Gordie. You can't be involved. You know that, right?"

He scowled. "I don't know that at all. I think I'm the best possible person to lead the investigation. I already have some background about the people. Some insights."

"Like what? Hit me with an insight."

"It's highly unlikely that Jack Fraser would bother to kill Gretha. What would be his motive? The house is gone and killing the new owner wouldn't get it back."

Roxanne waited for more. "That's it? I don't have to tell you that logic doesn't always define a motive. You said yourself that he was angry. He didn't like the changes she was making. He was jealous that she was doing something that he didn't bother doing himself. Maybe he thought she ripped him off in some convoluted twist of thinking. Gordie, you've already got blinders on here."

The detective stood to rinse out his mug before refilling it with fresh milk and tea. He felt older than his 54 years of age. He sighed as he returned to the table. "I'm not stepping aside."

"Did you tell Sarge that you knew the victim?"

His voice was defensive, "yes. I told him. I'm not a complete idiot."

She reached over and laid a hand on her partner's arm. "I'm not saying you're an idiot. Far from it. I just hate to see anyone accuse you of some kind of bias."

Gordie closed his notebook. "Let's call it a night. We'll meet with the boss in the morning." He narrowed his eyes at Roxanne. "Do you have my back?"

"Always."

"So, you'll support me when I tell him I can do this investigation?"

Roxanne chewed her lip before answering. "I'll support you."

*** 

After his partner left, Gordie went out back. He needed to call Vanessa to give her the news before she heard it on the local radio station, but he wanted a few moments to gather his thoughts before talking to her. The fall night had closed in; the smell of decaying leaves mingled with woodsmoke. A neighbour had a small bonfire burning, and the laughter and music Gordie heard were at odds with his melancholy mood. He longed for a cigarette but had been off the smokes for months now and wouldn't give in. He watched Taz wander the perimeter of his half-acre yard, sometimes sniffing against the ground and at other moments lifting her muzzle in the air.

"Taz, I'm going in."

The great white head lifted, and she looked at him. For a moment, he thought she would stay outside, but she seemed to sense his mood and trotted over to push her nose into his hand. When he turned to re-enter through his kitchen door, the dog left the night sounds and smells and followed him inside.

Gordie picked up his cell phone and wandered into the living room to make himself comfortable on his brown leather recliner. Taz stretched out on the floor beside him, content to be near him. He looked down at his dog. "If Gretha had only had someone like you, she would probably be alive right now." He shook his head and tapped the contact number for Vanessa.

# CHAPTER FIVE

MACLEAN SAW ALBRIGHT'S JACKET on the back of her chair when he came in. He was early, but she had arrived earlier, as she often did. He set down the cup of green tea that he had bought for her at the Tim Hortons coffee shop near the office and went to his own desk.

*I should see if Sarge is in to just let him know I'm here.* Gordie sighed, knowing that he had an uphill battle facing him about this investigation. Despite MacLean's success rate with previous investigations, Sergeant Arsenault always seemed determined to sideline his detective at the best of times, preferring to have younger, more like-minded men on a case rather than his aging bachelor detective and his 'girl' partner. There was never any bias that Gordie could take to a tribunal, but it was an attitude thing. The scowl on his boss' face. The small cutting remarks.

He walked down the hall but stopped before he reached the open door, pausing for a moment out of sight. He frowned when he heard his partner's voice in conversation with his boss. *What the hell?*

He felt his heartbeat increase, and he took a couple of deep breaths before moving forward to enter his supervisor's office without knocking. "I didn't realize we had a meeting scheduled." Gordie sat down in the other chair in front of Arsenault's desk, avoiding Albright's eyes. "Sorry, I'm late."

Sergeant Arsenault's voice was calm. "Now that you're here, we can begin."

Gordie gritted his teeth at the implied criticism they had been waiting for him, and hardly heard Roxanne's quiet explanation. "Gordie, Sergeant Arsenault saw me in the parking lot and asked me to come to his office right away. I've only been here a couple of minutes. I haven't even turned on my computer yet."

He turned to his partner. "Your green tea is sitting on your desk, getting cold. I would have brought it along if I realized you two were meeting already."

She flushed. "Thank you. I'll still enjoy it."

Arsenault drummed his fingers on the desk. "Can we get on with it?"

MacLean pulled out his notebook and his pen and then stared at his boss. "Of course."

"MacLean, you have to realize you are in a position of conflict of interest." He held up his hand to forestall MacLean's protest. "We all know it and there's no point arguing the fact."

Gordie turned his head a fraction to slant his eyes at his partner, who caught the look and shook her head as if to indicate she had said nothing to their boss.

It took everything MacLean had to remain silent.

Arsenault continued. "I thought about this last night. I take your point that you know the community and there can be some value in that. It's why we have you down there, after all. You're the man on the spot. I get it."

"So then…"

Again, Arsenault held up his hand and Gordie stopped in mid-sentence.

*One of these days someone's going to cut that hand off him.* Gordie felt his blood pressure pound in his ears.

"I have no choice but to assign someone else as lead to avoid even the appearance of bias. When this gets to court, you know a defence lawyer will find any reason to throw doubt on the evidence. You don't want that, and I sure as hell don't want that."

Gordie took a deep breath. "No."

"Here's what I've decided."

Gordie waited to hear whether it would be Detective Rob Norris, which wouldn't be too bad, or the newest favourite of Sergeant Arsenault's, a young pup called Detective Jason Ahearn who recently transferred in from Arson. Gordie secretly felt that Ahearn only came to Major Crimes because it was just too much trouble to say 'Ahearn of Arson' over and over again. That fellow was cocky, with a similar attitude to his boss'.

Gordie was so preoccupied imagining what he would do if he had to work with Ahearn that he almost missed it.

"It's time that Detective Albright take the lead."

He turned to look at his partner as she inhaled a quick gasp of breath.

"Me, Sarge?"

"If you call me Sarge again, I'll change my decision."

She widened her eyes. "Sorry. Are you sure?"

"Why? Aren't you up to the challenge?"

"I am. Yes, I believe I am. But I'm working with Detective MacLean, right?"

"Will that be a problem?"

"No, not at all. Not for me."

Arsenault drilled MacLean with his stare. "What about you MacLean? Will it be a problem?"

His mind spun. *Is it a problem? Anything's better than Ahearn.* "No, Sergeant. Of course not. We work well as a team."

Sergeant Arsenault nodded. "A team, yes. But remember that she gets the final decision if there's any kind of dispute." He waved a pen toward Roxanne. "If you have an issue, Detective Albright, come and see me. We need to be squeaky clean here. No shortcuts. The victim is a foreign national and I don't even know what that means yet as far as the politics of it all."

"I will, Sergeant, but I'm sure it won't be necessary."

Arsenault nodded. "Well then. As the lead, tell me what you've got so far."

Detective Roxanne Albright slid her notebook from her breast pocket and proceeded to brief their boss.

*** 

They walked down the hall to the open area that housed their workstations.

Gordie picked up the paper coffee cup sitting on his desk, took a sip, and grimaced. "Cold."

Roxanne nodded. "Let's log in and check our email, see if there are any forensics reports in already from John Allan's team and then we'll go over and get fresh drinks."

"You buying, boss?"

She gave a small, uncertain smile. "I'll buy."

He nodded, and they spent half an hour getting set up. There were no new reports, so when Roxanne came to his desk and raised her eyebrows, he nodded, picked up his jacket and followed her outside to the parking lot.

She hesitated. "My car or yours?"

"Yours, I'd say."

They got into her car and were silent for a moment as she pulled out of the parking lot.

Gordie folded his arms and looked around. "I haven't been in this car much. It's nice. What year is it?"

"2019. Look, Gordie. I never imagined he'd do this. Make me lead. I never asked for it. I never said anything. I promise."

He closed his eyes for an instant. "I know you didn't. Don't worry about it. It's probably the best possible solution. For me, for you and the investigation."

The drive to the coffee shop was short. She parked and by silent agreement they didn't discuss it any further until they had gone in, ordered their tea and coffee with an oatcake and pat of butter for him and a cruller for her.

As the server handed the oatcake over to Gordie, she nodded. "Enjoy it. That's our last batch. They're discontinued."

Gordie scowled. "I heard the rumour but hoped it wasn't true. How come?"

The server shrugged. "Who knows?"

While she paid, he carried the tray to their favourite corner table.

When they sat down, she resumed the conversation. "You're not mad at me, are you?"

"No, of course not. It took me a minute to get over the shock, but like I said, it's fine."

She sipped her tea and then frowned at him. "You think this is the best thing for the investigation because you can't be objective?"

He laughed. "No, that's not why. I think that, as much as I hate to admit it, Sarge is right that when the case comes to court, we can't even have the perception of a problem with the investigation."

He paused to take a sip of coffee before continuing.. "Whatever I think of Sergeant Arsenault, he's no dummy. I'll give him that. The big reason that this is good for the investigation is from the political perspective. This case is going to turn into a media circus. It won't just be our local papers and stations that want briefings, it'll be the nationals as well. As he pointed out, the victim was a foreigner, and that will make it a much bigger story than just a domestic argument or whatever gone wrong in our little corner of the island. Arsenault will already be planning his press conferences and he'd much rather show the world that the Cape Breton Police Service is an equal opportunity place. It looks much better to have you there beside him on the podium than me, or one of the other guys."

Roxanne flushed. "That's harsh. You don't think that my ability has anything to do with this assignment?"

Gordie put down his cup of coffee. "I didn't mean to sound so jaded. Of course, he knows by now you are extremely capable and well able for the assignment. He wouldn't take a chance otherwise. You've proven yourself. I just don't know if he would have been ready to acknowledge those abilities if it had been any other case. So, here's my advice to you. Make the absolute most of this opportunity. I'll admit to you, I am emotionally involved in the case, and you'll have to pull me up on it if you think it's colouring my judgement, but I sure hope you'll talk to me as a partner and friend and not go straight to the boss if it happens."

She grinned. "That goes without saying. I would have backed you if he asked me. You know that, right?"

He drained his cup. "I know that, and I'm behind you on this. When you're at the top of the hill in your career, look down on me kindly. I'm pissed that this very nice woman was murdered by someone, but at least I'm glad that you're going to go places because of it."

As they walked back to the car, she added one more thing to the conversation. "Don't ever call me boss again."

He opened his mouth to say *yes, boss* but saw her wrinkled forehead. "OK, partner."

*** 

Back in the office, Roxanne and Gordie went to the team briefing room to start a case board. The long meeting room had rows of chairs, an eight-foot table along one side and a screen that descended from the ceiling when you pushed the right buttons on the remote. Along the opposite side from the table were two six-foot whiteboards on wheels. The front was the formal part of the room with the brightly coloured flags of Canada, Nova Scotia, and Cape Breton in their stands as a backdrop to a podium. This is where the brass held the occasional press briefings.

Roxanne Albright took her place in front of a whiteboard and scribed the name of the victim. Below 'Gretha Braun' she wrote the name of the realtor, 'Linda Hickson' and the name of the former homeowner 'Jack Fraser'.

Gordie sat on a chair facing the board, with his notebook in hand. "There's also Mia White who owns the bakery, and Henry Davis, the contractor."

She added the names. "I can't see putting any of the neighbours down, can you?"

"Not at this point. Let's start with these people who seemed to know her best."

Beside the column of names, Roxanne started a new list and headed it: 'Motive'.

Gordie nodded. "That's always the key, isn't it? We have this woman who comes from her homeland somewhere in Germany and falls in love with our corner of the world. It appears that she's doing the right things, making friends with the neighbours, and giving business to the community stores like the bakery and the building supply place. She hires local tradespeople to work on transforming a decrepit house back into something the whole neighbourhood is happy about."

"Not quite everyone was happy."

He nodded. "True. Jack Fraser. I admit I may be wrong," smiling when his partner raised her eyebrows. "But I just can't see Jack boiling out with that much rage. For one thing, it would take more energy than I've ever seen him display."

"But we can't rule him out."

"No. You're right. Too soon for that. But seriously, I met Gretha. She was a nice, intelligent, enthusiastic woman who was excited to be starting a life here. How is it possible she made someone so angry they'd stab her?"

"Was she snooty? Maybe she got someone riled up without meaning to? A cultural misunderstanding maybe?"

He tilted his head. "That's a good thought. She was different, for sure. I don't know if I'd say snooty, but someone may have taken something the wrong way." Gordie rose and went to the second board. He picked up a pen and wrote 'Next Steps.'

Roxanne began ticking items off on her fingers while Gordie noted them down. "Get the autopsy report to get as much information as possible about the murder weapon. Interview the contractor and the friend, Mia. Take a closer look at the realtor's statement. Why was she there so early in the day?"

Gordie spoke as he wrote. "We need to make an official notification. Hopefully, forensics found a phone book or something. I suppose we need to reach out to the German Consulate. That may be one that you throw over to Sarge."

She wrinkled her brow. "I think there's only an honorary Consul in Halifax. It seems to me the actual Consulate General is in Ottawa or Toronto. I read something about that a while ago."

He turned from the writing on the whiteboard to look at her. "You're a fountain of information."

Roxanne shrugged. "The internet is a fountain of information. Once I figure out who to talk to, you're right, I'll push it up the chain."

Gordie grinned. "I wonder how Sergeant Arsenault's German is." He sobered again and turned back to the board and wrote: 'talk to relatives at home.' "Once we know the notification is done, we need to consider that some problem followed her here. We don't know who it was that came visiting late at night, but it may have nothing whatsoever to do with her life here. In fact, maybe that's exactly why she was here."

Albright nodded. "Because she was trying to get away from a problem at home, you mean?"

"Yes. That would make more sense, wouldn't it?"

"It does, but that's going to be tough to figure out."

He wrote again. 'Get German police contact.' Gordie turned to Roxanne. "We need to go through the house ourselves. Forensics would just be looking for evidence regarding her death. We need to examine her life."

"True. Let's start with that tomorrow. We'll meet there first thing. By then, hopefully, we'll have the forensics report, and we can build up a picture of her. Right now, I'll start with researching what government agencies we need to get in touch with, and if you can go see John Allan about forensics, we can make a start." She hesitated then. "Does that make sense to you?"

"Definitely."

"You'll say something if you think I'm going wrong, won't you? I know you like to keep your thoughts to yourself."

He shook his head. "I've gotten better at sharing. The one thing I'd say is to make sure you see Sarge later today to brief him. You may suggest that we might need help once we get a handle on what needs doing."

She frowned. "Do you think we need more bodies?"

"We will soon and it's always good to plant the thought early. We're going to have a lot of moving parts here, and once the media really gets involved, which I imagine will be today, there'll be a lot of pressure to get results."

"OK, thanks. Maybe I'll write out some lines of inquiry and run it past you before I go see him later."

Gordie left her at her desk, chewing the end of a pen, as he went down to the basement to visit the forensics lab.

# CHAPTER SIX

MACLEAN STROLLED INTO THE basement lab. The bright white fluorescent lighting always made Gordie squint when he first came in as his eyes adjusted. Doctor John Allan stood before a lightbox studying a set of x-rays.

Gordie joined him with his arms folded across his chest. "Are we looking at the victim's x-rays or your Aunt Edna's gallbladder?"

The tall, thin man peered over his black-rimmed glasses at Gordie. "For one thing, I don't have an Aunt Edna, and for another, if I was interested in a gallbladder, I'd use an ultrasound, not an x-ray."

"OK, I'll keep that in mind. So, can I assume this is our victim?"

"Yes." Allan pulled a stainless steel pen-sized instrument from the breast pocket of his white coat and extended it to point out the injuries on the images. "There are two stab wounds. The first was more of a scratch, but deep enough to start excessive bleeding, and then the killer drove in a deep thrust. That's why there was so much blood at the scene."

Gordie frowned. "The first one was tentative. Maybe they didn't even mean it, but then it was too late. There was no going back, and they gave it everything they had."

John nodded. "I suspect you're right. There was blood on the victim's hands. She probably touched herself, maybe screamed, maybe looked like she intended to run off, and then the killer made the second, final lunge."

"Stabbed in the heart?"

"Close. The thoracic aorta. The major artery that takes the blood from the heart to the rest of the body."

"What about the weapon?"

"It was what most people call an eight-inch stainless steel slicing knife. Extremely sharp with a Damascus pattern. Not actually eight inches, but near enough. The blade was 20 centimeters long with a twelve-and-a-half centimeters long woodgrain style handle. Three centimeters wide blade at its widest."

"That's very precise."

Allan smiled. "We found the weapon in the victim's dishwasher. The killer was very clever and ran the dishwasher cycle."

"Was the dishwasher full?"

"Two cups and the knife."

Gordie sighed. "No prints then, I guess?"

"Some smudges, but nothing usable. It's a new Bosch dishwasher, and the killer set it on the hygienic setting. We were still able to recover some blood residue, which appears to be the victim's, but the fingerprints were gone. And before you ask, the door and controls of the dishwasher were wiped down."

"Wow. Very thorough on the part of our killer. Are you prepared to declare it for what it obviously is, then?"

John Allan clicked his tongue to make a tsk sound. "You know better than that. Only the Medical Examiner can make the pronouncement of cause and manner of death after their investigation."

"Have they seen these x-rays from the Port Mulroy morgue?"

"They got the autopsy results from the morgue before I did. All right, let me put you out of your misery. I've already spoken to the M.E. in Dartmouth and while they won't have the report out for a couple of days yet, they are in no doubt that the cause of death is a sharp force trauma, and the manner of death will be ruled a homicide."

Gordie nodded. "Great, thank you."

John Allan switched off the lightbox and led the way to his office. "One more thing. You'll see for yourself from the crime scene photos, but the knife was one of her own. There's a knife block in the kitchen with seven other knives from a set and then this one."

"Huh. A weapon of opportunity, then. But she didn't die in the kitchen. How did the knife get from the knife block to the living room?"

"I'm guessing it might have been right there in the room already." John Allan picked up a file from his desk and flipped to the autopsy report. "She had tea and cake shortly before she died." The head of forensics peered at Gordie. "There was a cake on the dining room table."

"I know she had wine and pastries late afternoon."

"No, this was right before she died."

Gordie nodded. "OK. Overall, she was in good health?"

"Oh, yes. She was a 42-year-old woman who was in the physical condition of someone years younger. Not particularly muscular, but she obviously looked after herself in terms of diet and basic exercise."

"OK, thanks, John. Did your team collect any artifacts like a phone book or any documents?"

"No. We strictly focused fingerprints, blood evidence, and we took a single wine glass that was on the kitchen counter away to check for poison if we need to. We sent blood samples to the lab. I'll email you when the report gets loaded up and the M.E. has given their official word about cause and manner of death."

Gordie returned to his desk, deep in thought.

***

They had burgers delivered and ate in front of the whiteboard.

He picked out a couple of fries from the paper pouch. "OK, take me through the lines of inquiry you've got."

Roxanne swallowed her bite and wiped her mouth with a brown paper serviette. "OK. First, we need to go through the house and see what we can find in the way of papers like banking information, contacts, schedules, or diaries. That kind of thing."

"Good."

"Then, we need to talk to the immediate people who we know had contact with the victim. So, the contractor, the realtor, and the former owner of the house."

"And the bakery owner. They were friends."

Roxanne made a note on her pad of paper. "I keep forgetting about her. While that's going on, someone needs to contact the German Consulate. As I thought, there's an Honorary Consulate in Halifax that reports to the real consulate in Toronto, but we might as well start with her. Their office is on Grafton Street in Halifax, and I have a phone number for them."

"If we don't find any next of kin information at the house, hopefully, they can find that."

"I think there's an easier way. As a foreign citizen, she would have had to provide bank information and proof of income to get a mortgage here to buy the house, so with any luck, we'll find a file with all that information to give us some clue, or at least tell us who holds the mortgage and maybe they have some further details."

Gordie nodded; his mouth full of burger.

"So, once we know where to go, we'll make the notification, or maybe get them to do that in Germany."

He swallowed and pointed to Roxanne's meal. "Eat your lunch and let me tell you about the autopsy."

She grinned and dug in while he flipped open his book and reviewed the findings John Allan had given him.

When he finished, he gave her a final observation. "At first, I thought we must be dealing with a man because I figured it would take a lot of strength to stab a woman but that's probably sexist. This weapon is darned sharp, and with just a bit of luck or determination, anyone could do it."

"I agree. Women are stronger than they're given credit for." Bundling up the wrappers, Roxanne stuffed all the garbage into the bag the lunch had come in. "Just like with everything, we keep an open mind. What other lines of enquiry do we want to add?"

"As always, we need to check her financials and phone records. The mortgage documents will help with that, but we need to get a full picture of the victim, aside from the details around the house. Was she very wealthy? If so, where did that wealth come from? Maybe she had some risky dealings that we need to pursue. The phone records will help as well to figure out who else we need to talk to."

"Right." Roxanne put it down. "Thanks for all this, Gordie. I'd get there eventually, but I appreciate the help."

He shrugged. "We're a team, right?"

Roxanne read over her notes. "I think asking for extra resources isn't a stretch. We can't do all this on our own."

"I agree. You should make up your mind what pieces you want to assign and, based on the skills you're looking for; suggest those people you think would be best suited."

She tilted her head. "Will Sarge go for that?"

"You won't know until you ask. One last thing I suggest you do before you meet with him. Put down some bullet points on a piece of paper to give to him. He'll have to put out a press release soon, so give him something to say."

Roxanne shook her head. "Did you do all this for our other cases?"

"Pretty much. Of course, Sergeant Arsenault didn't trust me in the beginning, so he was forever looking over my shoulder, and I just figured I might as well be prepared and hand him something to read before he asked me. It seemed to work well."

"I never knew. What do I put down at this point? We don't know anything."

"That's essentially what you say. '*A German national in her early forties was found deceased in suspicious circumstances in a home she purchased months ago on Isle Madame. Her identity will be released after notification to her next-of-kin. We are waiting for the Medical Examiner to pronounce the official cause and manner of death. Our team is busy investigating, and more information will be made available as soon as possible.*' Something along those lines. I know Sarge can come up with that himself, but if you hand it to him, he'll be happy."

"Thanks. Gordie."

"Right. Let's get to it. I'm going to call the ReMax real estate office in Port Mulroy and see what they can tell me about that house." He ticked off the questions on his fingers. "When exactly did the victim buy it? What mortgage papers were filed?, What does the office manager know about the relationship between the victim and the realtor? Things like that."

"And I'll get all these notes put into the system and meet with Sarge. Are you up for going out to the house this aft?"

"Definitely. The sooner the better. I'll see if John Allan's crew has a key or what they did about securing the property."

She nodded. "Sounds good. I'll let you know when I'm ready to leave."

# CHAPTER SEVEN

ONCE GORDIE WAS IN the privacy of his Santa Fe and settled in for the hour and a half drive from the office to the crime scene, he called Vanessa.

Her voice held tears. "Hi, Gordie."

"How are you doing?"

He heard the sniffle. "Not great. I've just been sitting here all morning trying to wrap my head around it. Gretha and I only met once, but we clicked immediately. I can't imagine why anyone would want her dead."

"I know. I'm gobsmacked as well."

"You're in the car, aren't you? Are you on your way there now?"

"Yeah. I'm meeting Roxanne at the house."

"That beautiful house. I wonder what will happen to it now. She had such passion for restoring it. Oh, Gordie. How can a thing like this happen here? Do you think it was that man? The one whose family owned it before?"

"I don't know, and I really can't talk about the details."

"No. Of course not."

He couldn't help himself. "What I can tell you though is that I'm not lead on the case."

"What? I don't believe it. You're the perfect person for the job."

"Not according to Arsenault."

Now her voice was indignant. "Oh, my God. Who is lead, then?"

"Roxanne."

There was a pause the length of a breath. "Oh, my goodness. How do you feel about that?"

There it was. Sometimes Gordie felt that Vanessa read his mind and spoke his own thoughts out loud.

He sighed. "I'm trying to be an adult about it."

"That doesn't answer my question."

"I guess the truth is, I'm annoyed. I prove myself over and over and still it seems I can't be trusted."

"Sergeant Arsenault doesn't trust you to do a good job, but he trusts your partner. That doesn't make sense."

"I guess it's not that straightforward. He thinks I have a conflict of interest."

"Because you live nearby? That's ridiculous."

Gordie smiled. "I love you for being so outraged. If I'm completely honest, I get it. There's going to be a lot of publicity and therefore politics around this case. Sarge isn't going to take any chances that there's even a sniff of bias. It isn't that I live near the victim. It's because I knew her. Because we went to visit."

He heard her sigh, and her voice was calmer. "I can see that, I suppose. But he knows you. He must realize you aren't biased."

"Even if he knows that, and I'm not convinced he does know it, he can't have anyone accusing us of it."

"It sounds like you agree with him?"

"I suppose I do. I'm still annoyed, though. Is that allowed?"

It was nice to hear her laugh. "That's allowed as long as you don't take it out on Roxanne."

"I was a little pissed at first, but I'm getting over it. I'm probably going to lose you soon."

"OK. Before you go into the dead zone, do you want me to go get Taz? Will you be late?"

"I'm not sure how late I'll be, but how about you go over to my place and instead of taking Taz, you just bring yourself and be there when I get home?"

"That makes more sense. All right. Don't rush, though. Do what you need to do, Gordie."

He hung up, feeling lighter than he had when he left the office.

***

Roxanne pulled up and parked behind him in the long double-wide driveway. As she opened the trunk to get out her crime scene kit, she called out to him: "I assume you got the key?"

In one hand, he held up a ring with two keys on it. "Forensics took this off a hook in the hallway when they were here yesterday." In the other hand, he carried his own kit with gloves, bags, and other forensic basics.

They walked around to the back and let themselves in. Already the house had a vacant, damp feel to it, even though it had only been empty for a day.

Gordie saw Roxanne gaze around. "This is your first time inside the house, isn't it?"

She nodded. "Nice kitchen. At least it would be if everything wasn't covered in fingerprint dust."

"It is." He frowned. "There's a towel missing."

"You sure?"

He pointed to a linen tea towel hanging on the handle of the stove. "There's a mate to that. One for dishes and one for hands. Same pattern with little boats on it."

She shook her head. "You are one observant guy."

"I only know because Vanessa mentioned how much she liked them, and Gretha said they were from Germany."

He led the way to the large room that served as the living room and dining room, and they stopped for a moment to study the stain on the hardwood floor where Gretha Braun had bled out.

Roxanne shook her head and then pointed to the steps. "Bedrooms are upstairs, I assume. How about I take them, and you go through everything down here?"

"Sounds good. When I talked to the manager of the real estate office, he told me that Gretha definitely had a mortgage on the house. The realtor is also a mortgage broker, and she helped make the arrangements, so if we don't find anything here, she'll have copies."

"Did the office manager shed any light on what was going on between them? The nature of the unfinished business?"

"No. As far as he knew, it was all done and dusted. He did say Hickson hadn't been happy when Gretha decided to go with a house that was auctioned off for back taxes instead of buying the house Linda had shown her. The manager didn't seem to think it was the end of the world, though. These things happen, is what he said. They still got some business through brokering the mortgage."

Gordie started with the desk. It was an antique with a fold-down top which converted the piece into a desk with pigeonholes and three drawers. He sat on the swivel chair and felt how long Gretha's legs must be compared to his own. The top was tidy. A laptop computer had been here, which was bagged and removed by forensics. The pigeonholes contained typical desk accessories. A stapler, a small tray with paper clips, a pair of scissors.

The top drawer contained files. *Yes.* Lying on top of the small stack of manilla file folders was an 8 x 10 photo of two women. He lifted it carefully by one corner. The image of Gretha laughing into the camera, her tidy bun falling to pieces with windswept strands partially obscuring her face, showed a side of the woman that Gordie hadn't experienced. The other woman appeared to be several years younger and was obviously the photographer; her arm stretched out in the way of selfies. She too was laughing as if they had just shared a wonderful joke together and needed to capture the moment.

Gordie placed the photo in a plastic bag and went back to looking at the files, each neatly labelled with a black felt tip pen. Using an app on his phone, he translated the names from German to English. Receipts. Insurance. Contacts. Projects. In an unlabeled one, he found her German passport. He opened the one for contacts and flipped through business cards for window installers, septic service, tree cutting, driveway paving and other trades offering services. There were also hand-written notes with names and numbers such as *Sandy Ryan, firewood,* and next to it in European style numbers with a cross through the number *7: 275/cord. 18 inches.* Nothing in the file gave him the names and numbers of her family. This set of files seemed to be ones that would get regular use as Gretha collected new receipts and information.

He pulled open the last drawer and muttered aloud. "Damn, nothing." This one held several files that appeared to be work-related. Photocopies of paintings, grainy articles, and booklets from museums and galleries filled the drawer. On top lay a brown leather portfolio with her initial *GB* embossed in gold on the front, which contained a pad of yellow lined paper with pages of notes in her neat handwriting.

"It's a start." They'd follow up with the mortgage company, but these documents didn't shed light on anything.

By now, Gordie knew that the computer and phone were more likely to provide useful information. Still, he quickly went through the buffet, which held only towels, cutlery, and wine glasses. The end tables didn't have drawers, so he moved back into the kitchen. One by one, he opened the drawers and cabinets but found only items that belonged in the kitchen. Small appliances and more cooking and baking implements than even Vanessa owned were all tidied away in orderly arrangements. Pots, pans, casserole dishes and baking sheets filled the lower set of cabinets. He just closed the last one when Roxanne joined him.

He saw her hands were empty but asked, anyway. "Anything?"

She shook her head. "I've never seen such an organized house. What about you?"

"I have her passport, so that will help trace her next of kin, I hope. I found the mortgage papers, but I'm not really sure now what that will give us. There's a photo that's interesting, though." He led the way back to the desk where the plastic bag with the photo lay.

Roxanne picked it up. "She looks so happy." She flipped it over to see if the name of the other woman was noted on the back, but it was blank. She studied the faces again. "Maybe she's a relative."

Gordie shook his head. "I don't think so. This was taken here. Look." He pointed to a ship in the background harbour. "This is North Sydney. The Newfoundland ferry terminal."

"You're right. Huh. Maybe it's Mia, the bakery friend."

"We'll take it with us when we interview her. If it is her, they must be pretty good friends by the look of the photo. If it isn't her, maybe she'll know who it is."

Roxanne looked around. "Well, nothing to be gained here, then. We might as well call it a day."

Gordie stopped on the way to the door. "The laundry is upstairs, right?"

"Yes. Between the bedrooms."

"Any sign of the missing towel?"

"No. I checked the hamper, the washer, and the dryer."

"Interesting. OK."

They left with the agreement that they would each spend time entering their notes in the system when they got home. Roxanne also planned to draw up a tentative list of assignments for the team to work on the next day, while Gordie promised to create a list of priority questions needing answers.

# CHAPTER EIGHT

ROXANNE ENJOYED THE FISH chowder her Nana had made for supper. When the detective arrived home to the house in Big Pond, she shared with her grandmother, Helen Albright, she always breathed a sigh of relief. In theory, Roxanne was there to keep an eye on her Nana, but they both knew it was really the other way around.

Once Nana had cleared up the supper dishes, she wagged a finger at Roxanne. "Don't sit there at the computer all night. You need to be fresh for the morning, Miss Lead Detective. I'm taking Sheba for a walk, and I might pop in to see Vera on the way home."

Roxanne laughed. "You mean Sheba will take you to see Vera because she knows very well there's always a cookie or two waiting for her there?"

Nana smiled down at the golden retriever. "Yes, I'm afraid so. Come on, missy. Let's get out of Roxanne's way."

Roxanne typed for a few moments and then stopped to pick up her phone and pushed the contact number for Eddy Tomah. She smiled unconsciously when she heard his voice, soft and mellow like melting butter. She pictured him with his round face, short black hair, strong nose, and soft lips. Like many other Mi'kmaq, his almond-shaped eyes were the colour of dark chocolate. She thought him quite beautiful, but she didn't say that to him. He'd feel it wasn't very manly.

She answered his greeting. "Yes, I'm home and have been fed. I need to get some reports done, but I can take a few minutes off to have a little catch-up with you."

"You're working on this new case of the German tourist, I guess?"

Her voice rose even though she tried to stay cool. "Eddy, I'm not just on the case. I'm the lead!"

There was a pause and for a second Roxanne thought she might have lost the connection and then he came back to her. "You're the lead? Wow! How did that happen?"

"Gordie and I were the first ones assigned to the case but then, you'll never believe it, but it turns out Gordie knew the woman. Sarge figured it put Gordie in a position of conflict of interest, but he didn't want to take us off the case, so he made me lead."

"That's incredible. Why not one of the other more senior guys, though?"

Roxanne considered what Gordie had said about the optics of having a woman but didn't repeat his comments. "I suppose he feels I'm able for it. Don't you think I am?"

"Well, sure, I guess so. I don't really know enough about what's involved in being the lead."

Roxanne frowned. "I have to decide who is doing what, and what our priorities are, things like that." She smiled. "I may even have to be on the podium for press briefings."

"Sounds like a lot of stress to me."

"I'm sure it will be, but I think it'll be worth it. I like the challenge."

"I guess this means I won't be seeing you on the weekend."

Roxanne stifled a sigh. "That's several days away. Maybe we'll have it solved by then. Let's just play it by ear."

"You're optimistic."

"You're usually optimistic too."

"True. OK, well, good luck with it, then. I better let you go back to your reports."

"OK, Eddy. It's nice.." the phone disengaged before she could say "to talk to you."

She stared at the phone and shook her head, muttering aloud, "What the heck's with you tonight?"

Roxanne finished her reports and sent off her tentative list of actions to Gordie for feedback, all the while feeling disheartened after her phone call. *Am I being naive? Am I really able for this or is it like Gordie said, and they picked me just because I'm a woman? Even my boyfriend has doubts.*

Nana came home and went to bed, leaving Sheba curled up on the sofa next to Roxanne.

When her email pinged, the young detective took a deep breath before reading Gordie's note entitled 'Feedback'.

*R - Well done. You've captured a lot of what needs to be done and you're right to put Rob Norris on chasing some of these things down, but I think he'll need help. I wonder if Andrew DeLorey is avail? Give Rob the usual - phone records, mortgage/bank records and work with the tech guys to see if there's anything useful on the computer. I probably would put DeLorey on contacting the German consulate to try to get next of kin info and a contact at the appropriate German police department. If he can put together a background for us on Gretha Braun, it could be helpful. That leaves you and me free, as you've noted, for the interviews to start with, of the contractor, the bakery friend and the realtor. Again, great job–just a little tweak to give Norris some help, but totally your decision. G*

She responded with a quick note. *Thanks for this. Really appreciate your input. R*

Roxanne closed her computer and went to bed, automatically sliding over when Sheba jumped up. The dog settled with her back against Roxanne's which the young woman found comforting, and still she tossed and turned for a long time, her mind unable to switch off.

# CHAPTER NINE

GORDIE RAISED HIS EYEBROWS when he saw Roxanne walk into the office the next morning. He took in the sleek Helly Hansen white jacket over green cargo pants. "Where's the hundred-year-old black leather bomber jacket?"

Roxanne sniffed. "It's not a hundred years old. And I just felt like a change."

"Didn't you tell me that jacket once belonged to your dad?"

"Yes, and I'm very attached to it. Don't disrespect it."

He grinned. "I'm just teasing. You look great. Very lead-like."

She took off the jacket to reveal a neat red shirt and ivory sweater. "How did you get here ahead of me today?"

"I had help. Vanessa made me breakfast and pushed me out the door nice and early." He grumbled. "I didn't even get my morning walk with Taz. Vanessa told me she and Taz are planning a nice long walk in the picnic park. I've been replaced."

"I'm glad Vanessa and you are good again."

When she sighed, Gordie tilted his head. "Everything OK?"

"Oh, yes." She was silent, so Gordie just kept looking at her until she continued. "I talked to Eddy last night. I told him that Sarge made me lead on the case."

"And? Eddy didn't react the way you thought he should?"

She shrugged. "I'm just feeling a little insecure, maybe."

Gordie nodded. "It happens. The best way to get your confidence up is by doing, so, let's go get the briefing room ready."

They lined up the chairs to face the whiteboards and Roxanne set out boxes of donuts she had picked up on the way to work.

Gordie helped himself to a plain, old-fashioned donut. "It's always an excellent strategy to have food for the team."

Roxanne looked up from the notes she had printed out. "I can use all the help I can get."

"You've done this a hundred times."

"It's different this time. You'll jump in if I miss anything, won't you?"

"Sure. But you won't miss anything."

The room filled with the members of the Major Crimes Unit. Everyone took a pastry and found a seat, talking amongst themselves. When Sergeant Arsenault walked in, the room grew quiet.

Her boss nodded, and Roxanne began the briefing. She took them through a review of what they knew so far, pointing to the crime scene photos and the murder weapon to punctuate her words. Most of the six men and two women were already working on other cases, including a rape case and a couple of domestic violence cases, but Arsenault believed it was good departmental policy to have everyone informed about new cases.

Roxanne concluded her background presentation by waving the whiteboard marker in Gordie's direction. "Detective MacLean will now take you through the next steps and then will discuss action assignments."

After he finished going through the first priorities that Albright and he had worked out, Gordie sat down again.

Roxanne looked around the room. "Does anyone have any

comments to add? Anything you think we need to look at that hasn't been included?"

No one commented, so she continued. "Sergeant Arsenault, I'd like to request the help of Detectives Norris and DeLorey to help run some of this information down." She ticked off the items on the list on the whiteboard.

Arsenault stood and came to stand beside her. He looked at the board and then turned to the room. "Norris, you're on this now. Hand off your current work on the IPV to Detective DeLorey." No one needed to be told that IPV stood for Intimate Partner Violence, but Roxanne looked puzzled that Norris had been directed to hand over his work to the very person she had expected to join her team.

Arsenault pointed to the young man sitting off to the side on his own, with his arms folded across his chest. "Ahearn, you're on Detective Albright's team now."

Gordie and Roxanne both turned to look at Jason Ahearn. The man in his late twenties was muscular with a handsome face. He wore his thick auburn hair brushed back to reveal a distinctive widow's peak. His heavy brows and wide eyes were all variations of the same rich brown colour.

Ahearn blinked and sat forward on his chair. "Right, Sergeant."

Gordie clenched his teeth but thought he did a good job of keeping his face neutral. He didn't know Ahearn well, but it was obvious to everyone in the department that he had arrived as a protégé of the boss.

Roxanne nodded to Ahearn. "Welcome to the team." She turned back to the room. "That's it for now. Detectives Norris and Ahearn, can you please stay behind with Detective MacLean and me and we'll lay out our plan."

Arsenault gave Roxanne a short nod. "Come see me when you're done here."

Gordie risked a glance at Rob Norris who gave him a slight shrug. *This just gets better and better.*

Roxanne continued to stand at the board, so the three of them joined her there. "Rob, I'm counting on you to do your magic in getting the victim's phone records. We may find the person she was expecting that night, or there may be text messages or emails that will lead us to someone with whom she was arguing. The tech guys have her phone, but if they can't get into it, you'll have to find out who her provider was. I assume she got a local phone. I imagine that using a phone from Germany would cost her an arm and a leg." She turned to MacLean. "You didn't find any phone bills in your look through her desk, did you?"

"No. She probably gets all her bills emailed."

"Right. Rob, when you're with the tech guys, you'll also see about her computer. Same thing; emails, contacts, bank records if possible."

Rob nodded. "Got it. I'll meet with Andy DeLorey and do the handover first, and then I'm on it."

Ahearn had his pen poised over a fresh page in his notebook. "What about me, Detective? Where shall I start?"

She smiled. "Start by calling me Roxanne. Do you have anything you need to finish up?"

"No. I was shadowing Detective DeLorey, but don't have anything specific assigned to me."

"Great." She handed him a page from her notes. "We need to find out everything we can about Gretha Braun before she came to Nova Scotia. The priority is to find her next of kin. Right now, there's a family out there wondering why they aren't hearing from Gretha, and we need to put that right."

He scanned the page. "I'll start with the German Consulate, then. Do I come to you when I have anything, or do we get back together at the end of the day? How does this work?"

Roxanne looked at her watch. "Let's meet in interview room B at four for a debrief."

Gordie waited until Norris and Ahearn left the room. "Well? How're you feeling?"

She heaved a deep sigh. "A bit shaky, but otherwise OK. What did you think?"

"You were born to it. Even when Sarge threw you the curve ball of Ahearn, you didn't even flinch. Good job."

She shrugged. "I'm not quite so anti-Ahearn as you seem to be. I think he'll be good. Fresh eyes and all that."

"Yeah, but whose eyes? I just feel like he's got some kind of connection to Arsenault that we don't know about. Maybe he's a nephew or something."

"Then we'll just have to be on our best behaviour. Speaking of which, I better go see the boss. I'll come see you afterwards. Then we can make a start on setting up interviews."

***

MacLean looked up a short time later when Albright returned to the detectives' open plan area. His workstation was close to hers which meant that often one or the other would roll their chair over for a quick chat. She sat at her desk, wearing a frown.

Gordie used his feet to pedal his chair over to her desk. "What's going on? You look rattled."

She chewed her bottom lip. "At two o'clock there's a press briefing."

Gordie gestured towards the room they had used for the team meeting. "Here?"

"Yeah. He wants me beside him."

"Do you have to prepare something?"

"No. Matthew Lee is doing that."

Gordie raised his eyebrows. "Who?"

"The P.R. guy."

"Right. I've seen him around. You can relax, then. You probably won't even have to say anything. Sarge will do the talking."

She shook her head. "Inspector Lang is giving the briefing."

Gordie whistled a low breathy sound. "I shouldn't be surprised that it's the boss' boss that will be giving it. I knew it would be big. What's your role, then?"

She shrugged. "That's why I'm nervous. How do I prepare for something when I'm just supposed to stand there? I'll look like an idiot."

He smiled. "You never look like an idiot and especially scrubbed up like you are today. You'll be fine. Don't smile. Just look serious. Maybe frown a little."

Roxanne frowned at Gordie.

"That's it. You're a pro. Come on. I'll buy you a tea."

They took his car to Tim Hortons. He grumbled as he led the way in. "I don't know why I still come here now that they did away with the oatcakes."

"Have an oatmeal raisin cookie, maybe."

"Tried it. It isn't the same."

He studied the glass case and finally selected ham and cheese on a tea biscuit to go with his coffee. "I don't need lunch after this."

She laughed. "You think that now, but it's early still. By three o'clock you'll be starving."

"By then you'll need to get out anyway, so you can run out and pick something up for our four o'clock meeting."

Roxanne rolled her eyes while she waited for her green tea and cheese croissant.

They sat down and Gordie pulled out his notebook. "I've looked up the numbers for the bakery lady and the contractor, so I'll call them and set up appointments for tomorrow. I'm thinking we start with the realtor because, depending on what she has to say, we may want to go to the office as well to talk to the manager. What do you think?"

"They're all right there on Isle Madame, right?"

"The office is actually in Port Mulroy."

"OK. Yes, set up all the Island appointments first. I'm not fussed about what order we do them in. Whatever works for them, I think. What are we looking for? Any known enemies, and out-of-character behaviour, I guess?"

"I'd still like to understand more about the victim. When we met her and asked her about what brought her here, she seemed a bit evasive."

"Like she was trying to hide from someone?"

"I wouldn't go that far, but she just seemed vague. I hope these people will have known her better and can give us a feel for who she was. That might help us figure out what might cause someone so much rage."

"You figure it was spontaneous, don't you?"

"I do. They used a knife that was part of Gretha's own knife set, so they didn't go there planning to kill her."

"Unless they knew she had a perfectly functional weapon there waiting."

"True."

"They wiped down the dishwasher with one of her own towels and took it away with them."

"Again, a person's going to look pretty strange if they show up at the door carrying a towel or rag."

"I agree, but you know that some killers do have a kit with them. They might carry a briefcase or some other perfectly reasonable carrier."

She nodded. "Fair enough. I'm just playing devil's advocate. I think if you were intent on killing someone, you wouldn't leave it to chance and rely on the right knife to be there and available when you want it."

Gordie nodded. "It was someone she knew because she let them in after dark. From the crime scene photos, it looks like they had cake and coffee together."

"A friend, then."

"Certainly, an acquaintance. Not someone who stopped to

ask for directions. Another line of enquiry we need to look into is her work."

Roxanne tilted her head. "She was an art historian. Surely that can't be contentious?"

Gordie shrugged. "Maybe she discovered that some famous painting was a fake, and she was about to blow the whistle. Who knows? She had a lot of notes in her desk, but I didn't read them carefully. I took the folder back to the office and I'm going to spend the afternoon trying to make sense of it. I'm guessing, though, that if there had been evidence of a forgery, the killer wouldn't have left the documentation behind."

"OK, maybe you'll find a name to contact to get more information on what she's been working on."

Roxanne rose and stacked her mug on her plate. "Let's head back. I want to take another look at the reports just in case I'm suddenly called upon to answer something."

# CHAPTER TEN

MACLEAN RUBBED HIS EYES at 3:45 and closed the file. He had taken a break at two o'clock to stand at the back of the room during the press briefing, but Detective Albright had not been called upon. Inspector Lang had done most of the talking based on the scant information they had, with Sergeant Arsenault filling in for the occasional question. He had introduced Detective Roxanne Albright as the lead detective on the case, but when a question was addressed to her, Arsenault was quick to respond. The whole briefing took less than fifteen minutes and then the Public Relations Advisor, Matthew Lee, closed the session, promising to schedule another briefing for the next day.

Gordie met Roxanne with a cup of tea when she came out of the briefing room. "You looked appropriately solemn the whole time. Do you want one of these carrot muffins from the canteen?"

She took the proffered tea and muffin and led the way to her desk. She set the cup down and dropped into her chair. "Thanks." Peeling the paper from the muffin, she pushed her in-tray aside to make room for Gordie to perch on the corner of her desk. "There were more questions than answers there."

"Bound to be. We've only just started."

"But tomorrow we have to do it all again. That's crazy. Why did Lee have to schedule another briefing so soon?"

Gordie nodded. "We knew it would be like this. Tomorrow we'll be out of the office, so you won't have to be there. Surely Sarge doesn't expect you to be at every briefing?"

"No, it doesn't sound like it. If I'm in the office anyway, then yes. Otherwise, only when we have *significant breakthroughs*. His words."

He chuckled. "And I bet he gave you that frown along with the words to let you know he expects those breakthroughs to happen quickly."

She nodded. "You got it."

MacLean stood. "Then we better get to work. I'm learning more about art than I ever imagined I would. I'll be able to impress Vanessa with all this stuff."

Roxanne raised her eyebrows. "Anything useful to the case?"

He shrugged. "You'll have to wait for the meeting."

***

At four they gathered in Interview Room B, otherwise known as *the small meeting room* which had a six-foot white table with a round speakerphone positioned in the middle and a retractable screen, which was generally left down.

Roxanne began. "OK, what have we got? Rob, do you want to start?"

"I'm afraid I haven't gotten too far. After I cleared my desk, I went down to the tech guys. They've been working on trying to crack the password on her computer. They're running a type of software program called a dictionary attack, but not having any luck so far."

Gordie cleared his throat. "I assume they're using a German version?"

Rob frowned. "I didn't ask. But I will."

"What about her phone?"

"They're waiting for a warrant and once they get that, they'll be able to unlock it with their GrayKey device."

Roxanne widened her eyes. "Was I supposed to apply for the warrant?"

Norris shook his head. "No, I've done it. I sent it over this afternoon, but there's no one available to sign it until tomorrow. It won't be a problem. Getting a warrant after an arrest is sometimes an issue and the case really needs to be made to allow the violation of a person's privacy, but in the case of a murder victim, it'll be signed without delay."

"Sounds like we're in a holding pattern until tomorrow for those things, then. What about you, Jason?"

Ahearn straightened up and pressed his notebook open to flatten the page. "I first contacted the Honorary Consul in Halifax. I had to leave a message, but she got right back to me and gave me the number for the Consulate General Office in Toronto. I finally got a call back from an administrative person there, but when he heard the details of why I was looking for the information, he said that had to be handled by the embassy in Ottawa. He gave me a number but I had to leave another message. While I was waiting for these call-backs, I searched for Gretha Braun online and found her."

Roxanne nodded. "Well done. What did you find?"

Ahearn flipped the page. "I found a bio for her when she was the keynote speaker at a gallery fundraiser in Switzerland. She has a PhD in Art History and has worked on several important historical projects to trace the provenance of paintings, especially those found after the war."

Gordie furrowed his brow. "Dr. Braun. Wow."

Jason Ahearn nodded. "She was quite a respected expert in her field."

Albright made a note of her own. "Did you get any personal information that will help track down her family?"

He sighed. "Not a lot. I tried Facebook, but although there are piles of G. Brauns, none were for her as far as I can tell. They're pretty security conscious over in Europe, so, unlike here, you can't see photos or what their job is or other personal information. You need to send a friend request, and I wasn't about to do that."

Rob Norris chuckled. "Not likely you'd get a response."

Ahearn flushed. "No. Obviously. The one thing the bio said is that she was raised in Baden-Wurttemberg, which is a state in Germany. The capital of the state is Stuttgart, and that's where she got her BA in Art History, but then she went to the U.K. and eventually got her PhD at the University of Essex."

Gordie nodded. "No wonder her English was flawless."

Jason flipped the page. "That's the other thing the bio said. She speaks…" he shook his head and corrected himself, "spoke German, French, English, Italian, and Spanish fluently."

Roxanne waited until Ahearn closed his book. "Good work, Jason. I expect it shouldn't take long to get a next of kin once you get through to the right person at the embassy. You've got her passport, so that should help get us what we need."

Gordie smiled. "My turn. I've been working my way through the notes that Gretha had in a file labelled *Colville.*

Roxanne raised her eyebrows. "As in Alex Colville?"

He nodded. "There are a few printouts of paintings done by Colville. There's one that she seemed especially focused on." Gordie pulled out an eight-by-ten colour photo of a nude woman on a beach and held it up for his colleagues to see. "This painting is called *Coastal Figure,* and Greta took different parts of it to enlarge. It looks like the paintings are created with little dots instead of brush strokes, and it seems like she was studying that."

He put the print down. "She did the same with this other one called *Two Boys Playing.*" Pulling out another eight-by-ten, Gordie held it up. "These are well-known Alex Colville paintings, and it looks like she was comparing them to this other painting."

The third picture showed a little girl on a beach, like the other two Gordie had already held up.

Rob Norris shrugged. "How do you know it isn't just another one of a series?"

"I Googled them. In 1950, Colville started this style, moving from subjects like trains to human figures. There's a lot of information about it. This is when the world started to take him seriously as an artist and when he himself felt that he had found what he calls 'his voice'. He used a type of material called tempera on board. Apparently, it's got egg in the paint."

Ahearn picked up the picture of the little girl. "And is that what this is? Tempera?"

Gordie shrugged. "It doesn't say on the printout and since I couldn't find anything that looks like this on Google, I don't know."

Roxanne nodded. "Are there any notes about where this little girl painting is? Like who owns it?"

He shook his head. "Nothing like that in this file. There are enlargements of some parts of the painting and little notes written on them, but I can't understand them. She's drawn squares on some of them, sort of like grids with measurements, but I don't know what all that means."

"OK, anything else in there?" Roxanne pointed to the file.

"No, that's all I could make out. I sure hope the computer gives us more information about her client or where this painting is now."

Norris asked one last question. "Any idea what a painting like that is worth?"

Gordie smiled. "In 2009, *Coastal Figure* sold for somewhere around 300,000 dollars. I couldn't dig out the exact amount, but that's the figure that showed up in one article."

Jason Ahearn whistled. "If this is a lost Colville from that same era, it would probably be even more."

Roxanne bit her lip. "This might be the motive. Whoever has it doesn't want anyone else to know about it yet. Maybe it's stolen."

Gordie returned the printouts to the file. "We'll see what her email gives us, but meanwhile, I'd say we carry on with the rest of the interviews as planned."

Albright closed her notebook. "Of course. I'm going to brief Sarge, but we'll meet tomorrow morning Gordie, as arranged."

The meeting broke up with the team feeling some progress had been made.

# CHAPTER ELEVEN

GORDIE ROSE EARLY TO take Taz for a run on the beach. For a change, the wind was still, and the sheltered North Atlantic water was like glass, reflecting the bright fall colours, making the surface a bright orange-green. The white plume of the dog's tail flowed behind her as she loped along the rocky shore. Taz paused regularly to turn and assure herself that Gordie still followed. The autumn smell of decaying leaves was less pronounced here on the shore, replaced by the usual pungent salt fish tang of the sea. The blend of visual beauty and smells of the sea filled Gordie with peace and enabled him to think.

Gordie called for the dog, and Taz turned reluctantly to come to him. "Let's go home, Taz. I have a full day, starting with the realtor." They walked side-by-side back to the beginning of the trail that cut through a patch of forest leading to where he left the car on the side of the logging road.

"What do you think about Hickson, Taz? Is she capable of the sort of rage it takes to stab someone to death?"

Taz cocked one ear and looked up at him.

Gordie nodded. "Yeah. I'm not sure either, although it's impossible to know what a person is capable of when you see them in normal circumstances. It couldn't have been over a dispute about commission, though. That wouldn't do it. What about this painting thing, then? Do people kill over a painting?"

Taz left him to trot ahead as they entered the woods.

The leaves rustled and floated down on them in the soft morning air as they left the sea behind.

Taz leapt up into the back of his car and settled down for a short nap while Gordie felt energized from the walk and ready to meet with the different people who had each played a role in Gretha Braun's life.

***

Gordie saw the bright blue of Roxanne's car outside Linda Hickson's house as he drove up. She climbed out of her car and leaned against it, waiting for him to join her.

He nodded. "Mornin' How did your meeting with Sarge go yesterday?"

"Good."

"Was he all over this Colville thing?"

"No, actually. I heard him on the radio this morning. They had the briefing already, and he kept it short, just saying that there were a number of leads we're following, but he used some of what Jason found out. He said that the victim was a highly respected professional who had ties to Germany and the U.K. and that we were investigating all avenues to determine what happened."

"I'm surprised he didn't say anything more."

"He's waiting until the official notification happens so he can be more open. I think he's a bit skeptical about the link to the art world, anyway."

Gordie saw the living room curtain twitch. "We better go in. You'll take the lead?"

Roxanne blinked. "Right. Yes, sure."

Linda Hickson waited for them to knock before opening the door. "I wasn't sure you were coming in."

Roxanne ignored the sour look on Hickson's face and showed her identification. "Ms. Hickson, I'm Detective Roxanne Albright, and you've met Detective Gordie MacLean already."

Linda waved towards the forest green leather sofa and loveseat in the living room while she took the matching easy chair. She didn't offer them a drink. "I don't know what I can tell you. This has all been very upsetting for me, but I have no information that can shed any light on Gretha's murder."

Roxanne sat on the sofa, which made a *poofing* sound of escaping air, and again when Gordie sat beside her. "Often people know more than they realize. Let's start with your relationship with the victim. How did you meet her? What happened with the transaction of the house purchase? Things like that just to give us some background."

Gordie sat ready with his notebook and black pen.

Linda took a deep breath. "Gretha first contacted me by email to ask about a house I had listed."

Roxanne nodded. "When was that?"

"In March, I think."

Gordie made a note. *First contact - 7 months ago.*

Albright also made a note. "OK. After that, you communicated. Did she tell you why she was looking for a house around here?"

"She just said she had visited and found it lovely and wanted to buy a vacation home."

Gordie frowned. "Did it seem like she might be looking for a more permanent residence, or was it always just supposed to be seasonal?"

"In the beginning, it was just seasonal, so I sent her information on little cottages. The place she first enquired about was a proper home, but it sold pretty quickly, and we moved on. Then it became obvious she was looking for more than just a cottage because she sent me listings she found on different real estate sites or Kijiji." Linda shrugged. "Once I saw she was open to a proper home, I sent her better or bigger house listings. She was very cagey about her budget, so it was hard to know what to send her. It was only by her feedback that I got a better sense of what she liked and didn't like."

Gordie looked up from his notes. "She ended up finding a place on her own, though, didn't she?"

Linda pursed her lips. "I found the perfect place for her. A beautiful view with 150 feet of water frontage. Three bedrooms, two bathrooms. In good repair, but some things needed updating, so she would have had a chance to put her own stamp on it. The price was excellent. It was everything she wanted. First, she was interested, and I started drawing up the paperwork, and then suddenly, she sent me a note to instruct me not to proceed. She found a place that she liked better. When I asked her for more information so I could write up an offer, she told me she had bought it by auction. A tax sale auction. It was a done deal."

Roxanne frowned. "That takes time and lots of paperwork, doesn't it?"

"Exactly. While I had been searching for the right home for her, she had been doing all the research to buy this place by auction. She hired a lawyer. She had the title search done for liens and encumbrances. The whole nine yards. What really galled me was that she even came over to look at the place and to open a bank account in enough time before the date of the auction, so she was ready to go with a bank draft. Here was I, emailing her cheerful notes about the beautiful weather in the area, thinking she was in Germany, and she was right here, holed up in some rental place over in Guysborough, half an hour away."

Roxanne glanced over at Gordie before continuing with Linda. "That must have really made you angry."

"Damn right it did. I put a lot of hours into it and all for nothing." Her face reddened as she remembered the conversation.

"If she didn't buy the house through you, what business did you have with her then? What took you to the house that morning?"

The realtor sighed. "I had been furious. You're right, but I had it out with her as soon as she told me about the auction house. I told her about the risks, and she kept saying she understood, but she felt confident it was going to work out. She was so happy about the place, and she kept apologizing. She said she really didn't believe she was going to get the place, so felt the sensible thing was to carry on with having me look for something. She was shocked when she got it and for so little money. It was hard to stay angry with her, especially when she said she was going to use my services to get her a mortgage."

Roxanne raised her eyebrows. "I thought she bought the place with a bank draft?"

Gordie nodded. "That just pays the back taxes, right? There are still any outstanding liens, like a bank mortgage."

Linda nodded. "That's right. The mortgage had been paid off years ago, but when Jack Fraser inherited the property, he financed it. It wasn't a huge amount, but Gretha wanted to get a loan to cover the cost of paying out the mortgage plus improvements. I had a feeling that if she had to, she probably could have paid for everything with savings, but she didn't want to cash in investments if it wasn't necessary."

"So, you made up with Gretha? That still doesn't answer the question of what took you there. The mortgage was obviously in place months ago, and you must have received your commission directly from the mortgage company or bank." Albright prompted.

Hickson closed her eyes and took a deep breath. "In addition to getting the mortgage commission, Gretha had promised me a sort of bonus of twenty-five hundred dollars to cover some of my wasted time."

Now it was Gordie's turn to raise his eyebrows. "You guilted her into believing she owed you. She didn't know how things work around here and you took advantage."

Linda flushed. "She offered, and I accepted."

Roxanne continued. "But the money didn't come as promised."

"No. I don't know if someone told her she shouldn't or if she was just so busy. She never said she *wasn't* going to pay, and I just bought a new car. I needed the money."

Gordie shook his head. "You better rework your budget now."

Linda opened her mouth and closed it again without speaking.

Roxanne closed her notebook, but Gordie continued.

"This wasn't the first time you tried to chase her down for the money. When you spoke with her before, what did she say?"

"She always had other things on her mind. She was very polite and nice, and we had tea together at that damned mausoleum she bought." Her eyes widened when she realized the house had, in fact, become Gretha's tomb. "I mean, she was really making something of the place, but she didn't have the time to think about me and my issues. The contractor was always there asking about this trim or that flooring, which made it hard to talk."

Gordie continued with his thought. "When you were talking, did it seem like she had something other than renovations on her mind? Did she talk about problems back at home, or arguments she had gotten into here?"

Linda shrugged. "Gretha said that the former owner came by a couple of times and was upset that she bought his house. I told her to call the police if he became a real nuisance or if she felt threatened."

"Had she, in fact, been threatened by him?"

"It's hard to say. Like I told you, Gretha Braun was one to keep things to herself."

Gordie scrolled through his phone and held up an image of the photo of the two women. "Do you know who this is with Gretha?"

"No. We weren't really friends. I didn't know her circle."

MacLean nodded, tucked his phone back into his pocket, and closed his notebook.

"Is there anyone that you can think of that may have wanted Gretha dead?" Roxanne closed the interview with this familiar question.

"God, no. Really, she was a nice woman and while I was very upset to start with, I got over it quite quickly because she had that way about her. She went out of her way to soothe you."

# CHAPTER TWELVE

THEY SAT IN ROXANNE'S car for a few moments. Gordie looked through his notes. "What did we learn there?"

Roxanne frowned. "Not to recommend Linda Hickson as a realtor?"

He laughed. "You're right there. After listening to her, I think we're pretty safe to take her off the list. We know now why she was there and why she was cagey about it. Her office clearly didn't know about this private arrangement Linda believed she had with Gretha."

"Maybe Gretha did in fact tell Hickson she'd changed her mind. She had no intention of paying out that so-called bonus. That would make her angry all over again, wouldn't it?"

Gordie nodded. "I agree, but to where she'd kill Gretha? And then go there first thing in the morning to call it in?"

Albright shrugged. "Yeah. Seems like a stretch. I just don't like her."

"Careful. Someone might say you're biased."

She shot him a sharp look. "OK, we'll put her low on the list. You made an appointment with the contractor next, right?"

Gordie looked at his watch. "We've got about 40 minutes. Let's swing by La Goelette A Pepe, and I'll buy you a tea and a cinnamon bun or whatever."

The small coffee shop was busy, and they sat at a table outside, she with a pomegranate mojito organic green tea and he with something called Prosperity, his favourite organic coffee. She inhaled the fragrance of her tea as she broke off a piece of her bun while he buttered his cranberry scone.

Roxanne glanced around appreciatively, "What a great spot. I've never been here."

"Isle Madame is a secret haven with all sorts of treasures."

"And a killer."

He furrowed his forehead. "They're long gone. Most likely in Halifax by now."

"Do you really think so?"

He shrugged. "I don't like to imagine I have a murderer as one of my neighbours."

She nodded. "This contractor…"

"Henry Davis."

"Right. Henry Davis. What do you hope to get from him?"

"More background, I suppose. It sounds like he spent a lot of time there. He may have heard her on the phone arguing with someone or met people we don't know about. He might even be a friend after all this time and maybe she confided in him."

"OK. Why don't you take this one and I'll make notes?"

Gordie nodded, careful to keep the smile of satisfaction off his face. "It's not far from here. Do you want to leave your car here and come in mine?"

"Sure. Makes sense."

They arrived at the two-storey, blue-sided home. It was a large sprawling property backing on to a private waterfront. Well away from the main house was a black steel arched-roof garage. One of the double doors stood open through which they heard the buzz of a power saw. Gordie parked, and they walked towards the sound, but before they got there, the whining stopped and a man in his late thirties or early forties stepped out into the sunshine, brushing sawdust from his red flannel shirt. He pulled off his work glove and stretched out his hand to shake Gordie's as he approached, and then Roxanne's. "You must be the detectives."

They both pulled out their identification, and Roxanne spoke first. "I'm Detective Roxanne Albright and this is Detective Gordie MacLean."

He was handsome in a rugged way. Henry Davis wore his dark blond hair brushed upwards, in a spikey long brush cut, and he sported several days' worth of beard stubble. "I'm Henry Davis. Let's go to the house." He led the way through a side entrance. "Leave your shoes on. I'm in and out all day and damned if I'm taking my boots off every time."

Gordie stood looking out through the wide sliding doors, admiring the view of the water. "Beautiful spot you have here."

Henry called from the kitchen. "Thanks. What can I get you? Tea? Water?"

They both answered with a *no thank you*, Gordie explaining they had just come from the coffee shop.

Henry came into the living room, drying his hands and carrying a bottle of water for himself. He waved them to sit down on the dark blue sectional sofa while he sat opposite on a matching loveseat. Together with a second loveseat, the furniture created a horseshoe shape focused on the glass wall overlooking the sea. There was no television obvious in the room, although Gordie suspected that a large built-in cabinet discreetly housed it. There were pieces of artwork dotted around the room that appeared expensive.

"You're here about Gretha Braun. I couldn't believe it when I heard she was dead. Terrible thing. I'm not sure I can help you, but I'll do my best."

Gordie nodded. "Thank you." They went through the usual

identification questions and then he began. "How did you hear about her death, Henry?"

"Someone called me. Who was it now? Since the first call, I've talked to half a dozen people. I guess it was Joe Black from the hardware store who called me first."

"When did you last see Gretha?"

"Sunday. I went over late in the afternoon for a few moments."

"And why was that? What did you talk about?"

"I just wanted to let her know that I had to take a few days off." Henry paused; his head lowered for a moment. When he looked up, he bit his lip before continuing. "My dad just died, and I needed to help my sister make all the arrangements. The funeral was yesterday."

Roxanne looked up from her note-taking. "I'm very sorry to hear that. Are you all right to continue? Would you prefer we come back another day?"

Henry took a sip of water. "No. I'm fine. To be honest, my father was quite elderly, and he had a stroke a few years ago that left him quite fragile. I wouldn't say this to my sister, but quite frankly, I'm sure my dad hated the way he was. It's probably for the best."

She nodded. "But still not easy. Thank you for meeting with us."

He gulped down some more water before continuing. "No problem."

Gordie continued. "How did she seem when you saw her on Sunday?"

"She was just as always. Pleasant, cheerful even. She'd seen her friend that has a bakery and had a pile of baked goods. She offered me a cake to take with me for the funeral, but when I said it wasn't until Tuesday, she said she'd get something fresh." His voice caught. "She planned to come." He hurried on. "That's how she was. She would have come for my sake and for my sister. Just to support us, you know?"

Gordie tilted his head. "You were quite friendly with her, then. Your sister knew Gretha also?"

"My sister met her, yes. I'm not sure Gretha and I were friends but sure, I liked her. We got on."

You spent a lot of time in that house. Did you ever hear Gretha arguing with anyone?"

"No, but for one thing, I was always working with power tools, or on another floor. That place is one solid house, and if she was on the phone, it's not likely I could have heard anything. I definitely never heard her arguing with anyone in person. I'd have noticed that. But I have to say, for another thing, she didn't seem to me to be an arguing kind of person."

Gordie nodded. "What about Jack Fraser?"

"Oh yeah. I forgot about him. No one takes him seriously, though. He's just full of hot air, especially if he's been into the rum. I don't think he bothered Gretha that much. She seemed sympathetic to him if anything. More than I was."

"You were there when he came by?"

Henry nodded. "At least a couple of times."

"How serious were the arguments?"

He paused for a moment, seeming to relive the encounters. "Both times that Jack came when I was there, he'd been drinking. He was loud and obnoxious. The first time was the worst. I heard him and I was on the second floor. He stood outside shouting until Gretha went outside and I went down as well."

Roxanne looked up. "Were you afraid for her safety?"

Henry Davis shrugged. "I didn't know what to expect. I didn't really think that Fraser would take a swing at her, but you never know with someone like that."

Gordie encouraged him. "Go on. What happened?"

"We all just stood out on the front lawn. Jack was saying things like 'I'm Jack Fraser. This is my house. You have no right to it.' Nonsense like that. I tried to tell him to go home, but Gretha just held her hand up to stop me and said, 'let him speak,' so I just took a step back and it's like Jack ran out of steam then. He was ready for a fight, but when she wouldn't fight, he didn't know what to do."

Roxanne was fascinated. "What then?"

"When Jack stopped, Gretha said to him, 'Mr. Fraser, I understand how much you must care for this home. Sadly, it seems you don't have the means to look after it anymore, so now I will do so.' Something like that. She was very firm, but she didn't tell him to get lost. He grumbled some more, and she said to him, 'It's enough now. You are keeping us from our work.' And with that, she turned and went back inside. I stood there for another minute to make sure Jack wasn't going to follow her in, but he seemed deflated, and he got back in his truck. He shouldn't have been driving, of course, but I didn't call the cops. I knew he didn't have far to go."

As Roxanne made some notes to capture the incident, Gordie continued questioning Henry. "What about the second time?"

"That was just a few weeks ago. Jack wasn't as aggressive as the first time. Personally, I think he was more curious than anything else, but again, I knew by his voice he had drink in him. It was late in the afternoon, and I was sweeping up. I had been working on trim work around the windows, so I saw him drive up. I called out to Gretha, who was in the kitchen, to let her know Fraser was back. She told me to carry on with what I was doing, and she went out to meet him as he got out of the truck. I heard him. He said, 'Lady, I've been talking to the bank, and they say I can get my house back, so you may as well pack up and leave. Go back where you came from.'" Henry shook his head. "She was as cool as a cucumber. She said to him, 'well Mr. Fraser, until the lawyers tell me I no longer own this house, I will continue to stay here, and will carry on restoring the home. If you should end up with the house ultimately, you will be the beneficiary of my efforts, so you might as well leave me in peace in the meanwhile.'"

Before Gordie could ask, his partner jumped in. "Could that really happen? Could Jack Fraser get his house back after everything Gretha had put into it?"

Henry shook his head. "I asked her that, and she said no. She was very thorough and researched the entire process. Once it goes to auction, it's done. Fraser had months before it got that far to work with the bank, but he didn't. He just lived in his trailer and ignored all the notices until the bank foreclosed. Gretha told me that most of the time the lender is the only bidder at an auction like this, but she went herself in person to bid. She didn't tell me all the details, but once you are the winner in the auction, and you pay the court costs and back taxes, and then you pay the outstanding debt, that's it. You own it."

Gordie nodded. "So, like you said before, Jack Fraser was full of hot air. Aside from being a nuisance, did you ever have any sense that Gretha was worried about anything? What about money? She had you doing a lot of work. Did she pay you regularly?"

"Every two weeks. We had a list of the projects that I am... or *was* I guess, working on. I had given her an estimate for each major project, and she paid against that. If the cost changed for some reason, we talked about it and either she took something off the list, or we agreed to the new price. She had a budget. That was obvious, but I didn't ever have the feeling that she was stressing about where to find the money."

Gordie nodded. "Just for the record, where were you on Sunday night?"

"I was here at home and before you ask, I was alone. My sister called to see if I had any photos to add to the series she was putting together for the funeral home, but aside from that I watched TV."

"What did you watch?"

Henry raised his eyebrows. "I was distracted, thinking about my father and channel surfed. Watched some football and then a pre-season hockey game with the Senators. I can't for the life of me think what else."

Roxanne closed her notebook. "OK, thank you. Anything else you can think of? Did she ever talk about home? Maybe she expected a visitor or there was work there that caused her some concern?"

He shook his head. "Nothing she ever discussed with me. I can't think of any reason for someone to kill her. She was a nice lady."

Roxanne and Gordie stood, and Henry rose to walk them out. At the door, Gordie pulled out his phone to display the photo of Gretha with the unknown woman. "Did you ever see this woman?"

If he hadn't been watching Henry's face, Gordie would have missed the slight hesitation and ripple of a frown that creased his forehead before the young man smiled. "That's my sister Ellie."

# CHAPTER THIRTEEN

ROXANNE POINTED TO THE road. "Let's drive away and then pull over somewhere quiet, and we'll give Ellie Davis a call. Good of Davis to give us his sister's number, but I don't want to do it here while he's watching from the window."

Gordie had already started the engine and pulled out. He drove along Rocky Bay Road until highway 320 was in sight and then pulled off on the shoulder. This road saw little traffic, and he knew they were unlikely to be disturbed.

Roxanne keyed in the mobile number Henry had given them and put her phone on speaker mode. A woman answered on the first ring.

"Hello? Ellie Davis speaking."

"Ms. Davis, this is Detective Roxanne Albright calling and I'm here with my colleague Detective Gordie MacLean."

"Yes, Henry told me to expect your call."

MacLean looked up from his notebook and nodded at Roxanne. Henry had called his sister as soon as they left the house.

"First, let me give you our condolences on the death of your father. I'm sorry to call at such a time, but as I'm sure you heard, we are investigating the murder of Gretha Braun, and we understand that you knew her."

The young woman's voice was teary. "I can't believe it. It's just too much. First Dad and now Gretha."

Gordie had written 'station?' down and held it up to Roxanne, who nodded.

"Ellie, am I right in understanding that you live in Sydney?"

"Yes."

"Rather than talk to you now, can you come into the station tomorrow to meet with us?

"Yes, all right. I can come after school. I'm a teacher. Is four o'clock, OK?"

"That's perfect. Roxanne confirmed the address, and they signed off."

He closed his book and wrapped the elastic band back around it. "She sounded pretty rattled. Surely, she heard about the murder before Henry called her a few minutes ago?"

"Maybe, but then again, if she's been wrapped up in sorting out her father's affairs, maybe not. Whether she had or hadn't, she seems pretty upset, which fits with the photo of the two of them together. They seemed close."

Gordie nodded. "What about Henry Davis? What did you think about him?"

"He seemed genuine enough, but who knows? He's handsome. What if Gretha took a liking to him as more than a contractor?"

"Wouldn't that end up with her killing him if he rejected her? She was older than him and he may have laughed at the idea, so she'd be angry. Let's imagine she made a pass at him. Is Davis likely to be so enraged, he'd strike out at her?"

Roxanne shrugged. "Yeah. Seems unlikely, unless she attacked him, and he fought back in defense. Let's turn it around. What if he wanted more from her than just a working relationship? He was smitten, but she wasn't interested. She may have hurt his ego. She was snooty, right?"

Gordie shrugged. "It's possible. We'll keep him in mind, but he just didn't give me those kinds of vibes." He started the car again. "Now we're off to the bakery to meet with Mia White." During the twenty-minute drive into Arichat, they talked about Henry Davis a little more.

Roxanne's voice was warm when she spoke of him again. "I admit I liked him. He seemed forthcoming. It does look like he got along with Gretha."

"I think they did get along. In fact, when Vanessa and I visited with Gretha, she mentioned him because I admired some of the carpentry work. She was quite enthusiastic about his work."

"You don't think he's a serious contender, do you?"

"Probably not. The only thing was when it came to the sister. He glossed over how well Gretha knew his sister. Remember, he mentioned Gretha planned to go to the father's funeral to support him and his sister? That would have been the time to just add the fact they had become good friends."

"Maybe he didn't know?"

"Could be, I guess. That would account for the look on his face when he saw her photo."

"I didn't see that. What sort of a look?"

"It was just for a split second, but he seemed surprised."

"Do you think there was more than just a friendly connection between Gretha and Ellie?"

He sighed. "Hopefully we'll find out tomorrow, but if there was, that could provide a motive. Again, let's say one person was interested in more than a casual friendship, but the other wasn't."

Roxanne shrugged. "That happens every day, though. Imagine if every person who gets rejected turns to murder."

"True. I'd have a string of dead bodies in my past."

She laughed. "You can't fool me. You probably did the rejecting more often than you've been jilted."

"I'll take that as a compliment, even if you don't really believe it. Anyway, we'll find out more tomorrow when we meet Ellie Davis. Maybe this Mia White can even shed some light on the situation."

The bakery café was on the main street with the name *die Bäckerei* drawn in chocolate brown calligraphy above the door. Inside, the aroma of freshly baked bread with an underlying sweetness enveloped them.

Gordie inhaled deeply. "I wonder why I've never been in here."

There was a glass case to the right of them filled with pastries. On the wall behind that, two shelves filled with wire baskets of different loaves of bread made a delicious-looking edible display.

Scattered through the deep room were small wooden tables, some with four chairs and some with two. On the back wall was a double-swinging door beyond which Gordie heard voices, their sound mingled with the whirr of mixers and clatter of crockery.

A tired-looking woman wearing a white cap and coat, similar to a lab coat, smiled at them from behind the glass counter. "What can I get for you today? Coffee? Tea?"

Roxanne showed her identification. "Are you Mia White?"

"Yes. That's me." She held up a finger then. "I need to get someone to come out and look after the counter. She waved towards a back table with four chairs. I'll be out in just a moment."

They went to the table Mia had indicated. It was a quiet corner. Today's Cape Breton Post sat on the table, folded up and left behind by a patron who must have come to read the paper and enjoy the café's wares. Roxanne moved it to one of the chairs.

A young man came from the kitchen and took his place behind the counter, and a moment later Mia backed out through the swinging doors carrying a tray loaded with a large Brown Betty teapot, three mugs and spoons, a small matching brown jug of milk and a sugar pot. Besides all that, there was a plate with three large double-layered, jam-filled sugar cookies. She set the tray down. "I took the liberty since I'm ready for a cup of tea. These are Linzer cookies; almond shortbread with local strawberry jam."

Gordie smiled. "I won't say no. The cookies look delicious."

They waited as Mia poured tea into all three cups, and then they each helped themselves to the milk.

Mia took a sip and sighed. "What do you want to ask me about Gretha? I can't believe she's gone. We had become so close already." She had a hint of a German accent, revealed in the way she pronounced 'believe' as 'belief.'

This time Roxanne took the lead while her partner took notes. "Let's just confirm your details. Your name is Mia White?"

"It's Maria, but I've always gone by Mia."

"Your date of birth?"

"The fifth of September, 1977."

"How did you meet?"

"Here, of course." Mia appeared older than forty-four. She turned her head to look around the room as if searching for her friend, and the sunlight drew shadows in the creases of her face. Her pinned-up dark blond hair was streaked with grey. "From the first moment, when she came in here and spoke to me, we hit it off. It was as though she had found a long-lost relative, to find me, another German, in such a faraway place." Mia smiled at the memory. "It's refreshing to speak your first language sometimes, although I came here when I was just a teenager, so by now, my German is antiquated. English is my language now."

Roxanne nodded. "You may have known her better than anyone else, then. Did she seem worried about anything lately?"

"No. Not at all. She was happy and excited about how well the renovations were coming along."

"Did she have any arguments with anyone around here, as far as you know?"

"Not that she told me about. We were friends, but don't

misunderstand. Gretha was a very private person. She was more of a listener than a talker."

"Did she talk about home at all? You had that in common with her. Can you tell us about her family in Germany, or any worries she may have had about something there?"

Mia topped up her tea as she considered the question. "I did ask her, of course, but she wasn't inclined to talk about her home very much. She was an only child of a single mother, who died last year. I don't think her mother had much money, and lived in a rented flat, so there was no estate to inherit. She has a cousin that she was fond of, although I'm not sure they had seen much of each other in the last few years. She spoke of the woman, Ida, more in the context of her childhood. Ida has siblings, but I only heard Gretha talk about this person and what fun they had when she went to stay with the family during school holidays."

"There was nothing more recent? Business worries, perhaps?"

"No. I might as well tell you." Mia glanced around to ensure no one was within earshot.

They all leaned in a little.

"I told you Gretha was a good listener. I told her my own worries about keeping this place running. My husband, Mickey, is very keen for me to sell it. He would like to use the money to upgrade his boat and equipment."

Roxanne raised her eyebrows. "But you don't want to sell."

Mia shook her head. "No. This place is everything to me. I love being here, but Mickey wants me home. It's not just about the money. He doesn't like me here."

Roxanne nodded. "So, how does this connect with Gretha?"

She licked her lips before answering. "Gretha came up with a good solution. It was my birthday not long ago, and she presented the idea as a gift. Such a kind, wonderful gift. She offered to buy a half share of the business. She loved baking, but more, she was a businesswoman. She looked at my books and decided it was a good investment. She said that it was the perfect solution because Mickey could have his money, but I was to stay on and run it just as I always have." She looked around the room again. "I created this place five years ago. We never had kids, and I needed something for myself. At first, Mickey was fine with it, but over time, he didn't like how much time it took me away from home."

"When was this business arrangement to take place?"

Mia swallowed, her eyes filling with tears. "She already had a lawyer drawing up the papers. Any day now we expected she'd have the documents for me to sign and then she was going to give me a certified cheque. She intended to make the payment out in my name, and I could then give as much or as little as I wanted to Mickey. I know what she was saying. She didn't have to say it out loud, but she thought I should just leave him."

Gordie tilted his head. "That sounds extreme just because your husband wanted you to spend more time at home. Is there something else?"

She chewed her top lip before answering. "Once in a while, Gretha saw I had bruises I couldn't easily explain. She never asked, but I know she saw them."

Roxanne exhaled loudly. "Gretha sounds like she was a true friend to you and wanted the best for you."

"She was. But now that's all done." Mia brushed her knuckle under her eyes.

Roxanne nodded. "Mia, we have to ask. Did Mickey know about this plan?"

Her eyes widened. "No. Absolutely not. I never spoke about it. If he knew, he would have…" she hesitated before finishing with, "told me."

"We'll need to talk to him, Mia."

"Oh, God. Do you need to tell him about the plan? He'll be angry."

Roxanne rested a hand on Mia's arm. "He won't hear it from us, if we can possibly help it."

Gordie nodded. "But why do you believe he'd be angry? He was going to get the money he wanted. Maybe he would have been very supportive?"

"No. He likes to be in charge. If there was a chance to sell the place, he would have expected to be involved and do the negotiations. He wouldn't have agreed to keep me on as manager."

"Fair enough. Where can we reach him, Mia?"

She gave him a phone number and gathered the empty mugs on the tray.

Roxanne nodded to Gordie's phone. "One last thing. We have a photo to show you and wonder if you can tell us anything about the woman in the photo with Gretha."

Gordie opened the photo and held up his phone for Mia.

"Yes, I've met her. She's such a nice girl. Younger than Gretha and me. We were only a couple years apart, but Ellie, that's her name, Ellie, is a bit younger. They became great pals, though." Mia smiled. "Ellie took her places to show her around, and Gretha always seemed to have fun with her." She touched the screen of Gordie's phone when the screen darkened to bring it up again. "I never made her laugh like that. I'm glad she had Ellie as a friend."

"This is a delicate question." Roxanne hesitated. "Do you think there was more than just friendship between them?"

Mia frowned, and then Roxanne's meaning dawned on her. "You mean as in some kind of sexual relationship?"

"Yes."

"Oh God, no. I don't think so. I mean, I don't know for sure, of course. Like I said, Gretha was very private, but when someone likes a person in that way, there are always little signs, aren't there? A little touch, a secret smile, whatever. I never saw any of that, and they came here together quite a few times."

"OK, thank you. That's helpful." Roxanne handed the woman her card. "If you think of anything else, please call me. Feel free to call me, even if you just want to talk. I can be a good listener too." She smiled at Mia White and then they rose to go.

# CHAPTER FOURTEEN

THEY BARELY GOT IN the car when Roxanne growled. "This Mickey guy sounds like a real peach."

"Yeah. Do you think he knew that Gretha had cooked up this plan with Mia? Would he really be that angry if he did, to want to kill the woman?"

She shrugged. "There are men like that. It isn't just about getting what he wanted with the money. He wants to control his wife. That's the main point. So, if Gretha was giving Mia support with a plan that didn't include him, he might have gotten very annoyed. Maybe he goes over to let Gretha know he isn't having it, and she stands up to him. She won't allow him to bully her, and he loses it."

Gordie nodded. "It's possible. Let's go find out. Give him a call and find out where he is."

Mickey White was at home. It took them only a few moments to drive to the outskirts of Arichat to the White family home. The house was a typical Cape Breton home; one and a half storeys with a steep roof. Two small windows upstairs and two matching windows downstairs on either side of an enclosed doorway that most likely led down to a root cellar. The main entrance was on the side through a small, enclosed porch.

He was outside repairing a lobster trap when they drove in. He straightened up and nodded to them by way of a greeting.

Roxanne held up her identification as she walked toward him. "Mr. White?" When he nodded again, she continued. "I'm Detective Roxanne Albright, and this is my colleague, Detective Gordie MacLean."

Mickey White was stocky, about five feet nine inches, with a mop of unruly grey-brown straight hair that needed a good wash and trim. He had a beard and mustache that may have been intentional or may have been a result of not being in the mood to shave for a week or two. His wide forehead had lines carved between his eyebrows that hinted at a perpetual frown. He wore a faded dark green work shirt with a rip under his right arm.

Gordie put away his identification after showing it to White, and he and Roxanne followed Mickey into the house. White steered them into a cramped living room. Stairs leading to the second floor took up space at one end. A faded brown sofa, two easy chairs in different hues of taupe, along with a large television completed the décor. White sat in an easy chair, Roxanne took the sofa and Gordie took the last chair.

Roxanne perched on the edge of the sofa. "Mickey, can I call you Mickey?"

Mickey shrugged. "Everyone else does."

"As I explained on the phone, we're here as part of our investigation into the death of Gretha Braun. I understand you knew her?"

"Hardly at all."

"But you met her several times, I think?"

"I met her a few times." He corrected.

"Right. Was this at the bakery or did she come here, or perhaps you went to her home?"

His frown deepened. "I never went to her home other than to

drop Mia off once. Mia's car was in the shop and she and the woman were doing some baking together one afternoon."

Gordie wrote down: *Knows where the victim lived.*

"OK. And was she ever here?"

Shrug. "Yeah, I think so."

"So, you must have spoken to her a few times, then. What did you think of Gretha?"

"What do you mean?"

"Well, did you like her? Did you find her interesting?"

He shook his head. "Can't say I liked her or didn't like her. She was a foreigner, and I didn't have much to say to her."

Roxanne raised her eyebrows. "A foreigner? Your wife is also from Germany, Mickey. Do you think of her as a foreigner, too?"

Mickey's face reddened. "Mia grew up here. She's Canadian."

"All right. Mia and Gretha were good friends, though. Even if you didn't have much to say to Gretha, your wife did, didn't she?"

He nodded. "They were always yakking together. I didn't pay attention."

"Did you ever feel like Mia spent too much time with Gretha?"

Shrug.

"Was Gretha a bad influence on Mia?"

This time he scowled. "You could say that. Mia and me got into more arguments since she started hanging out with Gretha. I think that woman criticized me behind my back, and it was making Mia think less of me."

Gordie noted: *Resentful/jealous of the friendship between Mia and Gretha.*

"That must have made you mad. Did anything else about their friendship bother you?"

"Like what?"

"Mia mentioned that you'd like her to sell the bakery. Is that true?"

Mickey seemed confused by the change in subject. "I think we'd get a good dollar from selling it. She's built up the business and now's the time to take the money and reinvest it. That's just a good business decision. But what's that got to do with anything?"

"Maybe nothing. We're just trying to get a full picture of the relationships that Gretha had, so that includes with Mia and with you."

"Relationship? I didn't have any kind of relationship with that woman."

"I'm sorry. I didn't word that very well. I just mean we want to talk to everyone who knew Gretha."

He folded his arms across his chest. "I don't know what else I can tell you. She was my wife's friend, and maybe I didn't like her that much, but I didn't have much to do with her, so it doesn't much matter, does it?"

"Based on what you knew, or what you may have been told by your wife, can you think of any reason why someone might want to kill Gretha Braun?"

"No. I didn't know enough about her life to say, and Mia said nothing. Maybe she pissed someone off with her stuck-up ways."

"Is that how she seemed to you?"

"That's how she was. She had a great education, and she obviously knew I didn't, and it showed on her face whenever she talked to me."

"One last thing, Mickey. Where were you last Sunday night?"

"I was right here. So was Mia. We watched a Netflix movie."

"Do you remember what the movie was?"

"*The Harder They Fall*."

"OK. I think that's all for now." She looked over at Gordie. "Anything to add?"

Gordie closed his notebook. "No, I don't think so."

"Thank you for your time." Roxanne stood up and handed over a business card. "If you think of anything to add, feel free to call me."

Mickey took the card, but Gordie saw that he immediately crumpled it in his fist. Roxanne made her way to the front door and Gordie lingered, pulling out one of his own cards, he laid it on the armrest of his chair. He shook his head at Mickey. "Strong women. Think they rule the world, don't they?"

Mickey smirked and nodded. "I don't know how you put up with it."

Gordie sighed. "Not easy sometimes, but what can you do? There are times I feel like going outside and kicking something."

"I know what you mean. Mia used to be a nice, quiet woman before that one got in the middle."

"Did Gretha interfere with things, you figure?"

"Course she did. Couldn't help herself."

"Like what? At the end of the day, Mia came home to you, so how could Gretha interfere?"

"Made Mia mouthy. Can't abide that."

"Right. Well, I better get on before my partner gives me an earful. Great meeting you. Anything comes to mind, give *me* a shout." Gordie nodded down to where his card lay on the chair.

"Right you are." Mickey picked it up and tucked it into the breast pocket of his shirt.

*** 

Roxanne sat in the car with the door open, slamming it shut when Gordie climbed into the driver's side. "Well? Get anything useful after I left the room?"

Gordie shrugged. "He's an angry guy and sure didn't like Gretha. Apparently, she inspired his wife to be *mouthy*."

"Heaven forbid a woman should be allowed to speak her mind."

"He certainly didn't confess anything to me about being violent with his wife, but he thawed out a bit. If we need to follow up with him, I think he trusts me."

"Well, that's something. What do you figure, though? Can you see him going over and having it out with Gretha?"

Gordie started the car. "I can. Yeah, he may not have intended to kill her, but I suspect that if someone riled him up, he'd have it in him."

\*\*\*

It was close to four o'clock when Gordie returned Roxanne to her own car. "Do you want to come to the house, and we can go through things?"

"I better get home. I have a call with Sarge at five and I'd like to be at home to take that with my notes in front of me."

"Fair enough. I'll write up my reports and shoot them over to you before loading them into the system. Call me if there's anything you need after your call with the boss."

They parted ways, Gordie deep in thought about the interviews they had gone through during the day, wondering which, if any, of those people were a murderer.

# CHAPTER FIFTEEN

ROXANNE HAD SPOKEN WITH Sergeant Arsenault and gone through the updates. He wasn't thrilled to know there was no real breakthrough, but realistic enough to know it was early days yet. She had completed her reports and sent the drafts over to Gordie for a second look before entering them into the system. Nana had one of Roxanne's favourite meals in the oven, but the cheesy chicken and mushroom casserole needed another forty-five minutes to bake.

Roxanne changed and called out before leaving. "I'm going for a run, Nana."

"All right. Be careful." Nana's voice floated through the house from the kitchen.

Before she started running, she punched in the number for Eddy. When he answered, she adjusted her ear buds, slid the phone into the pocket on her sleeve, and started to run. "Heya. Are you OK to talk?"

She heard the smile in his voice. "Yup. We went to a chimney fire, but back now at the station and cleaning up."

"Anything serious?"

"No. Just the usual at this time of year. People start up their woodstoves or fireplaces without getting someone in to clean the chimney. In this case, there was a nest up there. Lots of smoke, but nothing serious."

"That's great." She paused, waiting for him to ask how her day was going.

"Are you out running?"

"I am. Just a short run while supper is cooking."

"I thought you'd be too busy with the big case."

It wasn't quite the enthusiastic interest that she anticipated, but it was enough. "We spent the whole day on Isle Madame interviewing people. Tomorrow I'll be back in the office. Did you see me on TV yesterday?"

"Were you on TV?"

"Just in the background during the press conference. Inspector Lang and the PR guy did all the talking, but still. I was there. Nana saw it."

Eddy changed the subject. "I miss you, baby. Will you be able to come out to Port Hood on the weekend?"

Her rate of breathing increased, and she found herself panting. She pictured her boyfriend's beautiful dark eyes and full lips. His soft laughter was like music in her ears. "I hope that heavy breathing is for me?"

She took a deep breath in through her nose and out through her mouth. "I'm panting because I'm running up a hill." She was glad he couldn't see the flat stretch of road in front of her.

He laughed again. "OK. I'll let you finish your run. I'll call you on Friday and see what the plans are."

"OK. Take care. Eddy?"

"Yeah?"

"I miss you too."

They never said words like *love*. It was too soon for that. Most of the time, they kept things light and easy, but Roxanne cared about this man. She had since their first encounter. That's when she saw him in action as a volunteer firefighter on the last big case she and Gordie had worked on. At times, she felt it was time to move the relationship on to something a little less casual but didn't know how to bring that about.

Somehow, she felt a little let down that he hadn't asked anything about how the case was going. *He probably thinks I'm not allowed to talk about it.*

Roxanne focused on her breathing and pace as she sprinted the last stretch back home. Nana would make up for Eddy's lack of questions by wanting to know every detail and Roxanne trusted her grandmother to keep everything she heard to herself.

***

Both Roxanne and Gordie were in the office early the next day. She had already updated the board with a couple of bullet points for each interview they had conducted.

Gordie had his travel mug and perched on the corner of the table, sipping his coffee. "Don't forget to write down that Gretha was going to buy out half the business."

"Right, thanks."

She wrote it down and then stepped back to review the notes.

Gordie stood and picked up a red marker. "Let's boil it down to a plausible motive for each of these people to make it easier to prioritize."

She nodded and moved to sit where he had been.

Gordie went through the list and wrote beside each name:

Linda Hickson: money

Henry Davis: ? (love?)

Jack Fraser: jealousy

Mia White: ?

Mickey White: control-freak

Ellie Davis: ? (love?)

Art client: money

A German? Money?

He set down the marker. "We'll find out about Ellie Davis today, but as it stands right now, I think we need to take a closer look at Mickey White and Jack Fraser. Let's start by calling Mia to see if she verifies Mickey's alibi."

Roxanne looked at her watch. "I'll do that. She's probably at the bakery right now."

"OK, and after the briefing, I'm going to give Floyd Sanders a call. He's the farmer that owns the land Jack Fraser has his trailer on. I want to see what he knows of Fraser's behaviour and whereabouts on Sunday night."

They left to make the most of the half hour before the morning briefing.

Rob Norris had arrived and taken a seat in the briefing room when Roxanne returned. He held up his hands in a gesture of *where is it?* "Detective Albright, I'm disappointed. You used to bring us donuts. Now you're a boss, you don't have time anymore?"

She smiled. "I expect the underling to bring the snacks, Detective Norris. You let me down."

By now several other detectives had filed into the room and good-natured laughter targeted Norris.

Norris grinned. "Next time, boss."

The room quieted when Sergeant Arsenault entered the room and walked to the front to study the board. He nodded and turned to Albright. "OK, where are we with this?"

Gordie stood back a few paces from the front, ready to step forward when Roxanne gave him the sign.

Roxanne gave a brief update of the interviews they had conducted and then called on her team one by one to update the group on their progress.

"Detective Ahearn, have you heard back from the German embassy?"

Ahearn stood to respond. "I did. I've got a next of kin name now. It's a cousin who lives there in Germany by the name of," he studied his notebook, "Ida Zimmerman. She lives in Frankfurt. I called the City Police of Frankfurt and they agreed to go right out and make the official notification." He sat down.

Roxanne nodded. "Well done. Do you have an actual phone number for her?"

"I do."

"Excellent. I hope she speaks English. We'll want to talk to her."

Arsenault nodded. "At least now we can release the details about the victim to the press. They've been howling for information. I'm amazed the victim's name hasn't made it into the papers yet."

Albright pointed to Rob Norris. "Any progress on the phone records or computer?"

Norris opened a manilla file folder. "Luckily, she bought a phone here and signed up for a plan, so I've gotten her phone records for the past month here. It would have been a pain to try and get this from overseas. They're still working on the computer." He smiled wryly in Gordie's direction. "They had been running software to break her password, but it was an English version. They got a German version late yesterday and they've started again."

Roxanne shook her head. "What do the phone records tell us?"

"Nothing jumps out at me so far. There were no calls late on Sunday evening, I'm afraid."

Gordie nodded. "Meaning her killer didn't call her ahead of time to say they were coming over, unless it had been prearranged a day or two ahead of time."

Norris nodded. "I'm going through the numbers now to put names against them. There are a lot of long-distance numbers from all over the place. U.S., Germany, Vancouver, the U.K."

Roxanne tapped on the bullet for 'Art Client,' on the white-board. "Call them. Find out which one she was working with right now. Give Jason half of them. He has all this international calling experience now."

She turned to Gordie. "Anything from the farmer in regard to Jack Fraser?"

He shook his head. "No answer." Gordie turned to the other detectives to explain. "I'm hoping that the owner of the land on which Fraser has his trailer parked will have seen Fraser on Sunday. We have yet to interview Fraser, but I wouldn't mind knowing ahead of time if anyone saw him that evening."

Roxanne pointed to Mickey White's name. "I spoke with Mia this morning. She said that Mickey was home, and they did start watching a movie, but she was tired and not interested, so she left him to it. She had a bath and went straight into bed with a book. She fell asleep before he came in and has no idea what time he came to bed." She smiled with satisfaction. "So, no confirmation of his alibi."

Putting the pen down, Albright turned to her boss. "Anything you'd like to ask or add, Sergeant?"

"No. Come and give me an update after lunch. And be here for the press briefing at two o'clock."

"Right. That's it, then. Jason, can you shoot me the phone number for the cousin? We'll want to talk to her as soon as possible to find out what she knows about Gretha's life, both here and at home. What time is it there right now?"

Ahearn looked at his watch. "They're five hours ahead. It's a little after three in the afternoon."

"Will the police have made the notification by now?"

Jason looked at his phone to check his emails. "They have. The duty sergeant said he would let me know, and yes, I have a note here from him."

The detectives went back to work, leaving Gordie and Roxanne alone in the briefing room.

Gordie raised an eyebrow. "Ready for a tea?"

"God, yes, but I don't really have time to run out. I'll have to stick the kettle on here, and then I want to call the relative of Gretha."

They made do with an instant coffee for him, and Roxanne used one of her own King Cole teabags to make a cup of strong tea which they took to Interview Room B to use the speakerphone in privacy.

Roxanne dialed the number. "What if she doesn't speak English?"

He shrugged. "Then it'll be a short conversation."

A woman's voice answered with a crisp, "Zimmerman."

"Mrs. Zimmerman, this is Detectives Roxanne Albright and Gordie MacLean calling from Nova Scotia, Canada. Do you speak English?"

"Yes. Not excellently, but enough to understand. Please call me Ida."

Gordie made a mock swipe gesture across his forehead in relief.

"First, please accept our sincere condolences on the loss of your cousin Gretha Braun. We were very shocked by her death. My colleague here knew her personally."

"Thank you. Yes, it is very shocking."

"I'm sorry that we are calling so soon after you just found out the news, but we want to pursue our investigation as quickly as we can to find the person who did this terrible thing."

"I understand, but I don't know how I can help you."

"Ida, when did you last hear from Gretha?"

"I had a short note by email from her just last week. She seemed so happy."

"Did something special happen to make her happy? A business deal, perhaps? Or a new friendship?"

"She didn't say much. She sent me photos of her house. She said I must come to visit when the work is complete."

The catch in Ida's voice was clear, and Roxanne waited for a few seconds to allow the bereaved woman time to compose herself. "Did Gretha say anything else in that note or previous ones about any problems she had?"

"No. She said nothing about problems."

"I see. Nothing to do with her work or any of the people she met here?"

"Nothing. No problems. Only she seemed happier than I've ever known her. She was usually very serious. Since she was there, she seemed... lighter. Can you understand?"

Gordie spoke for the first time. "This is Gordie, Ida. I met your cousin and yes, she seemed rather serious. We found a photo of her, though, with a friend here called Ellie. In the photo, she's smiling, and I understand exactly what you mean when you say *lighter*. I think the word describes her mood very well."

Roxanne nodded and took over again. "Ida, did Gretha ever mention either Mia or her husband, Mickey White, to you?"

"Ah, yes. Mia was a German woman, no? She and Gretha baked together, I think."

"Yes, that's her. Did your cousin mention any difficulties with the husband?"

They heard the frown in Ida's voice. "No. Is this the man who killed her?"

Roxanne spoke quickly. "We don't know that, Ida. We're just exploring all the possibilities right now." She looked at Gordie and shrugged, at a loss for where to go from here.

Gordie continued with the questions. "Will you be going to her home? Do you have a key?"

"I do not have a key, but I know she has a neighbour that does. That woman always waters Gretha's plants. I suppose, yes, I must go and make some sort of arrangements. I can't think what to do with everything."

"When do you think you will go?"

"Not this week, certainly. I will try next Sunday. I must find her address book and start letting people know." Ida sighed. "She knew many people."

Gordie tried to make his voice sound casual. "Ida, do you know who Gretha's beneficiary is?"

When she didn't respond right away, Gordie took a breath to explain what he meant, but then she spoke. "The last I heard; it was me. I was to benefit from her death. Gretha told me this several years ago, and perhaps she changed her mind. I didn't want to speak of it. I didn't want to know."

Roxanne widened her eyes at this revelation and waved at Gordie to continue.

"Thank you for your honesty. We know this is difficult. When you go to her home, please look for her will or the name of her lawyer who will have the up-to-date information. Also, when you go, can you please see if there are any documents concerning a painter named Alex Colville? Perhaps there is a file there with information about a business client, or research. And of course, if you see anything else that might help us figure how who did this or why this happened, please let us know. Can you please give us your email address? I will send you a note with our contact information to make it simple to reach us."

They heard tears in Ida's voice now. "We were once so close, but when she moved away and I had my family, things always got in the way of us spending time together. I should have made the effort. Life got in the way, and now...death is in the way."

Ida gave them her details and, with further murmurs of how sorry they were for the family's loss, Roxanne disconnected.

Roxanne looked glum. "Aside from the will, which may or may not still be the case, I had hoped we'd get some clue from her, but we're no further ahead."

Gordie tilted his head. "I'm not so sure about that."

# CHAPTER SIXTEEN

ROXANNE THOUGHT ABOUT WHAT Gordie had said when she quizzed him on what he meant. He suggested *Gretha was lighter. She was happy. We need to figure out what made her so happy. Maybe something changed. Somewhere in that is the motive that led to this killing. And I bet it isn't just a house that made her happy.*

He might be right. Roxanne knew that and hoped that Ellie would unlock the secret this afternoon.

The team was busy with their assigned tasks and Roxanne took the time to craft a one-page summary of what they knew to hand over to Sarge. Her stomach churned when she saw how little was really on it. *How did Gordie do this without getting an ulcer? Eddy's right. I'm out of my depth.*

Thinking about Eddy made her stomach churn even more. The strong tea she had consumed earlier coated her throat. Roxanne went to the vending machine in the hallway and bought herself a juice box. Stabbing the straw through the small foil-covered hole in the box's top, she considered telling her boss she felt overwhelmed. Lost in thought, it took her a couple of moments to realize Gordie leaned against the wall with his arms folded across his chest, a few feet away, studying her.

She started and then took a long sip of apple juice to cover her confusion.

"What's up?"

She shook her head. "Nothing. Just thirsty."

"Hmm. You were deep in thought there. Want to talk about it?"

She shrugged.

"Come on outside for some fresh air."

Roxanne followed him without argument.

He stood in the October sunshine and took a deep breath. "God, I'd love a cigarette. It was always a great excuse to come out here and get some fresh air."

She laughed. "Not very fresh anymore once you add cigarette smoke."

He smiled. "Probably not. It was always a pleasure, though. At this time of year, anyway. Not so much in February. So, what were you thinking about up there?"

After another long sip that finished the juice box, she sighed. "I think you're better at this than I am. There. I've said it."

Gordie studied her for a moment. "What's brought that on? You're doing fine. People respect you. You ask the right questions, so what gives? Did someone say something? The boss, maybe?"

"No. No one's said anything. It's just that I feel lost. I don't know where to go next. When *you're* the lead, it feels like you always know the next step without, I don't know, without thinking about it."

He laughed. "We all just fumble around in the dark, Albright. The case reveals the next step as you move along. Like today. You spoke with the cousin. OK, she didn't tell us anything that solves the case, but you can tick it off now and move on to the next thing. You'll cycle back to Norris and Ahearn and see what they're getting out of the phone blitz. I got a hold of Floyd Sanders and he tells me that Jack Fraser was acting erratic all weekend. Remember, I ran into him in the hardware store, and he shouted at Gretha? According to Floyd, he was drinking a lot. Tomorrow, I intend to run Fraser to ground and question him. See? This is a slow process. There's no easy or clear path."

She nodded. "I guess I'm just not as confident as you are."

"You'll get there."

"Thanks, Gordie. I appreciate the support. I'll meet up with you tomorrow to meet this Jack Fraser guy."

"You sure? No weekend plans?"

Roxanne shook her head. "Nothing more important than this."

*** 

At four o'clock Roxanne heard that Ms. Davis had arrived. She told Gordie and went to fetch Ellie while he gathered his file and notebook and went to the interview room. Roxanne brought the woman in. She was about five foot, seven inches tall and had a slim build. Her white turtleneck sweater accentuated her long, elegant neck and her straight chestnut hair hung in a long bob parted off-centre to hang just above her shoulders.

After introducing Gordie, Roxanne asked if Ellie wanted a hot drink or water.

When she nodded and asked for water, Gordie went to fetch it, returning to sit beside his partner, facing Ellie.

Roxanne started the recording equipment and began. They went through the preliminaries, confirming her legal name of Eleanor Davis, her age of 37 and her address in Sydney.

Roxanne's voice was gentle and kind. "We were very sorry to hear about the recent death of your father, Ellie. I believe he was ill for some time?"

Ellie frowned. "That's the thing. Yes, he had a stroke two years ago, but he'd been getting both physio and speech therapy and seemed to be making such progress. I just saw him two days before he died, and he was so upbeat."

Albright nodded. "When we spoke with your brother, it sounded like your father was still somewhat frail, though. I think sometimes people rally and the result can be misleading for their loved ones."

"*Pfft.* I love my brother, but aside from the usual Christmas and birthday celebrations, he never went to visit Dad, so I wouldn't take his observations as gospel."

Roxanne raised her eyebrows but then hastened to steer the discussion to the matter at hand. "It's been a lot for you, with your father's death and then the added shock of losing your friend so soon after."

The girl fished out a tissue from the sleeve of her sweater before answering. "I just can't believe it." She dabbed at her eyes as she tried to blink away tears. "When Henry first told me, I thought he'd got it wrong. It just doesn't seem possible."

Roxanne slid the photo of Gretha and Ellie across the table. "It looks like you were good friends."

She picked up the photo and smiled despite the tears sliding down her cheeks. "I think we were. Sometimes you just meet someone that you click with, you know?" She set the photo on the table but kept her hands on the edges, framing the picture with her fingers.

"Tell us about her, and your friendship. You met through your brother, I suppose?"

Ellie looked up. Her eyes were less teary, and she seemed to draw comfort from contact with the photo. "Yes. I went to see the house when he was working one day. He had asked Gretha if it was all right and she was fine with me seeing it. I often do that when Henry is working on a big project. He does such nice work. I'm proud of him." She smiled, her earlier criticism of her brother forgotten.

Gordie nodded. "I met Gretha and she talked about Henry's work when I commented on it. You're right to be proud. He's obviously a true craftsman."

"Oh! You knew her. That's so nice to know. That you met her and that she talked about Henry. He'll be pleased about that."

Roxanne nudged the woman again. "You went to see the house and you met Gretha. When was that?"

"I can't say exactly. Early summer. Henry had been working there a month or so. He told me about the floor upstairs that he'd refinished. It has these chevrons made of two kinds of maple. So pretty. Gretha took me around herself and we just talked and talked. We had coffee and cake while Henry worked upstairs and somehow by the time I left, we were friends."

Picking up on what she had said, Roxanne continued. "What did you talk about? Do you remember?"

Ellie frowned. "No. We've had so many conversations since then. I don't remember anything specific."

"OK, what about more recently? Did she give you any sense that she was worried about anything? Afraid, even?"

Her finely shaped eyebrows raised. "Afraid? I don't think that was in her DNA. But no. She never in all the time I knew her, talked about anything worrying her. In fact, just the opposite. She seemed delighted to be here and she said she felt that she had found her true home. She just loved everything about Cape Breton. She went for long walks, not just on Isle Madame, but she made it her mission to explore Cape Breton and even over on the mainland. She was familiar with Halifax because she'd been there before, but she planned to go on a trip to explore down towards Barrington Passage and then around to Wolfville. So, no. If she was worried about anything, she didn't share it with me."

As Roxanne looked at her notes for a moment, Gordie stepped in. "Did she talk about her work at all?"

A small smile. "She did. She had a great passion for art. It wasn't just a job for her. I'm smiling because my dad loved art too. You wouldn't think so because he made his living as a mechanic. He had two garages in Port Mulroy by the time he decided to retire. Even when he was still a mechanic, he used to say that what he did was a form of art. He wasn't doing the actual mechanics himself by the end, of course, but still, the day came when he wanted to be free of the responsibility. Henry wasn't interested so he sold up, and then he and Mom did some travelling, mostly to visit galleries. Mom could have lived without quite so many, but she went along for his sake. He invested in art as well. We have a Maudie at home you know, along with several other good pieces."

Gordie paused to give her the pleasure of her memories before bringing her back. "When Gretha talked about her work, did she talk about her latest project?"

Ellie blinked as if struggling to refocus. "You mean about the Alex Colville?"

# CHAPTER SEVENTEEN

ROXANNE FELT GOOSEBUMPS ON her arms when Ellie so casually mentioned Alex Colville, hoping this was the breakthrough they were looking for.

"If that's what she was working on most recently, then yes. What can you tell us about the job?"

Ellie frowned. "Not a lot. She was excited. I know that and we took a trip to Halifax, especially to go to the Gallery of Nova Scotia to look at a couple of Colville paintings on display there."

"Did she explain why she was excited?"

"She said she was working to authenticate a painting that a private collector had."

Gordie couldn't help himself. "And did she?"

"Did she what?"

"Did she authenticate the collector's painting as a Colville?"

Ellie shrugged. "I didn't hear. As far as I know, she was still working on it."

Roxanne shifted in her chair, leaning forward. "When was the last time you heard her talking about the work?"

"Oh, not for a couple of weeks now. Even then it was just something in passing, like 'I'm tied up on Sunday with work.' Nothing more."

"Did she talk about her client? The name of the person or where they lived? Had they ever had in-person meetings?"

Ellie shook her head helplessly. "She wasn't one to talk like that. When we were together, we chatted about things like what she remembered about school versus what I remembered. Stuff like that. She loved to compare experiences. Or likes and dislikes. You know, music, poetry, art. Or food. We both enjoyed going to the bakery her friend owns. The difference was Gretha enjoyed baking and I don't. I'm not even much of a cook." She smiled. "I enjoy eating though, so it worked out."

Roxanne tried a different tact. "Where else did you go together?"

The young woman sighed. "She went with me to visit my dad. She came a couple of times. She was so kind and thoughtful to do that, wasn't she?"

Albright smiled. "Yes. That was kind."

"I think it really bucked my father up to see a new face. The first time we went, I had to go out of his room to talk to the nurse for a few moments and when I came back in, she was holding his hand and he was smiling this big, goofy grin." Ellie smiled. "My Mom always said he had an eye for lovely things, including women. She wasn't jealous, though. They were so close."

Roxanne glanced at Gordie who nodded to encourage her to ask the difficult question. "Ellie, it's obvious you grew quite close to Gretha in a short period of time. We see in this photo of the two of you together that you both seem very happy."

Nodding, Ellie touched the photo again. "This was a really nice day. In fact, this was taken after her second visit to my dad. She was in a great mood and so was I. My father seemed so much improved. Gretha had said a few words in German to him and he seemed to understand. His speech was still hard to make out, but I think he said *Liebchen.*" She laughed softly. "He could say 'sweetheart' in about five different languages. Yes, that was a nice day."

Roxanne bit her bottom lip before continuing. "Ellie, was there more between you and Gretha than just friendship?"

Ellie tilted her head. "More?"

"Were you lovers?"

The young woman flushed, the white of her sweater contrasting with her skin. "Good God, no. We were friends. That's it."

"Did it ever feel like one of you may have wanted it to be more than friends?"

"Certainly not. I had a long-term boyfriend that I broke up with last Christmas, and I wasn't in any rush to get involved with someone again. I can give you his name and number if it is relevant to Gretha's death, but I can't see that it is."

"Are you sure that Gretha didn't harbour feelings for you that way?"

"I never got that vibe from her, and she certainly never put any moves on me. Are we just about done here?"

In the pause, Gordie spoke up. "We are just trying to get a complete picture of Gretha and the people she interacted with. I'm sure you want to help find whoever did this?"

"Of course. I really don't have anything else I can tell you, though."

Roxanne went back to her list of questions. "Did she speak of anyone from home that may have come to visit? Any problems that may have followed her here?"

The flush faded from Ellie's face. "I don't think so. She had a cousin that she hoped would visit, but as far as I know, nothing had been arranged. I never heard her speak of any problems at home. Gretha was a woman who seemed very much in charge of her own life. She knew what she wanted and went after it. I admired that in her. She inspired me."

"Did she talk about Jack Fraser?"

"Was that the guy who had the house before her?"

Roxanne nodded.

"She mentioned him. He came out to the house a couple of times. She seemed a bit sorry for him that he lost the house, but at the same time, she was critical of him. She didn't have a lot of time for people who, through their own doing, were down on their luck. She believed that people create their own destinies."

"What about the husband of her friend, Mia. Did Gretha mention him?"

Ellie hesitated. "Gretha told me he was a brute, but she seemed immediately sorry she said that to me. She asked me not to repeat it to Mia."

Gordie made another note in his book. "Did she tell you why she thought he was a brute?"

"No, but she didn't have to. I've seen bruises on Mia's wrist despite her trying to wear long sleeves. We both saw them, and when we left the coffee shop that day, Gretha said it. She was driving and it was like it slipped out unconsciously. I just said something like 'I agree, and don't worry, I won't say anything.'"

Gordie continued. "Do you know if she ever encouraged Mia to do something about changing her situation?"

"I don't know for sure. Gretha said it was something Mia needed to work out for herself, but she had an idea that might give Mia more options."

"OK, that's helpful. When would that have been?"

"Several weeks ago. She never mentioned it again, and we've been back several times for coffee or lunch. Nothing seemed any different to me, but Mia seemed happy enough, so maybe the bruises were a one-off."

Roxanne closed off their interview with Ellie Fraser. "Just for our records, where were you on Sunday night, Ellie?"

Her voice was cold. "I was at home, sorting through photos to give to the funeral home to prepare for Dad's funeral. No one was with me, but Stevens and McCauley Funeral Home in Port Mulroy can verify that I sent them the photos first thing Monday morning."

"Thank you." Roxanne slid a business card across to Ellie. "If anything occurs to you that might be helpful, however insignificant it may be, please call. Gretha Braun was a newcomer here and she didn't deserve this. We need to do all we can to figure out what happened."

Ellie Davis picked up the card and in exchange took one last look at the photo of her and Gretha before sliding it back to Roxanne. "You're right. She was a smart, kind woman who wanted nothing more than to fit in here and make it her home. I'm sure that eventually, she would have moved here permanently. I'll miss her." Her eyes welled up again as she stood to go. "I'm sorry if I was short with you. I just feel overwhelmed with everything that's happened over the last couple of weeks."

Both Gordie and Roxanne also stood, and he reached out to clasp Ellie's arm. "That's completely understandable. Are you all right to drive, or do you want us to call you a taxi to go home?"

"I'll be fine. It's only a few minutes from here. Tomorrow I'll go down to Isle Madame but tonight I'll go home to my own apartment."

Gordie escorted Ellie out and walked her to her car. By now it was already dusk, and the autumn evening held a damp, misty feel that chilled a person to the bone.

She stopped to shake his hand before getting into her small red Kia. "Thank you. You've been kind. If I think of anything helpful, I'll be sure to let you know."

He nodded. "We may contact you again with further questions."

Gordie watched as she drove into the darkening night and sensed her loneliness.

When he returned, Roxanne stood beside Norris' desk listening as he spoke and pointed to the phone records on his desk.

Gordie joined them. "What's up?"

Norris grinned. "A man named Robert Wilson who currently

resides in Vancouver, but who is originally from Waverly, Nova Scotia is the mystery man."

"The art collector?"

"Yup."

"And? What does he have to say for himself?"

Norris shrugged. "He seemed genuinely shocked to hear about Gretha, but he didn't have time to talk as he was just running to a meeting. We have a phone call set up for tomorrow morning." Norris looked up at Roxanne. "I assume overtime is approved?"

"Yes. I talked to the boss earlier. No worries there. He's very keen to see progress."

"OK. The boy-wonder" Norris nodded to Jason Ahearn who was listening "and I will come in here tomorrow. According to the techies, they should have a copy of the victim's hard drive available for us tomorrow morning."

"Great stuff." Roxanne looked at her watch. "Go on home now and we'll connect tomorrow. Gordie and I are going back to Isle Madame tomorrow to talk to the former owner of the house, and I want to go back to the scene again."

Gordie followed her back to her desk. "Anything, in particular, you're looking for at the house?"

"No. I'm just getting a better sense of her now and I feel there may be something there that we didn't catch the first time around. You said it yourself. Gretha was happier. Why?"

# CHAPTER EIGHTEEN

GORDIE CALLED VANESSA ONCE he was on Route 4 on his way home. "Hiya."

She seemed out of breath. "Gordie, hi. How are you?"

"I'm OK. Did I catch you at a bad time?"

"No, not at all. I just came in from planting tulips along the back walk. I'm not as young as I used to be and being down on my knees for an hour was maybe a little more than I should have done."

Gordie made a mental note to ask his sister about those gardening knee pads he once heard her talk about. *Is that a suitable Christmas gift? Or is it not romantic enough? Jeannie will know.* "It'll all be worth it in spring when they come up."

She laughed. "You're absolutely right. Are you finished work for the weekend?"

"Finished for the day. Albright and I are getting together tomorrow. A couple of the others will be in the office as well."

"Ah. Well, can I make you some supper tonight? Or would you prefer just a quiet night at home?"

"I'd like a quiet night with you if that's ok. So yes, a homemade supper would be great. Shall I go by home and pick up Taz and come to yours?"

"That sounds great. I've got a nice piece of whitefish I can panfry with some small potatoes and a salad. How's that sound? It's all very easy and won't take long, so I can wait to start cooking until you get here, so just take your time."

"Perfect. I'll see you in a bit."

Gordie thought about his relationship with Vanessa. They had come a long way from their first meeting when she found a skeleton in her garden. They had gone through some bumps along the road, mainly because he always felt he needed to protect her or look after her, but he now understood that's not what she wanted from him. Sometimes he still felt the compulsion to shield her, but so far, he always managed to recognize what he was doing and stop himself before he dug himself in too deep.

As he drove past the turnoff for Big Pond Beach, his mind turned to Roxanne Albright. It was in this pretty spot of Big Pond that she lived with her grandmother, a feisty woman named Helen. In theory, Roxanne lived there to look after Nana, but Gordie understood that in truth they looked after each other. Now, there was also a golden retriever named Sheba in the mix. They had gotten the young dog, not quite a puppy anymore, during the Covid isolation time to give Helen some company in the absence of her beloved card clubs. Now the clubs were back up and running, but Helen found plenty of time to walk the dog, loving the excuse to take her to the beach for a daily romp.

It wasn't Helen that Gordie mulled over now. It was Roxanne. She was doing fine as lead on the case and Gordie wasn't as upset about it now as he had been at first. He didn't feel as restricted as he had expected. No, it was more how she seemed in herself that had him worried. *She should be more excited and energized by this opportunity. Something's going on. I thought it was Sarge, but maybe not. It's me he dislikes, not Roxanne. I can't believe something's going on with Nana or the dog. She'd tell me. That only leaves Eddy.*

Eddy Tomah was the volunteer firefighter who had responded in the spring when Gordie had been in trouble on their last case. He was smart and gentle, and Gordie supposed he was a nice-looking young man. Eddy and Roxanne had become friends and lately, they'd been seeing a lot of each other. *So, what's wrong? Maybe he wants more than she does? Roxanne's a lot like Vanessa. Pretty independent. Should I have a word with him and explain that?* He sighed and decided he'd better try to get more information than just a feeling that she was down. He may be completely off-base.

***

Roxanne was also thinking about Eddy as she drove home. She had met with Sarge one last time before leaving the office to give him the latest updates and to confirm that the team would all be working on Saturday. She tried to focus on the case, but now her mind wandered to her boyfriend. She knew he wouldn't be too happy that she'd be working on Saturday. There was a televised concert of *The Men of the Deeps* scheduled to be shown at the Legion in Port Mulroy tomorrow night. There were limited tickets because they were still only running events at half capacity, and Eddy had two. She probably could still make it after working with Gordie, but it would mean driving back and forth from Isle Madame to home, and then from home to Eddy's place in Port Hood and from there to Port Mulroy and back. The idea of it all was exhausting. *I guess I can take a change of clothes to Eddy's and go straight there after Isle Madame. That's the sensible solution.* She sighed aloud. *I'd rather just spend the evening at home.*

She considered calling him now but decided that the service was sometimes in and out along here, so she'd wait. *I'll call after supper and then make up my mind.*

***

It was close to nine o'clock when Roxanne called Eddy. "Hi, Eddy."

"Hey, babe. I wasn't sure I'd hear from you when it went past eight o'clock."

"Sorry. I went with Nana to take Sheba for a walk. It's such a nice evening out and who knows how many we'll get before the weather turns rotten."

"No worries. It's good to get out and clear your head. So, how're things going?"

"All right, I guess. I had a few minutes there today that I felt a bit lost. I wasn't quite sure where we go from here because there's nothing obvious that has jumped out yet. Everyone liked her, she didn't have any obvious problems or arguments. That kind of thing."

"I can imagine it's overwhelming. I'm still surprised they don't have someone more senior leading the investigation."

Roxanne heard the defensiveness in her own voice. "I talked it over with Gordie and he's just as baffled as I am, but he said this is how it always goes. We just move forward step by step. If he or one of the other team members have some great insights, I'm open to hearing it."

"Whoa, Rox. I didn't mean anything. I'm sure you're doing the best you can."

Roxanne took a deep breath to calm herself. "Eddy, I better tell you now that I'm working tomorrow."

"Damn. I was afraid of that. You'll be finished in time for the show though, right?"

"I'm not sure. Rather than take a chance, I think you should find someone else to go along with you."

"It's not until eight o'clock. You won't be working that late, surely?"

"You're right. I'm sure I won't be out interviewing or whatever, but Gordie and I and maybe even the rest of the team might decide to do some brainstorming, and I don't want to cut it short. There's a lot of pressure on me to make some progress on this, Eddy."

His voice held irritation. "I knew this would happen. I thought we'd have a nice weekend. I was planning to make a curry dinner and then the night out and then back here. A nice relaxing Sunday morning. Maybe go out for breakfast. That's what I imagined when I bought those tickets. You're my girlfriend, Rox. I don't want to go with someone else."

"Eddy, I'm sorry. Really, I am. Under any other circumstances that sounds like a perfect weekend, but just like I wouldn't begrudge you if we were together and you suddenly were called out for a fire, you can't begrudge me now. I'll make it up to you when this is all over, I promise."

"By getting a big promotion and working even more hours, probably."

"People don't get promotions from one case, Eddy. I've got a long way to go before that happens. Come on. Don't be mad."

She heard the sigh. Was meant to hear it. "Fine. I'll see if Dennis wants to go along. He's a big fan. Maybe I'll just give him the tickets. The fun's gone out of it now."

Roxanne swallowed. "Well, I'll leave that to you. There'll be other shows. The curry sounds good too and I'll hold you to that for another time."

"Yeah. OK. Well, it's late. I want to go for a run tomorrow morning."

"Good night, Eddy. Send me a text tomorrow and let me know what you decided about the tickets. If you're home, I can call you tomorrow night."

"Sure. Bye, then."

She hung up and blinked tears from her eyes, second-guessing herself. *Why didn't I want to just go after work? I know it won't be a late night.*

Sheba licked Roxanne's bare toes and she leaned down to caress the dog's silky ears. She went into the kitchen and called out to her grandmother who was watching a musical reality show in the living room. "Nana, I'm making hot chocolate. Do you want one?"

"Oh yes please, sweetheart."

The idea of watching mindless television with her grandmother while drinking hot chocolate was just the tonic she needed.

***

The next morning Roxanne rose early, took Sheba and went for a run along the Big Pond Beach. The wind coming off the Bras D'Or Lakes was gentle but brisk enough to coat her lips with salt. She came home, had a shower and when she came down, she saw that Nana had cooked a mushroom and cheese omelette for her.

"Nana, you shouldn't have gone to the trouble. You know I'm fine with cereal and a banana."

"You have that every morning. You deserve a cooked breakfast on the weekend even if you are going to work."

Roxanne leaned in and pecked her grandmother on the cheek as the older woman handed over the plate. "You're the best. Thank you."

She felt better after a good night's sleep. The run and breakfast helped put her in a positive mood as she drove to MacLean's house on the North-East shore of Isle Madame. *I'll call Eddy later and make it up to him. I won't go out there, but he'll understand.*

Parking on the road in front of the house, Roxanne left room for Gordie to pull out. *He'll want to drive.*

The front door opened as she walked up the driveway and Taz came bounding out to greet her. The big white dog aimed her nose for a strong poke at Roxanne's crotch, but Albright was ready for her and put her hands down and clasped the dog's head to caress her. "Oh no you don't, madam. No snotty prints on my pants, please."

She let Taz go and followed her into the house. "Morning."

Gordie called from the kitchen. "Want a cup of tea before we head out?"

"No, thanks. Nana made me a massive breakfast and I need to let that settle." She glanced around the kitchen. "Are you just out of bed? I can't remember when I've ever come in and not smelled coffee."

Gordie smiled. "I'm not home long. I had breakfast, but not here."

"Ah. Vanessa was busy spoiling you."

"How do you know I didn't make the breakfast?"

"Did you?"

"No. But I could have."

Roxanne laughed. "Of course. OK, tell me the plan. Do we just drive out to this trailer of Jack Fraser's or have you told him we're coming, or what?"

"No, I haven't told him. I think the element of surprise is more effective. We'll go there first. I suspect he's not an early riser, but even if he isn't there, we can stop at the house and ask Floyd if he knows where Jack is."

Gordie settled Taz with a cookie, and they left. "Want me to drive?" he asked.

Roxanne smiled. "Sure. Sounds good."

They bumped along a rough track, coming to rest beside a dirty white and tan trailer.

Roxanne shook her head. "Wow, flashbacks to the 70s. I can see why he'd be upset living here instead of that nice house."

"Don't kid yourself. This was his choice. The house was way too much work for him."

The door opened and Jack Fraser stepped out, peering into the car. Gordie and Roxanne climbed out, Roxanne holding up her identification.

Jack nodded and folded his arms across his chest. "What do you want?"

Gordie pulled out his notebook and pen. "We need a few minutes of your time. You know me, but you haven't met my colleague Detective Roxanne Albright before."

Jack Fraser nodded but remained planted in front of his trailer. "Hey."

Gordie stepped closer. "Can we come in and sit for a minute, Jack?"

"It's a bit of a mess."

"We don't mind. We're not here to check your housekeeping skills."

Fraser shrugged and turned to climb back into the trailer with the two detectives following.

The front of the trailer contained a table with benches on either side. Above the table a wide pine shelf with a rail had been built and held a clutter of books, Tupperware and small cardboard boxes. Nearby a fairly new three-burner propane cooktop with a glass fold-down top was installed in a length of counter space with cabinets built in below. Beside that there was a small vintage refrigerator. Across from the fridge and stove was the sink. Deeper along the trailer was a futon and television. At the end of the narrow hallway, Roxanne saw a bed filling the full width of the trailer, and she presumed that between the bedroom and kitchen there was a small bathroom.

Albright slid into the bench on one side of the table. She moved the dirty dishes to one side, so they weren't right in front of her. "This is more spacious than I was expecting. It's cozy."

Gordie took the spot beside her and left Jack Fraser to take up the place across from them.

Jack looked around, as if seeing his home through the eyes of a stranger. "I did a lot of work when I first bought it. Replaced the stove. Built in the shelf above here. Things like that."

Gordie nodded. "You did a good job."

Jack thawed a bit, his face relaxing when he realized they weren't going to insult his home. "Thanks. So, I guess you want to talk to me about that lady that stole my house?"

Roxanne took over as Gordie prepared to take notes. "Gretha Braun. Yes. You heard she was murdered?"

"It's all over the news. I live in a trailer, not a cave."

"You were quite angry with her for taking over your house. You went to see her to harass her about it on more than one occasion."

"It's a free country. I'm allowed to express my opinion."

"What did you hope or expect would happen by harassing her like that, Jack?"

He shrugged. "Maybe I hoped she'd just give up and go back to wherever she came from."

"And then? She bought your property. You couldn't just move in, even if she had left."

Fraser frowned. "She didn't buy it fair and square. I never got any money for it."

"Ahh. You wanted to pester her enough that she'd give you money to go away. Was that the plan? It was never really about the house or wanting it back."

He ran his hand through his shaggy mop of dark unkempt hair. "I should have gotten some money when she bought it. That's the normal way of things."

Gordie shook his head. "But Jack, if you had just sold the house before the bank took it, you would have gotten money. I'm sure you know all this."

Jack clenched his fist. "Things got away from me. I'm sure that never happens to the likes of you, but for some of us, life isn't always a walk in the park."

Roxanne tried to soothe the man. "You ran into some trouble and because if it, the bank foreclosed. After a time, they auctioned off the house and Gretha bought it. OK. I understand all that. It's the past and I get it. So now, you saw this newcomer fixing up your old house and you thought she had lots of money and you wanted some of it, so you came up with this plan to make a general nuisance of yourself. First, you tried just bothering her at the house, but that didn't get you anywhere, did it? So next, you started bothering her in public. Detective MacLean told me about how you confronted Gretha in the hardware store last weekend. You shouted at her, you made her feel threatened. In other words, you escalated your campaign, didn't you?"

Fraser toyed with a dirty teaspoon, pushing it back and forth between his hands. "I guess."

"Did you hope she would just offer you money without ever having to demand it from her? You knew there'd be a fine line between legal 'expressing yourself' as you call it, and illegal threatening and blackmail behaviour. But she didn't do that, did she? She never said to you 'what will it take to make you stop this?' did she? She was a strong woman who just saw you as an irritation, but not enough of a nuisance to pay you."

He continued to study the spoon silently.

Roxanne looked at Gordie and raised her eyebrows, looking for confirmation that she should continue.

He nodded, took out his phone and opened the app to record their conversation. "Jack, we're going to record our discussion, just so there's no confusion in the future about what you say today. So far, you've admitted that you felt Gretha Braun owed you something since she bought your old house by auction, and you didn't get any money from that transaction. We talked about a campaign that you waged against her, whereby you hoped she would give you some financial compensation in exchange for you to end your harassment."

Fraser looked up. "Those are your words. I didn't say that."

"Do you deny it?"

Jack frowned and chewed his lip. "You make it sound worse than it was."

"OK, we're agreed on the general situation. Let's move on. Detective Albright, you were asking some questions."

She continued. "On Saturday you confronted her in public. Detective MacLean intervened and took you for a coffee after you accosted Ms. Braun in the hardware store. What happened after that?"

"Nothing happened." Fraser pointed at MacLean. "He made me

nervous when he read the riot act to me. Told me to stop bothering the lady, and I did."

"Simple as that? You didn't follow up to see how effective your escalation tactics had been? I find that hard to believe, Jack. You created this ruckus in a public place, and you had seen for yourself that she was more rattled than when you'd been shouting at her at the house, so why wouldn't you go see if you had softened her up enough for the final push? Doesn't make sense."

"Believe it or not, as you like."

"Where were you last Sunday night?"

Jack frowned. "Is that when she was killed?"

"You just told us you've been following the news, so you know that. Don't play the innocent now."

"I was here at home with a bottle of rum and the television."

"What did you watch?"

"Sunday night football."

"Who was playing?"

"Bills versus Chiefs."

"Who won?"

"Bills." He grinned. "I won twenty dollars, so I was celebrating."

Roxanne pursed her lips. "You spent a lot of time hanging around your old house, watching Gretha. Did you see anything that might be helpful in finding out who did this? "

Jack visibly relaxed. "That real estate lady was there as much as me. I heard her going on at Braun one day. She wanted money too. I'm not the only one. Everyone figured she was a cash cow. Even that contractor Henry. He acted like her great protector, but it was obvious he was fussing around taking forever with his tinkering. Probably got paid by the hour, so he was going to drag it out for as long as he could."

"Did you ever hear Gretha argue with him? Questioning how long it took for the work?"

"Nope. I wasn't standing there listening at the window or

anything, but that doesn't mean it didn't happen. I know the real estate lady wanted money because one day the two women were out on the front lawn talking and I was around the side. They didn't know I was there. I heard Braun say something like *'you don't need to remind me of my own words. I will pay you as we discussed, but right now I need to manage my budget.'* That's why I know it was about money."

Roxanne nodded. "We'll probably be in touch again Jack, but that will do for now."

He opened his hands to splay them in front of himself. "You know where to find me."

When they got back in the car, Gordie spoke as he navigated a small bumpy circle to drive out along the track again. "What do you think? His alibi isn't solid, but it has a ring of truth to it."

"I think it would be a simple matter to know who won a football game after the fact. I think he wanted money and after all his efforts, he wasn't about to give up that easily."

# CHAPTER NINETEEN

THE DRIVE TO HERITAGE House took only a few moments. Roxanne had the key and after letting themselves in, she locked the door again to keep curious neighbours from entering.

Roxanne stopped in the kitchen. "I want to look in every nook and cranny. I don't know what we're looking for, but there must be something in this place that will give us a clue about the person she argued with. You don't just kill someone without some lead-up, unless it was a stranger, but I don't think that's likely, do you?"

Gordie shook his head. "No. No one took anything as far as we can tell. Maybe that's a good point, though. No one's been in the house. Maybe we should get someone to come through to confirm that. Ellie or Henry. Maybe the neighbour or Mia. Someone who spent a lot of time here would know if it was something obvious. A valuable piece of art, maybe?"

"That makes sense. Who should we ask?"

"I say Ellie. In my opinion, she is the least likely suspect and she said she was coming here for the weekend, right? Maybe she's here now and could run over."

"You have her number?"

"Yup. I'll give her a call now, shall I?"

"You do that. In the meanwhile, I'll start going through the kitchen."

Gordie went into the living room and made the call before coming back to find Roxanne holding a small notebook.

Roxanne looked up. "Did you reach her?"

"She said she'd come right over. I'm going to get a blanket or something to cover the blood in the other room. It might be just a little less upsetting for her."

Gordie went upstairs and took the comforter off the bed in the smaller second bedroom, took it down and laid it over the stain on the floor.

He went back to the kitchen. "I don't know if that helps or just draws even more attention to the spot she was killed."

"I don't think it can look any worse than a big blood stain. It's not like Ellie will forget what happened here."

"True. What have you got there?"

Roxanne sat down at the kitchen table and lay the book down. "Gretha jotted notes down in it. Phone numbers, dates, and little reminders. Look here." She turned the book to face Gordie where he had taken the seat across from her.

"What am I looking at?"

"It looks like where she was trying out different names for the house. See? On one side in German, I assume, and the other is the English."

Gordie looked at the list with words written and lined out.

| | |
|---|---|
| *Familienheim* | *Family Home* |
| *Heimat* | *Home* |
| *Haus des Glucks* | *House of Happiness* |
| *Erbe Haus* | *Heritage House* |

"Interesting. It's clear she loved the place. House of happiness. That's nice too, although I think she made the right choice going with Heritage House. We talked about the name and the sign she had done up. Vanessa noticed it."

"What did she say about it?"

"I don't remember much. Not a lot. Just that she felt it must have had a great history as a family home and I think she wanted to honour that history with the name. Something along that line."

Roxanne flipped the pages. "She met Mia regularly by the look of this. *Mon lunch w/Mia, Sun baking M. Get apples.*"

"Any names or appointments with people we haven't talked to yet?"

She turned three more pages and then the rest of the pages were blank. "No. She's got the phone number for the pharmacy. The hardware store." She closed the book and stood to return it to the drawer in which she had found it.

Gordie sat watching as she went through each drawer, pulling out utensils, linens and small gadgets, and then, just as she started on the upper cabinets, they heard a car pull in.

"Will I go through the house with her, or do you want to?"

"No. You go ahead. I think you have a rapport with her. I'll carry on going through everything. We should arrange for someone to come in and clear out the perishables. It'll be a while before the cousin organizes anything, I guess."

"That's a good thought. Shall I ask Ellie, or maybe the neighbour?"

"Anne White seemed to be friendly. It might be better if we ask her. It might be too hard on Ellie, and let's face it, she isn't completely in the clear yet, so let's not leave her here unsupervised."

"OK, I'll leave it to you." He went to the door to let Ellie Davis in.

Ellie was already blinking back tears as she stepped inside.

Roxanne touched her arm. "This will be hard for you. We're very grateful that you are helping us like this."

"I'm sort of glad to do it because it gives me a purpose to be here and go around the house. As I was driving up to Isle Madame this morning, I dreaded even going past the house. This will serve to tear the band-aid off fast if you know what I mean."

"I do know what you mean. Detective MacLean will go around with you."

Gordie nodded. "We want you to look around each room and tell us if there's anything missing. We're talking about major things that might be worth stealing."

"Worth killing for, you mean."

"Yes, I guess I do."

Ellie glanced around the small kitchen. "Nothing obvious here. Everything looks the same." She shook her head. "Everything's the same, but everything's different."

Gordie nudged Ellie forward with a gentle hand on her back. "This will be the worst for you. Try not to dwell on the tragedy. Think instead of the nice times you shared here with your friend."

Ellie took three steps and then stopped. She put her hand over her mouth as she stared down at the bright sea-green comforter laying on the floor. "Oh, God. That's where…"

"Please look around the room Ellie." He pointed to a set of shelves built around the fireplace. "The shelves look rather empty. Was there anything of value there when you were last here that isn't there now? Even if it didn't seem of great value, perhaps there was something that might have value for someone even if it wasn't monetary."

Ellie forced herself to look where he pointed. "No. Gretha was a minimalist. She didn't go for clutter, so it always looked like that."

"OK, good. We know she was into artwork. Was there any piece of art hanging in these rooms before that isn't here anymore?"

She did a slow scan around the entire room. "No, nothing."

"Let's go upstairs, then. You're doing so well."

He encouraged her again with a touch on her back to move to the staircase.

At the top they went room by room, starting with the master bedroom. Ellie lifted her shoulders helplessly. "I was only in here once, and that was when Gretha gave me the tour that first time. If anything's missing, I wouldn't know for sure, but nothing jumps out at me."

One room was still in the midst of renovation. Empty of furniture, cans of paint stood against one wall, and the new drywall taped and sanded, looked incongruous in the old house. Ellie nodded. "Henry talked about this room. There had been water damage through the ceiling, so everything was ripped out and replaced once the roof was repaired. They were still discussing whether Henry should replace the flooring or refinish it."

They both looked down at the floor in silence. The old wooden floors had been painted previously, but now were bare in patches, showing the wear of years of hard usage.

She dabbed at her eyes with a wadded-up tissue she had been clutching since she arrived. "Who will make the decision now?"

Gordie didn't respond but steered her into the last room. He waved his hand across the span of the floor in this room. "This is my favourite room in the house, I think. This floor is spectacular, isn't it?"

Ellie nodded. "I never saw anything like it. Why would they spend all this effort to create a chevron floor out of maple in a bedroom? Why not the living room?"

"One day perhaps I'll ask the former owner, Jack Fraser."

The room was quite empty of furnishings again, except for a desk in front of the window, and an old-fashioned wheeled, swivel office chair. The wooden chair had spindles in a classic captain's-chair style, but with an oxblood red leather seat and back.

Ellie frowned and looked around the room.

"What is it?"

"I was here last week. This is where she had her computer."

"Yes, I'm sorry. I should have mentioned that we took that."

"Did you take the big accordion file thing too?"

Gordie frowned. "We took a few manilla file folders from the antique desk downstairs, but there weren't any files here."

"It was a big, black plastic thing that looked like a box with a handle but then when you opened it up, inside it was an accordion folder. That's where she kept most of her stuff. I think the files downstairs were just for quick reference things, but she kept most of her work and other important papers in this portable filing cabinet. That's what it was like. Probably fifteen inches wide because she kept legal size documents in it, and it opened to be, I don't know, maybe twenty inches or something. I don't know what all she kept in there. She was very private. She brought me up here last week because she wanted to show me something on her computer. She was considering buying a used car. She leased the one in the driveway, and she thought it might make sense to buy one and keep it here. I said she could park it at our place when she went away since we have garage space."

"She brought you up here and that file box was here at the time?"

"Yes, but she quickly closed it before I even came near, and she put it on the floor beside her desk."

Gordie walked around to the other side to be sure there was nothing there. "Let's do a quick walk around the house again in case we didn't notice it the first time. Maybe it's in the living room somewhere."

Ellie shook her head. "I would have noticed because it would be out of place, but sure, I'll look again."

They went around the house again, and this time Ellie carefully avoided looking at the spot with the covered bloodstain. Gordie walked her to her car and as she was getting in, she stopped. "Did you hear about the memorial?"

"No. Tell me."

"Some of her neighbours are organizing a memorial reception for Gretha for Monday evening over at the Legion. I'm taking the day off work so I can stay for it. I'm sure you'd be welcome if you want to come."

"Thank you. That's very kind. Of course, I'll be there."

When he came back in the house, Roxanne was waiting, perched on the edge of the kitchen table. "That's it, then. Someone killed her for whatever was in that file box."

"It sure looks that way. Now we need to figure out what was so important it was worth killing for."

# CHAPTER TWENTY

ROXANNE WENT HOME KNOWING that it was early enough that she could easily have changed and gone to Eddy's place, but glad she had cancelled. She wanted time alone with her thoughts. She had stopped at Gordie's place long enough for two pots of tea, a piece of home-baked-by-Vanessa ginger with rum cake and a video call with Norris and Ahearn.

Robert Wilson, the art client, had proven elusive. The scheduled call hadn't taken place, Norris' calls going straight to voicemail. They had more luck with the computer, though. The tech team had provided each of them with a copy of the hard drive, and Rob Norris was going through the documents and photos while Jason Ahearn was sifting through the emails, with Google Translate open in a browser to help him make sense of what he was seeing.

Roxanne had told them to call it a day. "We're done here for now, and you guys go on home as well. It'll be there on Monday morning, waiting."

She had yet to call Sarge with an update. but she'd do that when she got home, after making some notes.

Nana wasn't home. The radio played classical music softly to keep Sheba company, and Roxanne took a few moments to enjoy the peace of her home as she caressed the golden retriever and gave her a treat. When she'd gathered her thoughts and Sheba was out in the yard so she wouldn't bark and disturb the call, Roxanne phoned Sergeant Arsenault.

His clipped voice always intimidated Roxanne. "Arsenault."

"It's Detective Albright here." She said that even though she knew that *he* knew before answering the phone that it was her.

"Yes, what have you got?"

"I think we've made some progress today, Sergeant."

She took a breath to begin, and he barked "you think?"

"We have. We have made progress." This time she hurried on to tell him about the interview with Jack Fraser and the confirmation that Ellie Davis had provided about the missing file box.

"This Fraser character. He sounds like he had means, opportunity and maybe motive. You believe he wanted to get money out of her, but when he didn't get anything willingly, he killed her and took the files, maybe hoping to find pin codes or whatever to her bank?"

Roxanne hadn't thought this side through yet. "Well, maybe. Or he wanted to get his hands on the house deed papers. You hear of scams all the time about people selling houses that they don't own."

"Right. What's your next step, then?"

She licked her lips. "I want to bring him in for a formal interview."

"That's a start. Cozying up to him in his trailer isn't going to get him to talk."

Roxanne had a sudden thought. "I think we should get a search warrant for his trailer to see if he's got the file box. We should include any outside storage area that he might have on the farm itself. His trailer is pretty small. He might have a room in the farmhouse or a locker or something."

"You need to be specific. Find out from the farmer if Fraser has any stuff in his house or a barn or wherever. If he has a locker, you need to find that and then get a warrant. Include his vehicle in this warrant, though."

"Yes. Very good. I'll get on this first thing Monday."

"Good work, Detective. MacLean behaving himself?"

"Oh yes, Sergeant. No issue there."

"Monday, then."

He was gone before Roxanne had a chance to say 'have a nice weekend.'

Buoyed, she called Eddy. "Hi, hon. How's your day going?"

"Probably not as good as yours by the sound of you. Did you catch the killer, then?"

She laughed. "No, not quite but we are getting somewhere, so that's a good thing."

"I've given the tickets away now."

"That's fine. I'm sorry, I still wouldn't make it, no matter what. I have all my reports to complete from the day and I have some prep work to do for Monday morning. I could come up tomorrow though, if you like."

"Sorry, babe. I've got plans now. I assumed you were too busy to see me, so I'm meeting a couple of the guys and we're going up to the Margaree River for some fly-fishing."

Roxanne tried to keep the disappointment out of her voice. "That sounds great. It's supposed to be a nice day tomorrow. OK, well, have a nice day. Bring back a nice fat salmon and we'll do it up on the barbecue next week."

"No guarantees."

She laughed. "Of course not."

"I mean no guarantees there'll be anything left. If I get a good one, I'll probably take it over to the folks. My mum loves her poached salmon."

"Fair enough. Give me a call tomorrow and let me know how it went."

"Sure. Will do."

She hung up and wandered into the backyard where Sheba was busy digging a hole under the big blue spruce tree. "Oh, Sheba. No!" Picking up a yellow tennis ball Roxanne tossed it the length of the yard. The dog streaked to the back to snatch it up and run with it in her mouth around the yard several times before settling several feet away and dropping it.

Roxanne shook her head. "You're a great chaser. Not so great at bringing it back though, are you?"

They went back in together, and after making a cup of green tea, Roxanne settled at her computer to do her work.

*** 

Gordie arrived at the station before eight o'clock on Monday morning. He gave a cheerful wave to Roxanne who was already busy typing. He hung up his jacket and walked over to her desk. "Good morning. Do anything nice yesterday?"

She looked up, with a deep frown etched on her forehead. "Sorry, what?"

"Just wondering if you and Eddy had a nice day yesterday. Great weather."

"Yeah. Great weather for fly-fishing with his buddies. I stayed home and caught up on my laundry."

"Ah. What are you up to? You're hard at it already."

"Finishing off the form to get a search warrant for Fraser's trailer."

"What? Did I miss something?"

She shook her head. "You know everything I know, and in my opinion, it's enough to get Jack Fraser in here for a formal interview and to search his trailer. I thought he may have some stuff stored somewhere else on that farm; in the house or barn, but I talked to the owner yesterday and he says no."

Gordie crossed his arms across his chest and stared at Roxanne. He looked up and nodded as Rob Norris came in and called out a *good morning* greeting.

Roxanne stared back at Gordie for a moment and then looked back at her screen.

"What's going on?"

She kept typing. "What do you mean?"

"I mean normally we'd talk about something this big first. Figure out if all the ducks are in a row. Go through all the evidence that would prompt a move like this. What happened between the last time we talked on Saturday and now? Did Sarge put you up to this? Don't let him bully you into making a move before you're ready."

Roxanne stopped typing and stood up to face him. "No one bullied me into anything. I'm not you, Gordie. I get along just fine with the boss."

He flushed and saw Rob Norris swivel in his chair to look at them.

"So, without any pressure or discussion, you just decided to apply for a search warrant. Anything else?"

"Yeah. I called Fraser this morning and told him to come into the station for a formal interview." She looked at her watch. "He should be here at ten o'clock. While he's here, I hope to have Norris on the scene with a uniform out of Port Mulroy to execute the search warrant."

Gordie stepped back. "You figure Jack Fraser will actually come in?"

"I know he will. As I told him, he can come voluntarily, or I'll get the Mounties out of Arichat to pick him up and bring him in. If he gets to go home when we're done, he'd have to make his own way without a car. He decided he'd rather come in on his own."

By now Ahearn had arrived as well and stood beside Rob Norris, openly gaping at them.

Gordie took a deep breath. "I look forward to hearing what else Jack Fraser has to say to us, then."

"Actually Gordie, I'm going to have Detective Ahearn sit in on the interview. I think a fresh, unbiased perspective is called for."

Gordie's heart pounded. He gritted his teeth. He leaned in to speak so that only she would hear instead of the whole room. "Well done, partner. You've proven to the world that you're in charge. I hope the price is worth it." He turned and walked away, past his desk, down the hall and outside. He walked to his car and climbed in. His keys were in his jacket pocket and the jacket hung on his chair, so he didn't go anywhere. He slammed his hand on the steering wheel and let loose with a long string of foul language. He thought it might make him feel better, but the unaccustomed venting had the opposite effect. His heart still pounded, and his breath came in ragged gasps.

He tried taking deep breaths. In through the nose and out through his mouth. Vanessa taught him this when he quit smoking. He closed his eyes and focused. Long, deep breaths. *What the hell is going on with Roxanne? This isn't her. Sure, she wants to make her mark. She wants to solve this. We all do. She's taking something out on me, but what?*

He realized he had his phone in his shirt pocket and dialed. "Hi, it's me. Sorry to call so early. I didn't get you up, did I?"

Vanessa's voice was filled with concern. "No, of course not. What's up? I thought you'd be at work."

Gordie told her about the scene as it had played out.

"Good Lord. That doesn't sound like her. She said it wasn't because of your boss, but maybe it was. Is it likely that he pressured her?"

"Oh yes, he probably did, but this felt like more. If that's all it was, I would have expected her to say something to me like *the boss wants to see some action* or something like that. I would have understood that and worked with her."

"Then it must be something personal."

"I didn't do anything. Honestly, I've been doing my best just to be supportive and give my opinion when she asks for it."

Vanessa laughed. "I didn't mean you did something. I meant she's bothered by something, and you just happened to be the one to take the fall-out."

"Eddy."

"Maybe. Probably. But who knows? Everything ok with Helen? Or her folks?"

"I don't know. She didn't say anything."

"Maybe she's saying something now."

"Should I ask her? I mean I tried to. I said *what's going on?* What else can I do?"

"I'm not sure, Gordie. For a start, I'd go back in and do the job. Let her cool down and maybe later today you can have a quiet word in a private place."

He sighed. "And this is why I prefer working alone. This nonsense of trying to figure people out. Like the job isn't challenging enough."

"Cut her some slack, Gordie."

"The voice of reason. All right. Thanks for listening. I'll see you at my place around 5:30 so we can have a quick bite to eat before we go to Gretha's memorial."

Gordie took a few more deep breaths for good measure before going back inside.

When Gordie arrived back in the office, Roxanne was away from her desk. He sat down, turned on his computer and tried to gather his thoughts. *Forget about Jack Fraser. He's not our guy, and sooner or later Albright will know that too. So, where to go from here?*

He went over and stood beside Rob Norris. "Where's Albright?"

"Gone to file for a warrant."

"Right. Do you have a few minutes to tell me what you know about the art client?"

"Sure, pull up a chair."

Gordie wheeled his chair over to sit side by side with Norris who had his computer open to a Wikipedia page.

Rob read out excerpts from the page which described Robert Wilson as a Canadian business executive. It went on to give a short biography of his main accomplishments including his current role as a venture capitalist, and an art collector and then a series of bullets showing his work as a philanthropist, with links to various news articles.

Gordie nodded. "OK, he's a great guy. He's rich and likes to spread some of his cash around, but he seems like a slippery fish to me. Did you hear back from him yet to explain why he missed his scheduled phone call with you?"

"Nope."

"Have you got anything else on him? Especially about his art collection?"

"I've looked at a couple of the articles linked here, but they don't give us anything useful. To be honest, I've got too much on the go right now with looking through the documents on the victim's computer and the phone list. I never did call all the local numbers. I only made it through the long-distance ones." Rob raised his eyebrows at Gordie.

"Hand over the list. You're going out on a field trip to enjoy the pleasures of Jack Fraser's trailer. I'll work the phone for a while."

Rob glanced around. Jason Ahearn had left to get himself a coffee. "What's the deal between you and Albright? I thought you two got on?"

"You and me both. No idea. Saturday we were on the same page and today we're clearly not." Gordie shrugged. "This too shall pass."

"You seem to have calmed down, anyway. You looked like you were going to blow a gasket earlier."

"Calm and serene. That's me. Give me the list while I'm in this mood."

Rob handed it over. "Have fun."

Gordie took the list to his desk; prepared for several boring hours of telling the same story over and over: *This is Detective MacLean. I'm with the Cape Breton Police Service, I'm following up on a routine enquiry. Blah-blah-blah.*

He wasn't prepared for the one phone call that would change everything.

# CHAPTER TWENTY-ONE

ROXANNE GOT THE WARRANT signed, arranged for two uniforms to meet with Rob Norris and then took Jason Ahearn to the meeting room to explain the game plan. "You'll take the notes, but if something occurs to you, either note it down and pass it to me without Fraser reading it, or if it seems appropriate, go ahead and ask your question of the suspect."

Jason had printed out the report from the interview at Fraser's home as well as other information about Fraser. "It appears that he was stalking the victim. Do we have any witnesses to any actual threats?"

Roxanne frowned. "Detective MacLean had to come between Fraser and the victim the day before her murder. That's a pretty good witness, I'd say."

Ahearn fanned out the various printouts on the table in front of him. "I have that report here somewhere." He located it and skimmed through it. "That's what I thought. It doesn't come out and say Fraser was threatening. The man was angry and claimed that

Braun had no right to buy the house, but it doesn't sound like he threatened her with anything."

Roxanne sighed. "That's what we are going to get today, Jason. We need him to tell us how he escalated these incidents that went from stalking to threats to murder."

"I'm just trying to understand the situation. See what we have for leverage."

"If you're uncomfortable with this, I can get MacLean in instead."

He held up his hands as if to ward off her angry words. "No, I'm not uncomfortable. Just trying to get myself up to speed."

"I may say things that aren't completely true, but that's fair in this situation. I'm trying to rattle him, push him over the edge."

"OK. I understand."

Roxanne nodded. "Right. He should be here any minute. We'll leave him to sit in the waiting room for ten minutes after we hear he's arrived and then you'll go get him. He sees MacLean as an ally since he knows him outside of this case, so he'll already be off-kilter when his buddy isn't present."

They went back to their desks to wait until the front-desk constable called. Gordie nodded to Roxanne when she passed his desk, and she paused beside him. "What are you working on?"

Gordie slid the list over for her to see. "Since Rob went on a field trip, I took over the phone records to finish the follow-up on the local numbers. Put a name to each one and find out what they talked about."

"Right, good." She hesitated for a moment and when he picked up his desk phone receiver and started dialing the next number on the list she returned to her own desk.

Jack Fraser was fifteen minutes late, and then sat for a further ten minutes before Jason Ahearn fetched him and took him to the interview room. Only when they settled down did Roxanne ask if he wanted a cup of tea or coffee.

"No, let's just get this over with. I have no idea why you needed to drag me all the way in here after we went through everything on Saturday. I already told you everything I know. You even recorded it, so why go through it again?"

Roxanne nodded to the recording equipment. "Just to be clear Jack, this is a formal interview, and we are recording it again. It is my duty to tell you that you do not have to tell me anything about this unless you want to. Furthermore, it is my duty to tell you that whatever you say will be taken down in writing and may be used in court against you."

Jack bit his lip as he listened to her caution him.

When he didn't say anything, she finished by advising him that he had a right to counsel. "Do you understand these rights?"

"Yes, fine. Ask your questions. I have nothing to hide."

They sat in silence for a few heartbeats and then Roxanne began. "Mr. Fraser, I want to inform you that at this very moment a search warrant is being executed on the trailer you call home, located on the farm owned by Mr. Floyd Sanders."

Fraser's eyes widened. "They can't go in without me there. They'll wreck the place."

"The entire search is being videotaped and a copy of that tape will be made available to your lawyer, if and when that becomes appropriate."

He clenched his fists at the edge of the table. "I don't understand this. I haven't done anything wrong. You're trying to pin this on me just to save yourselves the trouble of finding out who really did it."

Roxanne waited until Jack Fraser ran out of steam. "What if I told you we have a witness who saw you near Gretha Braun's house on Sunday night?"

He shook his head, his face puckered with a deep frown and pursed lips. "Whoever told you that is either wrong or lying. Maybe they're lying because they did it. I was at home all night."

"Shall I tell you what I believe happened?"

"I don't care. You can have any theory you want, as long as it doesn't involve me."

"I think you ran out of patience with Gretha Braun. You thought she'd be a pushover because she wasn't from around here and didn't know you or your history. You hoped that just the constant harassment was enough to get her to offer you money, right?"

"I wanted compensation. I told you that already. That's no secret. She owed me. It was my house that she bought, and I didn't get a penny."

"Instead of following the process and appealing to the Government for a part of the sales money, you took a shortcut. You went right to the new owner."

Jack sighed. "Yeah, so?"

"So, when Gretha proved to be more stubborn than you expected, you escalated things. First, you went and threatened her in public. Then…"

Before she finished her sentence, Fraser interrupted. "I didn't threaten. You know that. Ask Detective MacLean. I never threatened her."

"Detective MacLean didn't witness the entire confrontation. He heard shouting and came to investigate. By then you'd already been yelling at the victim for a few minutes. You threatened her."

His eyes widened. "No. That's not true. Ask the guy who brings the carts back inside from the parking lot. He was there the whole time because he was offering a buggy to her. I was going out with my bag of charcoal, and I saw her. I thought I'd just give her another nudge since the opportunity presented itself. Ask him. He'll know."

Jason Ahearn made a note in his book.

Roxanne continued calmly. "Whether you used the exact words of 'I'll kill you' or not, is irrelevant. You used threatening behaviour, and that's the same thing."

Beads of sweat covered Fraser's forehead. "It's not. It can't be."

"MacLean's interruption cut your confrontation short, but the next night you watched her house. When everything was quiet, you knocked on her door. She believed that it was a safe neighbourhood, and she opened the door without question."

"Not to me."

"She opened the door to you and before she had a chance to close it again you stepped inside. Maybe you even lulled her by being calm. This was it; you had softened her up and it was time to have the conversation with her about what she could do to make the harassment stop."

"No."

"You went in, and she led you into the living room, but as you passed the kitchen table, you saw the knife lying there beside the cake. You picked up the knife and followed her. You didn't intend to kill her. Your lawyer can maybe argue that you had a moment of diminished responsibility, but I don't know that for sure. What I do know is that the conversation didn't go the way you expected or wanted it to go."

Jack Fraser had his arms folded across his chest and kept shaking his head. "No, no, no."

"You had the knife in your hand. She probably didn't even notice it as she told you that she wasn't going to pay you anything. It was clear then that your whole scheme wasn't going to be successful. You'd been working on it for weeks by then and you were so sure, weren't you? So sure, that she'd give you something because you'd been cheated out of the house sale money."

He laid his hands flat on the table and leaned forward. "You're making this all up. It's not true and you can't prove it because it didn't happen." He turned to look at Jason Ahearn. "She's just making it up. You can't make stuff up like this."

Roxanne's phone pinged with a text message, and she pulled out her phone to read the message from Rob Norris. *No joy. Nothing here. No bloody clothes or anything else, no file box.*

Roxanne looked up as Jack Fraser pushed himself away from

the table and stood up. "I came in of my own free will. And now I'm leaving."

Roxanne's heart pounded. "Sit down Mr. Fraser. We're not finished."

"Yes, we are. If you're going to charge me, then do it and get me a lawyer. If not, I'm out of here."

Both Fraser and Ahearn looked at Roxanne, who nodded. "Interview finished at 11:20 hours. Detective Ahearn, please escort Mr. Fraser out."

When they left the room, Roxanne sat for a moment collecting herself. The rush of adrenalin of the last half hour left her shaky and on the verge of crying. She had been so convinced he'd break down under the barrage, but he hadn't. *Now, what do I do?*

She swiveled as Gordie knocked and came in carrying a file. "Come to gloat?"

Gordie stopped and turned back to close the door. "I came to talk to you about the case. What the hell's going on with you?"

She scowled. "You were right. I didn't have enough to break Fraser and he knew it. The search was a bust."

"That's not what I'm talking about, and you know it. What happened between Saturday afternoon and this morning? You've never lashed out at me like you did this morning. If you have a problem with me, I expect you to treat me with respect and talk to me, not treat me like something you scraped off the bottom of your shoe."

Roxanne closed her eyes and sucked in a deep breath. When she opened them, she tilted her head back and looked at the ceiling. "I'm sorry."

"And?"

She remained silent staring up at the ceiling, trying not to let her tears fall.

"Are you going to tell me what happened on Sunday to put you in this mood?"

Quietly, almost in a whisper, she answered him. "Eddy broke up with me."

Gordie leaned towards her and squeezed her arm. "I'm sorry. I know how it feels, but from experience, I can tell you that it may all come out all right in the end. Do you want to tell me what happened?"

She had her tears under control and looked at him. "I hardly even know. He had tickets on Saturday night for a concert. A recorded concert, not an in-person one. I was tired and it was going to be a lot of driving here and there and I said I couldn't go. That's what started it. So then on Sunday he decided he was going fishing with friends. I didn't mind. It's salmon season, and I get it. I thought we left it that he'd call me later, after the fishing."

"But he didn't call."

"No. So I called him before I went to bed. I didn't want him calling after I was already asleep, you know?"

"Seems reasonable."

"He was just home watching TV. He had no intention of calling me. I felt like he was punishing me for not going on Saturday. When I said that, he got angry and said that we should take a break from each other since I was so busy anyway. And that's it. We're on a break."

"Can I ask you something?"

"Go ahead."

"How often does Eddy come to your place?"

She frowned. "I don't know. What's your point?"

"Over the past few months, it sounds like you are always the one that goes to his place. You're the one driving and making the effort. I have never heard you say that Eddy came down to hang out for the afternoon on a weekend or take you and your Nana out for a meal."

"Well, there aren't too many guys that want to spend time with their girlfriend's grandmother, Gordie."

"I'm not sure about that. Helen is an intelligent, interesting, and active person. More than that, she's someone that you care about and live with, so it seems to me that once in a while a fella could put aside his own comfort and spend some time in your space. You may not want to hear this, but I think Eddy likes you better when he's in charge of the place, the agenda, and you. Right now, this case has given you the opportunity to show him the strong, successful side of you, and maybe that's just not as much fun for him. I know what I'm talking about, because, as you know very well, Vanessa is a strong, capable woman and I need to tell myself regularly not to always try to be in charge. I've learned the hard way, it's not what she wants from me and I'm OK with that. I just remind myself sometimes to watch what I'm doing."

Roxanne frowned. "He's not a control freak."

"Maybe not, but maybe you both just need to learn how to work with this different situation. Maybe a break is exactly the right thing for both of you right now. Let you focus on the case."

She nodded. "I am sorry, Gordie. On Saturday, I gave Sarge the update and he kind of pushed me into moving on Jack Fraser. I should have said we weren't ready, and I fully intended to talk to you about it, but then with the whole Eddy thing, I just got steamed up and needed to shout at someone. I should have gone for a run instead."

Gordie nodded. "I get it. I know what the boss can be like, and he's very good at pushing people. We'll put it behind us. But Roxanne?"

She raised her eyebrows.

"Once was enough, right?"

"Right."

"And on that note, forget about the Fraser interview for a moment. Let me tell you about what I found today."

"Hope it's good news."

"It might be. I've been going through the local phone numbers and this one," he showed her a number he had circled in red. "A Halifax number. It's for a hotel. The Royal Basin."

"OK, I know it. Big, glass affair overlooking the Bedford Basin."

"Right. When I called the number, it went into the main switchboard. I explained who I was and what I wanted, which of course was to know who made the call. See? It's for Saturday night."

"Could they tell you?"

"It took some running around. The guy asked me to read off the number because for outgoing calls their system records that number so that they can bill the guest for appropriate long-distance charges, but incoming calls always go through the main desk. See how it ends in 1010? That means it's room 1010. That was the easy part. Prying the information out about who the guest was, took a lot more effort. The desk clerk had to talk to his manager, and I had to leave the number for the station so they could verify who I am. That done, the manager told me the whole blurb about how much they value the privacy of their guests, and all that until I finally had to tell her that I am investigating a murder. That shook her up enough to finally cough up the identity of the person who stayed in that room, arriving Friday afternoon, and departing Monday morning.

"You've dragged it out long enough. Who was it?"

"None other than the art client of Gretha's. Robert Wilson.

"The elusive, Mr. Wilson."

"The very one."

# CHAPTER TWENTY-TWO

ROXANNE LEFT GORDIE TO go through it all again with Rob Norris when he returned to the office, while she went to meet with the boss.

Sergeant Arsenault tapped his pen on the desk to punctuate his comments in an irritating manner. "In other words, you jumped the gun by bringing this Fraser character in for a formal interview." Tap "And the search warrant." Tap "It'll be harder to get the next one because the judge will think you're on a constant fishing expedition." Tap, tap.

Roxanne felt herself flush. "Yes, Sergeant."

"And MacLean was in favour of bringing this guy in now as well?"

"I didn't discuss it with him."

Arsenault frowned. "Why not? I thought we all understood that you were working as a team. Not that you were going rogue."

Roxanne bit her lip but couldn't help herself. "I discussed it with you, Sergeant, on Saturday on the phone. I believed you encouraged me to act. I understood that as support to get the search warrant and do the interview."

The tapping had stopped now. "Detective Albright, I'm not working the case. Any support I give you is of a general nature and not to be taken as inserting myself in the investigation."

"I see that now. In future, I'll ensure that Detective MacLean and I are on the same page before I take any action."

"All right, we'll put that down as a lesson learned. What other leads are you following since Fraser seems doubtful right now?"

Roxanne told him about Robert Wilson.

"You say that this man was a client of the victim's? What's his motive for killing her?"

"We're speculating that he hoped she would authenticate his painting as a lost Alex Colville and perhaps she wasn't prepared to do that. It would mean a significant difference in the value of the work."

"How much are we talking about?"

"I'm not sure, but in the order of hundreds of thousands of dollars possibly."

He widened his eyes. "Yes, people kill for less. What's the next step?"

"Detective MacLean left a message for him that unless we hear back from him either with a call or to schedule a call, we'll have no choice but ask our colleagues in Vancouver to take him in for questioning."

Arsenault frowned. "If I understand you, this man is an important and powerful person. I hope MacLean isn't overreaching with his heavy-handed approach."

"I was with him when he left the message. He was very polite. He asked nicely, but he did point out that we've been unsuccessful in our attempts to reach him, and we missed him the first time we had a scheduled call."

"What can we say at the press briefing this afternoon?"

She handed over a page with bullet points. "I've made some notes about people helping with our enquiries. Also, there is a memorial service tonight near where Gretha Braun lived. I thought people might like to know about that."

"Very good. Are you going to that?"

"Detective MacLean is. Do you feel I need to be there?"

"I leave it up to you."

Roxanne joined Ahearn, Norris, and MacLean in the interview room. "Did you hear back from Mr. Wilson?"

Gordie grinned. "His assistant has us rescheduled for a video call tomorrow morning, along with apologies for the missed Saturday appointment."

Rob tapped the list of phone numbers. "Sorry I missed this. I should have stuck with going through the list, but I did a few and all the local numbers were for services or stores, like a tile store in Sydney and the Habitat for Humanity place in Halifax. I abandoned the list in favour of looking at the documents on her computer."

Roxanne shook her head. "You prioritized your work. Look, we're all doing the best we can. I thought getting Jack Fraser in here and searching his place would get us some answers. I was wrong."

In the silence that followed that admission, Gordie pointed to an empty chair. "I was just finishing up telling the guys about my call with the hotel manager."

She sat down and listened as he continued.

"Where did I leave off? Oh yes, once we got past the whole 'we value the privacy of our guests bit' she was prepared to talk away to me. As I told you, Wilson checked in on Friday and checked out Monday morning."

Ahearn voiced what everyone was thinking. "So, he was in the province on Sunday night when Braun was killed."

"Yes, he was. Before I got too excited, I asked if anyone saw him Sunday night, but of course Manager McKillop protested that unless Wilson did something to draw attention to himself, it was highly unlikely that anyone would have noticed him coming or going. It's a busy place with the restaurant and bar right off the lobby."

Roxanne nodded. "I know the place. That's fair enough. It is busy."

Gordie held up a finger in a 'wait' sign. "So, I asked if she could check his bill to see if he'd charged anything to the room on Sunday evening."

The three pairs of eyes stared at him until he continued. "He wasn't there for supper, or at least, if he was, he didn't charge it to his room. He did; however, have a bar bill for Sunday night."

Norris shook his head. "Damn. That's it, then. If he was in Halifax drinking, he wasn't in Isle Madame."

Gordie smiled. "The bill was for one drink and was signed for at 12:45. If someone was in Isle Madame and left at, say nine p.m. and then hustled back to Halifax, ordered a nightcap because they needed to settle their nerves, it could be done."

Roxanne raised her eyebrows. "I don't know. It's close to three and a half hours."

Gordie shook his head. "I've done the trip a thousand times because my mother and sister live in Halifax. At night with no traffic, you can do it in three hours without even trying."

Ahearn nodded. "Yeah. I've done it faster too. It makes sense that buddy would stop for a drink to set up an alibi as well as for the nerves."

Roxanne chewed her lip. "OK, so Robert Wilson is now a person of interest. What time is the call scheduled for tomorrow?"

"Eleven our time, which is eight in the morning his time. I think we keep it easy to start with. Tell him his name came up as someone with whom she had recent contact. Talk to him about the painting and find out where that all stands. Is it real? Is it fake? Or was Gretha still working on it? Once we get through all that, he's maybe feeling at ease, and we ask him casually where he was on Sunday. If he tries to tell us he was at home, that's it. We call in the Vancouver police or the Mounties to go pick him up."

Albright stood. "Makes sense. Norris – you keep going through the files on her computer. Do a search for 'Colville' and find everything you can. Hopefully, we'll already know the answer to the question of the painting's authenticity before we even ask Wilson the question. Jason, you do the same with her emails. Also, find all the correspondence you can between Wilson and Braun. Maybe there's an email note setting up a meeting for Sunday night. Gordie, you're heading out soon to go to the memorial this evening, right?"

"Yup. Even though Wilson looks good right now, I'll be watching to see who shows up and how they act tonight."

Ahearn smiled. "Like Macbeth's banquet."

Gordie blinked. "'fraid my Shakespeare is a long way behind me."

"The man that Macbeth murdered came to the banquet and freaked him out."

"I'm counting on Wilson to reveal himself on the phone tomorrow, and don't count on Gretha turning up at the wake tonight to point someone out."

Ahearn flushed. "Sorry. I didn't mean to make light of it. It's nice that the victim's friends and neighbours are getting together to honour her."

Roxanne opened the door. "Yes, it is. Now let's do our part to honour her and get to work finding the killer."

# CHAPTER TWENTY-THREE

VANESSA FUSSED WITH HER hair in front of the hall mirror while Gordie pulled at his tie. She had done her shoulder-length hair in a French braid at the back, with the tail end tucked up underneath. Wisps floated loosely, softening the style. She looked in the mirror at Gordie standing behind her. "Does it look messy?"

"It looks very pretty. I have no idea how you did it, and I like it loose better, but I'm sure it's just right for this kind of thing."

She turned to him and pulled his tie straight again but loosened it a tiny bit. "Stop tugging at it."

"Let's get going. I'll forget about it if I'm busy."

She picked up her small black purse and slipped it over her shoulder to hang across her body. "I can't believe it's barely a week ago that we went to visit Gretha and saw her lovely home."

"I know what you mean." Gordie handed Taz a cookie and watched as the dog turned to go back to the kitchen and then they left the house.

They didn't talk much on the way to the Legion. The parking lot was already busy, and Gordie let Vanessa off at the door before going to find a spot. As he walked to the entrance, he saw people carrying trays of food. Vanessa slipped her hand into the crook of his arm and whispered in his ear. "I never even thought. We should have brought something."

"Don't worry about it. There'll be more food here than the crowd can possibly eat."

They went inside and then Vanessa released his arm. "I know you need to wander around. I'll be fine. Don't worry about me." Without a backward glance, she left his side and went to join a group of women standing chatting. He watched long enough to see the group widen to admit Vanessa into the circle before he turned to see who was present in the large room.

He walked over to the side wall where long tables were covered in white paper tablecloths. Mia White was busy slicing up a cake which a small handwritten sign proclaimed to be *Apfel Kuchen (Appel Cake)*. "That looks delicious."

Mia looked up and smiled. "I hope so. It was a favourite of Gretha's." Her eyes misted. "Only three weeks ago we spent an afternoon together and made one for her and one for me. We talked so much, we didn't even notice the work of apple peeling and mixing. The cakes seemed to make themselves." She pointed to the cake she had just sliced and one right beside it. "You see? She had her style and I have mine. She puts streusel on top of hers and makes it in a square pan, so this one I made to her recipe." She waved the knife at the other one. "I braid mine in a circle and dust it with icing sugar. Sometimes I also put whipped cream on top."

Gordie rested his hand on her shoulder for a moment. "You've created a real tribute to her."

She nodded and pointed further along the table. "I also made her a Frankfurter Kranz. It is a buttercream cake in the shape of a crown. To me," she swallowed hard and took a deep breath "to me she was a special friend and deserves a royal send-off."

Gordie nodded. "I only met her the once, but I can see why you feel that way. She did seem like a very special lady. Is your husband here as well?"

Mia nodded. "Yes, somewhere." She frowned. "Do you need him?"

"Oh, no. This is just a social occasion. I'm here with my partner, Vanessa." He pointed to her across the room. "I was just curious."

She looked relieved and then a woman approached with a platter of brownies. "Where should I put these, Mia?"

Gordie left them to it and continued his circuit around the room. He spotted Mickey White and Henry Davis together huddled over Henry's phone, studying something. He moved closer, wondering what had them so enthralled.

Henry tapped the screen on his phone. "You like hockey, right?"

Mickey nodded. "Sure."

"You can bet on the NHL or AHL. Like I said, do your homework, get to know the players, like this guy here. I'm watching Sam O'Reilly and his team. They're a winner."

Mickey hunched in further. "And can you make money on this, then?"

Henry closed off the screen. "Like anything, you win some, you lose some." He turned and saw Gordie close behind him. "Detective. How are you this evening? Here to pay your respects?"

Gordie nodded. "Just like both of you."

Mickey White took a step away as though to leave them.

Gordie shifted his stance to make it awkward for White. "I was talking to your wife. She's gone all out for this event. You must be proud of her."

Mickey stared as if trying to read more into the comment than was obvious. "Sure I am. Nothing she likes better than baking up a storm. In fact, now that you mention it, I'm ready for some of that fancy crown cake of hers." He nodded and stepped around Gordie.

Gordie turned to Henry. "You two looked like you were deep in conversation there. What was so interesting?"

Henry shrugged. "Just passing the time. These kinds of events aren't my thing. Gotta find something to talk about. Sports are always good. That and the weather." He smiled and gestured to the small platform that served as a stage. "Looks like Father Pat is going to say a few words. Better go listen."

Gordie found Vanessa and they stood listening.

"I only met Gretha Braun once. She wasn't part of my congregation, but she came to our strawberry tea in June and made a point of introducing herself to me. She was a well-spoken and interesting woman, and we spoke for quite some time, but what I remember most is how much she enjoyed being here. She told me that the strawberry tea was an example of what she loved most about our community. She loved the way people came together to share food and fellowship."

There was silence in the room as people thought about their individual memories of Gretha Braun, and then Father Pat continued. "Gretha told me that she had lived in many places, all of them large European cities, and London, England. She told me that she had never felt so at home before coming here. Gretha Braun wasn't part of our Isle Madame family for long, but she quickly made an impact. Thank you to all of you who helped put this evening together. I know she would have been pleased. I'll call now on a woman who had become a good friend to Gretha to say a few words. Ellie Davis? Where are you?"

Ellie stepped up beside Father Pat. Her eyes were red-rimmed, and she took a deep breath before speaking. "I just want to echo Father Pat's words and thank all Gretha's neighbours and friends who brought food and came out tonight." She turned and pointed to a man sitting on the piano bench behind her, and another man quietly tuning his fiddle. "Kenny and Roger have very generously offered their services tonight to give us a few tunes. Gretha came to a couple of dances here with me and although she wasn't a big dancer, she loved music, so I think it's a fitting tribute to her to enjoy yourselves." She nodded, pulled out a ten-dollar bill and threw it into the open violin case on the floor and left the stage.

Ellie came to stand with Gordie and Vanessa, who immediately introduced herself. "I'm Gordie's partner, Vanessa Hunt. What a wonderful evening you and the others have put together here. I only met Gretha once as well, but I just know she would be so honoured."

Ellie smiled. "Thank you. That's kind."

At that moment, as they watched and listened to the musicians begin their cover of *Orangedale Whistle*, a slow mournful violin intro replacing the Rankins' guitar version, Ellie's brother Henry joined them.

"Good job, Sis. Listen, I'm heading out. If you want a ride, you need to leave now."

"Oh. I didn't realize you'd leave so early. I should have taken my own car."

Gordie glanced at Vanessa who gave a nod. "We'll drop you home. It's no problem at all."

"I couldn't ask that of you. I'm sure there's someone here I could ask."

Henry said. "Right, then. See you later."

Ellie shook her head and *tsked*. "He's not a big social butterfly. I think it's even worse right now between Dad's death and then so soon afterwards, Gretha's. I think he's having a hard time with it all."

Vanessa nodded sympathetically. "I'm so sorry to hear your father died recently. I can see that it must be quite overwhelming for both of you. Gretha mentioned your brother and really admired his work."

Ellie smiled. "Yes, Detective MacLean told me. He doesn't say much, but of course, they had become friends during all those months of working on the house."

Gordie watched the young man leave. "Has he found more work yet? His job came to an abrupt end, so that must be a worry for him as well."

"You're right. It is a worry. I told him I can lend him some money until he finds work, but he's proud. Men."

Vanessa touched Ellie on the arm. "With his skills, I'm sure he won't be out of work for long."

"That's true, and of course, we have Dad's estate coming one of these days."

Gordie raised his eyebrows. "You make it sound like there's a snag?"

"No, no. God, I shouldn't even be talking about all this right now. It's nothing. Just that my father's lawyer is away in Kenya right now on a photo safari. He'll be back this week, though, so, as I told Henry, there's no point trying to work with another lawyer in the firm. John Michaels was one of Dad's closest friends and I'd rather just wait for him. He isn't very reachable right now, but he did send an email when his admin got a hold of him to tell him of my father's passing. I know he was shocked, just like all of us." She sighed. "It's no big deal to wait. Dad told us both a few years ago already that everything was coming to us, the kids, so there won't be any big surprises. I can wait, that's for sure. Somehow it feels so terribly final, thinking about dividing up his stuff."

Gordie nodded and raised his voice. "What you need is a bit of a dance." The music had picked up in tempo over the last couple of tunes and now there was a large crowd on the dance floor stamping and whirling to the music as couples step-danced in unison and others clapped with appreciation.

Ellie smiled. "Yes, maybe. I see a former dance partner over there just aching to get on the floor. Let me go and put him out of his misery."

"We'll be here for another while. We'll let you know when we're leaving, in case you're ready to go then."

She waved to acknowledge his comment and wove her way through the joyful crowd.

\*\*\*

After two cups of tea each and samples from the large selection of pastries, Gordie felt there was nothing more to be gained from staying longer. The evening showed no sign of ending soon.

He squeezed Vanessa's hand. "Are you sure you don't want to dance? I'm sure you'd find a partner, no problem."

She laughed. "This isn't the music I was raised with. I danced to Fleetwood Mac and George Michael at my school dances. This is a different world. No thank you, no dancing for me. It's been fun watching, though."

Gordie pointed to Ellie Davis standing talking to a few people near the kitchen. "Make your way over to the door then and I'll just go see if she wants a lift home."

Ellie saw him approach and said goodbye to the group she was with. "You're ready to go?"

"We are. What about you?"

"Oh yes, but I don't want to be a nuisance."

"Please. It's no trouble at all. Is there anyone else you want to say goodbye to?"

"Oh no. Let's just slip out."

"A girl after my own heart."

He led the way to the door and told the two women to just wait while he went for the car. There was a fine drizzle coming down which made the evening cold and gloomy after the heat and energy of the room. He pulled his collar up and took a detour down a different row of cars than where he was parked to go past an old black pickup truck. Through the gloom, he had seen someone sitting in the parked truck watching the door of the hall. He was close enough to recognize Jack Fraser, but as he approached to have a word with the man, Jack noticed him coming, started the engine and pulled out, taking the turn out of the parking lot with a spit of gravel.

Gordie watched for a moment and then carried on to his car. He put the back seat up, flinging Taz's duvet out of the way. He so rarely used the seats that they were relatively dog-hair free.

Ellie settled in the back with a sigh. "Thank you for this. I was quite ready to leave. I probably should have just gone with Henry. He had the right idea, but I felt obligated to spend some time with folks. They were so good to come. Some only knew Gretha to see her."

Gordie smiled into the rearview mirror at Ellie. "I don't think it was a hardship for people. They were enjoying themselves, and from the little I knew of Gretha, I think that would have made her happy."

"True. I'm so tired, though. It's been a hell of a couple of weeks."

Vanessa half turned in her seat to look at Ellie. "You're bearing up so well. Many people who went through a parent's death wouldn't have been able to do what you did tonight."

The young woman nodded. "I think I've been running on automatic. I feel like there's a crash coming. I don't know why. You would think I'd be glad that the worst is over, but somehow, I just have this sense that it really isn't."

They were all quiet for the few minutes it took to drive to the Davis family home.

When they turned in, Ellie exclaimed. "Oh. I assumed Henry would be home. Never mind. I'm sure the door isn't locked. I didn't bring my key."

Gordie put the car in park. "I'll come in with you."

"Oh, no. No need. Thank you so much for driving me. I really appreciate it."

"All right, well, we'll wait until you're inside safely."

Ellie nodded. "Thanks. Good night, then."

They watched as the young woman walked to the side door, opened it and turned back to wave, before Gordie started the car again to head for home.

Vanessa took a last look at the house as lights came on in the kitchen and living room. "Poor thing. She's really done in, and who could blame her?"

"I know. She's been through a lot. I wonder where the brother's gone. He seemed so keen to go, but he isn't there."

"Gone for a drive to clear his head, maybe."

"Maybe."

"Did you learn anything tonight?"

Gordie sighed. "Nothing that jumps out at me. Sometimes things need to percolate with me, though. In the morning after a good night's sleep, I'll know better."

"I know people were gathered for a sad reason, but is it bad if I admit that I enjoyed myself?"

"Not at all. That's why these events are so good. There are still people who wake their loved ones at home around here. The deceased will be in a room and right next door the fiddle will be playing and people singing and telling stories."

"I like it. That's what I want when I go, Gordie."

He laughed. "You better tell someone other than me, then. I'm guessing you'll be waking me before then."

She reached over and gave his knee a squeeze and then changed the subject. "I do feel sorry for Ellie. She does seem ready to collapse, doesn't she?"

"Hopefully her sense of foreboding will be conquered by some rest now that all this is behind her."

"Yes, hopefully."

# CHAPTER TWENTY-FOUR

GORDIE ROSE EARLY TO take Taz for a walk on the beach. He saw that Vanessa was buried deep beneath the duvet and didn't stir when he got up, so he resisted the temptation to kiss the top of her head before leaving.

"Right, Taz, let's go. We'll have our breakfast when we get back. Is that OK?"

The dog bumped against his legs in her haste to beat him out of the front door and then paced by the back of the car until he opened the hatch for her to jump in.

It was barely daylight when he parked by the beach. He stood and watched as the sun rose in a dramatic light show of red, orange, and yellow over the water to the east, the colours replicated on the surface of the water, which shivered with fish-scale-like ripples. The land mass of Red Island and Little Harbour formed a black, bumpy demarcation between sky and water. Gordie loved this time of day, and he breathed in deeply, the pungent, sulphurous aroma clearing his head.

Taz ran off to nose through soggy lumps of stranded seaweed

while Gordie followed, deep in thought. He walked for fifteen minutes and then called Taz back. "Come on, girl. Breakfast time, and then I must get to work."

Taz loped back to him, content to walk by his side for the return trip.

He took one last look at the rising sun over the water and then murmured. "Taz, I know this Colville guy was a great painter, but no human hand can create something as good as this, can they?" He looked down at his dog, who looked back up at him, tongue lolling in a happy grin.

*** 

Using a piece of toast to scrape up the last remnant of egg, Gordie nodded with appreciation. "*Mmm*. Thank you, Vanessa. That was delicious and such a treat to have a bacon and egg breakfast on a Tuesday morning. You spoil me." He watched as she gave a full piece of bacon to Taz and added, "and you spoil Taz."

"You're welcome. Everyone needs a little spoiling occasionally. Just don't get used to it."

Before he had time to answer, his phone rang. He studied the screen, shrugged, and then answered. "MacLean."

"Detective MacLean, it's Ellie Davis."

"Ellie. How are you today?"

"I'm well. I hope I didn't get you up?"

"Good Lord, no. I'm just about to leave for work."

"That's what I figured. I'm on my way as well. Those of us who want to stay in Isle Madame and work in Sydney know about early mornings. I won't keep you. Thank you again for taking me home last night. I was so weary, and was grateful for the kindness you and Vanessa showed me. She has a very comforting way about her. It was just what I needed."

"I'll tell her. Did Henry get home all right?"

Ellie laughed. "Oh, yes. I have no idea what time since I was sound asleep, but he got up to have a cup of coffee with me before I left this morning. I teased him about having a secret girlfriend. He was very non-committal, but he's always been a very private person. He'll tell me about her when he's ready."

"You sound more cheerful this morning."

"Oh, yes. I'm thinking of the kids and that always picks me up. I'm planning for Remembrance Day and intend to have the kids pair up to do research on Canadian veterans. Like me, many of the students have fathers or mothers, grandparents or great-grandparents who were in the military, so they can use a family member for the project, or just pick someone from history books. It'll be fun."

Her voice started to break up.

"That sounds great, but I think I'm going to lose you, so drive safe. I'm sure we'll be in touch."

The phone cut out without hearing Ellie say goodbye.

Gordie relayed Ellie's comments to Vanessa, who smiled. "She's a nice girl who has been through a lot, but she'll be fine. Now, you better get yourself going, hadn't you?"

He looked at his watch. "God, yes." He hustled out the door, leaving Vanessa to tidy up before she went home.

***

They had a department briefing prior to the scheduled call with Robert Wilson. Roxanne stood at the whiteboard and gave an update on their progress, or rather, lack of progress.

Detective DeLorey shook his head. "So, after all that hustle to get a search warrant, Norris, you came up empty?"

Norris shrugged. "Win some, lose some."

"Is that Jack Fraser out of the frame, then?"

Roxanne shook her head. "We aren't ready to say that yet. Inquiries are ongoing."

DeLorey laughed. "You've got the press-speak down pat by now anyway, Detective Albright."

She scowled and then turned to Gordie. "You went to the

memorial last night. Anything come of that, aside from copious amounts of tea and salmon and cream cheese sandwiches?"

"The quality of the food was at a much higher level than that with a professional baker in the group. But to answer your question, I saw Fraser there. He wasn't inside talking to people, he was just sitting out in his truck, watching."

Roxanne tilted her head. "Watching what?"

"Don't know. I went over to ask him exactly that, but when he saw me coming, he took off."

"Huh. Anything else?"

Gordie walked to the whiteboard and wrote beside Mickey White's name: *Gambler?*

Albright folded her arms. "OK, you have our interest. What did you find out?"

"I didn't find anything out for certain, but I overheard him talking to the contractor Henry Davis. Sounded like White was interested in understanding the gambling angle of some sports website Davis showed him, and it made me wonder how serious a problem Mickey White might have."

Roxanne nodded. "That would explain why he is keen to sell the bakery business."

Gordie added, "And why his wife was trying to do a secret deal with Gretha about selling half the business without letting him know about it. She must know about his problem and wouldn't want to hand over all that money just to see it disappear. She might have planned to just quietly use the money to keep the household afloat."

Roxanne looked at Sergeant Arsenault, who stood at his usual spot at the back of the room. "Do we have enough for a warrant to look at the White finances, Sergeant?"

"Based on Detective MacLean's eavesdropping? No."

Roxanne flushed. "Right."

MacLean, who still stood beside the board, pointed to Wilson's name. "Let's first see what Wilson has to say for himself. With any luck, we may not need to concern ourselves with White's interest in the odds."

Arsenault nodded. "Detective Albright, let me know how that goes before the afternoon press briefing."

Most of the group filed out with Ahearn, Norris, MacLean, and Albright staying behind.

"Sorry, guys. I was a little thrown off there. Jason, I meant to ask if you had any updates from going through the emails. Especially as it pertains to Wilson."

Ahearn nodded. "If I had MacLean's sense of drama, I would have gone to the whiteboard and done this." He picked up the red marker and wrote in capital letters beside Wilson's name: *FAKE*

Roxanne's eyes widened. "You found correspondence between them where Braun told Wilson the painting is a fake?"

He nodded. "It isn't a fake as such; it just isn't an Alex Colville. A student who had studied under Colville at Mount Allison University in 1947 did the work. His name is John Adam Culpepper, but he always signed his work just with 'AC'. He was apparently a huge fan of Colville's work, to the point of emulating even his later works. As Colville's style became more recognizable and consistent, Culpepper's followed a similar trajectory."

Gordie laughed. "You mean he copied Colville?"

Ahearn shrugged. "Being influenced by someone or copying them. Who knows? That's above my pay grade. All I know is that after Gretha Braun did all sorts of research, she concluded it was a Culpepper and not a Colville. She sent the report attached to an email note where she explained all this with little detailed images of similarities and differences. Looks like Colville was rigorous in the geometry of his work, whereas Culpepper was less so."

Norris shook his head. "I never heard of the guy. Obviously copying someone famous didn't make him famous himself."

MacLean raised an eyebrow. "And you're an art expert now, are you?"

Roxanne chided them. "OK, kids. That's great work, Jason. Now we really have the background we need. Was there any response from Wilson when Braun gave him the news?"

"Two words. *Very disappointing.* And then she responded with *Call me if you would like to discuss further.*"

She nodded. "And we know that he did call her. From right here in Nova Scotia."

Gordie had made notes as Ahearn spoke. "Did she copy anyone else on the email notes?"

"No. They were just direct notes between the two of them."

"And did you see any other emails to someone else during her research about the topic? Did she consult with someone to confirm her conclusions?"

"Not that I saw. I'll go back and sort emails by the subject line and see if anyone else pops up. I went by the dates and names so there may be someone else in there that I didn't see."

Gordie paused in his note-making. "When did she send him that report?"

"The week before she died. Tuesday, September 21st."

Roxanne rose. "I'm running out to get something from Timmy's. You guys deserve a treat. Give me your orders. Lunch is on me."

They gave her their orders for sandwiches, drinks, and desserts.

Gordie walked with her. "Do you want a hand?"

"No, I'm good. Can you write out the questions we want to ask, just to organize our thoughts before we start?"

"You got it."

By the time Roxanne was back with food and drinks, and she and Gordie set up in the meeting room with the speakerphone, and a large yellow notepad at hand, they were ready to grill Mr. Robert Wilson.

# CHAPTER TWENTY-FIVE

THEY HAD AGREED THAT Gordie take the lead since he had been the one who talked to the hotel. Roxanne would jump in as needed to follow up with questions or clarification.

"Mr. Wilson, you understand why we are calling?"

"Yes, I'm shocked to know that Gretha Braun is dead. I'm not sure how I can help. I only knew her in the context of work."

"We realize that. Please take us through what that entailed."

"I bought a painting, and I hired Gretha to research the provenance of it. I bought it at an estate sale and the auctioneer didn't know anything about its history. The style was very familiar to me, and the date of the painting was in the right ballpark, which made me want to pursue finding out more. That's really the start and end of it."

"Did Gretha Braun complete the research for you?"

"Yes, she did."

Gordie glanced at Roxanne. It was like pulling teeth.

"Can we ask what she concluded?"

They heard Wilson sigh. "Sadly, it didn't go the way I hoped." Having said that much, Wilson became more open. "I had hoped it was an Alex Colville, but although it was indeed from the Maritime School of Realism, it is by a student of Colville's."

"I suppose that affects the value of the piece significantly?"

"Yes, of course, although just like a piece by an artist from the School of the Group of Seven has its own relevance, so does this painting. Let's face it, no one would turn up their nose at an Emily Carr, and neither do I look down on my Culpepper."

"Of course, Mr. Wilson. I certainly wasn't trying to disparage your painting. I was simply trying to understand the impact of your realization that it was not what you had hoped. Perhaps there are insurance implications or whatever. Let's move on."

There was silence as Wilson waited.

"You may know that the murder of Gretha Braun took place on Sunday night, September 26th. Can you tell me where you were at that time?"

"Good Lord. I didn't exactly know when she died. This really is distressing. I was in Halifax at the time."

Roxanne raised her eyebrows with a shrug that meant *That's the truth anyway*.

"Halifax. What brought you to Halifax, Mr. Wilson?"

"I met with some businesspeople about a deep-water port in Guysborough County."

"I see. Since you were in the province anyway, did you meet with Gretha?"

"I thought I might get a chance to go and see her. I hoped to. Damn. If I had, maybe she wouldn't be dead. Good Lord. What a thought."

Gordie frowned. "Are you suggesting that you know something about her death? That it's connected to your business?"

"God, no! It's just that I talked to her on Saturday and explained that I was going to Melford Loop which isn't all that far from Isle

Madame, so we loosely arranged that, if possible, I'd go along to see her. I've only ever met her the once when she came to Vancouver to study the painting. We spoke many times and, of course, emailed, but since it was an end to our business now, I just thought it would be fitting to see her in person if I could. The thing is that I didn't end up driving myself. These business associates provided a driver, so then, of course, it really wasn't viable to go for a visit. I tried to tell them I had my own rental car and could easily drive myself, but they were keen to keep me captured to pitch their plan to me for those hours in the car. I was just thinking that if I had gone, maybe whoever did this might have been scared off because she had company."

"I understand. Can you take me through your schedule then for Sunday?"

"Their P.R. person and a driver picked me up at the hotel at eleven on Sunday morning. Prior to that, I had breakfast on my own and had a bracing walk on the waterfront. It's been some time since I've been there, and I'm impressed with the boardwalk. Very nice."

"Yes. Go on."

"We drove out to the site, met up with the other two from the company, and wandered around. They did their best to convince me of its potential. After we walked along with the three of them, taking turns to paint pictures of the great hub that might exist in the future, they took me for a drive to the town of Guysborough where we had lunch. Eventually, we went back to the office for more show and tell, and finally they took me back to the hotel. I had an hour to pop into the Art Gallery and then I went to a local place called The Old Triangle for supper. I stayed late talking to the owner of the place and listening to a live band. When the band finished at eleven o'clock, I walked around town for a little while to clear my head from the noise and think about the day's business. Then I went back to the hotel. I finished the night with a quiet drink in the hotel bar, and that was that. On Monday I came back to Vancouver."

Gordie nodded and raised his eyebrows at Roxanne to see if she had any questions. She shook her head and spoke for both of them. "You've been very thorough, Mr. Wilson. We appreciate you taking the time with us today."

"I apologize for missing our previous scheduled call. We had a business emergency and the call got lost in the shuffle. I was very impressed with Gretha, and while I was naturally disappointed with her conclusion about my painting, I don't for a moment doubt she was correct, and certainly didn't hold it against her for giving me that news."

"We understand. We won't keep you any longer, but if you can please email Detective MacLean the names of those business associates, you spent the day with on Sunday, we'd appreciate it."

Gordie rattled off his email address for Robert Wilson, and they signed off. He closed his notebook. "Well. To quote Mr. Wilson: *very disappointing.*"

"Very believable, though."

"Yeah. Afraid so." Gordie sighed. "Well, onwards, then. I think we can safely put a line through the whole artwork angle."

"Next step? We take a closer look at Mickey White and his gambling?"

Gordie nodded. "Makes sense."

"I better go give Sarge the news."

***

Roxanne kept her briefing short and to the point. It was obvious Sergeant Arsenault had things on his mind, and he nodded impatiently throughout her update.

"It sounds like you and MacLean can carry on looking into the gambling side of things. You don't need Ahearn and Norris anymore, do you?"

She blinked. "I can spare them for now, Sergeant."

"Good. There's been another murder and I'll put them on that case effective immediately."

"Oh no. What happened?"

"A man stabbed in Port Mulroy. A Syrian refugee by the sound of it." He picked up the phone as she was still rising from her chair, clearly dismissed.

She heard him bark into the phone. "Norris? Bring Ahearn and get in here."

Norris passed her in the hallway and raised his hands in a gesture of *what gives?*

She just nodded to Arsenault's office without trying to explain.

Gordie looked up when she came back by his desk. "How'd it go?"

"Ready for a coffee?"

He picked up his jacket and walked ahead as she grabbed hers and they walked together to his car. "Was it that bad? Sarge give you a hard time about getting it wrong, or something?"

She shook her head impatiently. "No, no. Nothing like that."

When they were in the car and Gordie was pulling out of the lot, he glanced over. "Well? What is it, then?"

"I think we may have someone going around killing foreigners."

"What?"

She explained what had happened. "I don't know anything more than what I've just told you. But what if they're connected? Did we even consider this a hate crime? What if we have someone who bears some kind of grudge against immigrants?"

Gordie parked in the lot of Tim Hortons but didn't make a move to get out. He chewed his lip, thinking about what she had said. "Why steal Gretha's file box, then?"

"Who knows? Maybe someone is even now forging her signature on cheques that were in that file box." She nodded. "We need to call the bank and make sure it clears nothing without confirmation."

"And we should flag her accounts for ATM use, too. Maybe she had bank cards and her passwords or pin numbers written and stored there."

He opened his car door, and the two went in to get their drinks.

"No point taking anything back to the boys. They'll be on their way to the scene."

"Let's have it here."

He had a roast beef and cheddar sandwich, and she ordered a chicken wrap. He took a bite and watched as she delicately nibbled off the end of her wrap.

When he swallowed, he made a moue of distaste when she took another bite. "How does anyone eat a wrap? It's like eating skin. It's not bread, it's just this flabby thing holding the insides together."

She closed her eyes. "Mmmm. Brings out the cannibal in me."

He laughed and went back to his own lunch. "It's good to see you back to normal."

"What's normal?"

"True."

The truth was, she had put Eddy to the back of her mind. She only allowed herself to think about him late at night. He was a problem she would deal with later, Roxanne told herself, trying not to picture his beautiful brown eyes.

When they got back to the office, Roxanne called Norris in his car to let him know she was interested in what he found at his crime scene.

Norris' voice crackled in and out. "I'll give you a call later. Right now, I only know the bare minimum."

"I understand. We'll keep working the White lead, but it may open a whole other avenue here."

"OK. Talk later."

The phone disengaged, but her mind busy with the implications.

*If we have someone who is on an anti-immigration campaign, this puts a whole different spin on things.*

# CHAPTER TWENTY-SIX

GORDIE AND ROXANNE SPENT the afternoon reaching out to Gretha's bank to ensure safety measures were in place. The bank confirmed there had been no activity since her death, so that both gave them comfort and perplexed them because they knew that if the purpose of the stolen file box was to take advantage of access to her bank, it would have happened by now.

Roxanne shrugged. "The person may not be especially bright. Maybe they thought they'd let the dust settle after her death before going after her money."

Gordie nodded. "Or they grabbed the file believing they'd get bank info there but didn't find anything. Of course, the argument against this line of thinking is the fact that they didn't take her wallet. That was the obvious way to get her money and bank card."

"They were so rattled after killing her, they didn't see it?"

"Hmm. Maybe."

They also scheduled another meeting with Mia White at the bakery for the morning. Gordie would go on his own while Roxanne planned to meet with Rob Norris.

Gordie looked through his notebook. "I may just take another trip over to see Jack Fraser while I'm there. I want to know why he was sitting outside the memorial last night, but didn't come in."

"And then took off when he saw you."

"Right. He's a watcher, but he doesn't like getting caught at it."

Roxanne perched on the edge of Gordie's desk. "If you were me, would you talk to Sarge about my theory about the anti-immigration angle?"

He shook his head. "I'd wait until you've spoken to Norris at least. See what his thinking is on this."

"Yeah. Good thinking. OK, I better put together something for his press conference, which got pushed out to five o'clock. People may not even be interested in poor Gretha Braun anymore."

"They'll be interested. It'll be a feeding frenzy with two murders on the go."

"OK, I'll send you a note later and tell you what we know about the murder in Port Mulroy.

\*\*\*

Vanessa had left a note on the table inviting him to come for dinner if he felt like it, but pointing out that there was leftover hamburger casserole in the freezer if he preferred to eat in. Gordie opted to stay home. He called her to thank her for the invitation, but he had work to do and better just stay put.

He changed into an old flannel shirt and worn-out jeans, took the casserole out to sit on the counter for a while, and made a pot of tea and some toast to keep him going.

"I know I shouldn't have the toast, Taz. Don't look at me like that." He stroked her silky white ears as she rested her chin on his knee. "I don't know which is better. The thought that we have someone out there targeting immigrants or that we don't. If we don't, we need to seriously consider that one of my neighbours is a killer. But which one? And the bigger question, why?"

The dog gave up and wandered to her bed in the corner to circle three times before flopping down with a grunt.

He reviewed his notebook and made new notes on a pad of lined paper. Questions for his meeting with Mia, and probably subsequent questions with Mickey White. He also jotted down a few thoughts for discussion with Jack Fraser. While he didn't believe Jack was guilty, he knew the man watched people and he may know more than he had told them. Maybe Jack didn't even realize the importance of something he'd seen. He moved to his easy chair and closed his eyes to put order to his thoughts.

The ping of an incoming email startled Gordie into wakefulness. He glanced at his watch. Seven o'clock. He blinked a few times and stretched to shake himself of his groggy feeling. He went to the kitchen table and sat in front of his computer to open Roxanne's email.

*Talked to Rob. The victim is an Afghan man. He and his wife and son have been here for five years and seem to be very well-liked in the community. He opened a Middle Eastern cuisine restaurant about 9 months ago despite the pandemic and it's been popular. The wife's sister, brother-in-law and 2 kids live in the basement. Sounds like the victim was home alone and then the brother-in-law came home to find him stabbed, mid-afternoon. The family are all staying with various neighbours. No one saw anything or know about any enemies or problems. Forensics and door-to-door have begun (busy neighbourhood – hoping for some security cameras). Nothing I heard moves me away from my thoughts about an anti-immigrant killer.*

Gordie agreed. So far, the similarities were strong.

Taz looked sadly at her dinner dish.

"All right. Sorry, big girl. I nodded off there." He got the dog's dinner organized and poked at the still-frozen casserole as he thought about the two murders. It must be someone who knew these victims.

*We're saying they were targeted because they were newcomers, but one in Isle Madame and one in Port Mulroy? What do they have in common?*

He responded with that very question to Roxanne and then put the casserole in the microwave oven, carefully lifting the corners of the plastic wrap first.

*Ping.* Roxanne replied.

*Delivery guy? Service guy? Real estate, bank, etc. The possibilities are endless.*

Gordie nodded and typed his response. *True. Fair enough. Do you want me to forget about the interviews tomorrow morning and go straight to the station?*

*No. They shouldn't take that long. Go ahead with them and hopefully by the time you get in, Rob will have more information for us.*

Gordie sent back a thumbs-up emoji. His dinner beeped, and he stirred it and continued reheating it. He went back to his notepad and made a list of all the possible people that Gretha Braun and the new victim could have in common. Roxanne was right. There were umpteen possibilities.

He called Ellie Davis. Her voice sounded tired. "Hello?"

"Ellie, it's Gordie MacLean. Sorry to bother you but I have a quick question."

"No problem. Go ahead."

"Did Gretha ever complain or comment about someone who was rude to her, aside from Jack Fraser? Maybe a delivery person, or bank clerk?"

"No. If anything, she complimented the service she received here. People were friendly and the idea that you could get something delivered the same day you ordered it, like the building supply place often did, well, she said that just wouldn't happen at home."

"All right, thank you for your time."

*That would have been too easy, I guess.*

This time when the microwave beeped, it was hot enough to eat. He ate it at the kitchen table while he continued making notes.

There were several lines of enquiry, and without Norris and Ahearn, they'd be busy. Maybe Roxanne could have Rob work on the angle that the two murders were connected because of anti-immigration sentiment while they themselves carried on with their current list. *Maybe that list is coming to a dead end, anyway.*

*** 

At eight o'clock the next morning, Gordie texted Mia to let her know he was in the parking lot. The kitchen staff were busy working, but the café didn't open until nine o'clock. He stood at the door, and although the sky was overcast, it wasn't raining. He waited and enjoyed the soft westerly wind carrying a hint of spruce and pine fragrance from Sandpoint and Hadleyville across Chedebucto Bay.

Mia looked flustered when she opened the door. "I'm sorry to make you stand outside."

"I'm enjoying the morning. I'm early and you're busy, so don't give it another thought."

They went inside, but before they sat at a table, Gordie touched her arm. "Do you have an office, Mia? Somewhere that we won't be in the middle of your staff coming and going. I know they're busy getting ready to open, so I'd rather stay out of their way."

She nodded. "Of course. It's messy, though."

"I won't even notice."

She led him through the kitchen to a small office at the rear of the building. It had a window giving visibility to the kitchen, but Mia shut the blinds after closing the door.

"Thank you." Gordie sat in the chair in front of the desk as Mia squeezed around the grey metal filing cabinet to sit in her swivel chair behind the old wooden desk.

He pulled out his notebook and pen. "Mia, I want to talk to you about Mickey."

She shook her head. "I told you already that Mickey and I were both at home the night Gretha was murdered. Besides, he is not a killer."

"Is he a gambler?"

She blinked several times before responding. "And if he is?"

"If he is, and he somehow knew that Gretha was buying half your business, he might be very keen to get his hands on the money. He might have gone to talk to Gretha about that." Gordie held up his hand before she protested again that her husband had been at home that night. "Mia, I believe you went to bed earlier than Mickey. With a business like this, you get up early, and go to bed early. Isn't that true?"

She nodded. "Yes, I don't stay up past nine most nights. But Mickey was on the couch watching the movie when I went to bed. He came to bed later when the movie ended."

"You woke up? You saw what time that was?"

She licked her lips. "No. I sleep very well and didn't wake up, but he was there when I got up at five o'clock."

"Yes. All right. Tell me about his gambling. How serious is it?"

Mia looked away, staring at the wall. "It was bad once. That's why this business is completely in my name. Even the boat is half in my name. Everything is half in my name."

"So, he can't sell anything without you knowing?"

"That's correct. Five years ago, he had to give someone his truck because he owed them money. After that, he went for help, and we changed everything so that my name is on all our documents. He agreed. He wanted to quit gambling, and he did."

"But lately?"

She sighed. "Lately he's slowly going back to his old ways. He has discovered online casinos which he likes very much. A month ago, I cut up his credit card. He wasn't happy."

"And you ended up with a bruised wrist somehow."

Frowning, she nodded. "He tried to stop me. He didn't mean to hurt me, but yes, in his effort to take the scissors and the card away, he wrenched my arm badly." Mia rubbed her wrist as if the memory brought back the pain.

"Does he owe a lot?"

"Nothing I can't manage." The woman hesitated and then continued. "He's also been going back to that club where he got into trouble years ago. That scares me more. It's in Port Mulroy, and not only does it have those video slot machines, but I know they run card games in the basement. That's how he lost the truck all those years ago. There are people there that will lend money to someone like Mickey." Her face reddened at the thought. "They're bloodsuckers, those people."

"And he's gotten back in with those people again?"

She shrugged. "I don't know that for certain. When he's working, it's fine. He can stay away. When it's the off-season though, he's bored, and he's not strong enough. He's trying, though. That's why he wants to get the equipment to go crab fishing as well. He's a good worker, is my Mickey. If only the deal with Gretha had gone forward, I would have put the money toward the equipment. You, see? Even if Mickey had found out, and I'm not saying he had, he would have gotten what he wanted. There was no need to kill the poor woman. Just from a financial point of view, we are now worse off."

"Yes, I can see your reasoning. I will need to talk to Mickey again though, specifically about the gambling, I'm afraid."

Another heavy sigh. "He'll think I complained to you."

"I'll assure him I heard from someone else. But Mia?"

"Yes?"

"Don't let him get away with any kind of violence. Call me, or Detective Albright, or we can give you the name of a counsellor. Please. Will you give me your word?"

A nod was all he got, and Gordie had to be satisfied with that.

"One last question. Are you aware of anyone who treated Gretha rudely because she was an immigrant?"

"No. And I think if anyone had said something, she would have told me because in that case I should be treated the same."

"You've been here for a long time. You don't even have an accent anymore. With Gretha, it was obvious she was from somewhere else, despite her flawless English."

"She said nothing, and I don't think she encountered any unkindness of that sort unless it was from that Jack Fraser man."

He stood. "Thank you. I've kept you from your work long enough."

"Are you going now to talk to Mickey?"

"No. I'll leave it for the time being. I'll call him first to schedule something when I need to speak with him again."

She was silent as she walked him out.

# CHAPTER TWENTY-SEVEN

H E PULLED UP TO the trailer and saw Jack Fraser behind the home, fiddling with a black hose.

"Morning, Jack. What are you up to?"

"Pumping out my septic tank. Care to help?"

Gordie didn't get too close. "You look like you have it under control."

Fraser hung the black corrugated hose with green end couplings on a large hook at the back of his unit, peeled off his yellow rubber gloves and rinsed his hands in a bucket of fresh water that stood ready.

He dried his hands on his jeans and then walked around to the front of the home to sit on the steps. "So, what do you want now? I've told you everything I know."

Gordie stood a few paces away and folded his arms. "I saw you at the memorial."

"I know."

"Why didn't you come in?"

"I thought about it, but I know what people are like. They think I did this. Even though I've known most of them all my life."

"You should have come in. No better way to convince them of your innocence."

Jack shrugged. "I couldn't be bothered. Is that why you're here? To bug me because I didn't go into the memorial?"

"No. I'm here because you're a watcher, Jack. You spent time watching Gretha Braun come and go. You saw other people come and go. Did you ever see her get into any arguments? Maybe someone insulted her just because she was a foreigner?"

Jack picked at a cuticle and then looked up. "You know it wasn't me, right?"

"I don't believe it was you, but I'm not sure my partner thinks the same way. Give me someone else. Am I right? Did you see someone hassle her because she's a foreigner?"

"Not really."

Gordie sucked in his breath to calm himself. "Not really isn't the same as no."

"There's lots of people who don't like foreigners."

Jack turned to look across the yard to the farmhouse.

Gordie followed his gaze. "Are you telling me that Floyd Sanders has said something along that line?"

Fraser shook his head. "I didn't say that, did I? He's good to me. Let's me stay here and use his septic and run the hose to his outside tap for water." Nodding again, he repeated. "He's good to me."

"But you aren't a foreigner."

"No. That's true."

"Did you ever hear Floyd threaten Gretha Braun?"

"No. Never."

The detective knew he wouldn't get any more from Fraser, but it was something. "OK, thanks, Jack."

"I didn't say anything."

"No, you didn't." He turned to his car but looked back for a moment. "Next time there's some kind of event with your neighbours, you should go on in."

"I'll think about it."

Gordie considered stopping at the farmhouse on his way past but saw the old red Ford 150 Floyd drove was missing, so he kept going. Instead, he decided to stop by and see Henry Davis, whose house was only a few minutes further along highway 320.

The garage door was open, and the familiar sound of a machine filled the air. Gordie went to the open door and stood for a moment while his eyes adjusted to the darkness in the woodworking shop.

Henry Davis wore safety glasses and a mesh mask with a valve to protect himself from the cloud of fine dust he created using his lathe. He saw Gordie at the door and turned off the machine. He took off his glasses and mask, laying them down on his workbench and came forward. He ran his hand through his hair to brush away some of the dust from his hair.

Gordie stepped inside to meet Henry half-way. "Sorry to drop in unannounced, but I was in the area."

Henry gestured towards the house. "No problem at all. I was just thinking it was time for a break, anyway. Let's get out of the dust. Can I offer you something to drink?"

"No, no. I'll only stay a moment. You saw Gretha Braun as much as anyone, and probably more. Did she ever mention anyone giving her a hard time because she isn't from here? Maybe you even saw or heard someone hassling her?"

Henry led the way to the house but stopped at the door. He stuffed his hands in the pockets of his blue hoodie and frowned as he considered the question.

"Maybe something as basic as a snide comment about foreigners?"

Henry tilted his head. "I'd forgotten all about it, but now that you mention it, there was something."

"Tell me."

"There was an incident at the building supply place. Getting materials has been a nightmare because of Covid. Long lead times and then you only get half of what you want." Henry shook his head.

"If you dare get annoyed, you're told it's because of the pandemic, right?"

Gordie smiled. "It's the same everywhere."

"I had a tipoff that a load of materials had just come in, so I recommended to Gretha that we stock up a bit. We had plans for several projects, like ripping out the walls and floor in that upstairs room, so needed lots of two-by-fours. Gretha went in and paid for the order by debit card. They like that because it's cash in hand without the 3% for credit cards."

"OK. Gretha was a good customer. Surely no one at the store gave her a hard time?"

"God, no. No, but when I went to pick up the load the next day, the lumber desk guy was in a big debate with a customer because it's first come, first served and this guy was pissed that they were out of two-by-fours, when he could see a stack of them on a cart ready to go out the door."

"Your load, I presume?"

"My load. When buddy at the lumber desk tried to explain that, and told the customer there was another shipment coming in a few days, the customer gave out and, well, he said some unkind things about Germans and that he wasn't a second-class citizen to those people. That kind of crap."

"*Huh*. Do you know that customer?"

Henry nodded. "Sure. I've known him most of my life. He's not usually like that. I mean, he's not a racist or anything. His right-hand man for years is a Mi'kmaq guy. It's just that he lost his father in World War Two over in France when he was just a baby. They didn't have it easy. Just him and his mother running a farm. People helped, of course, but still. It left him resentful, I guess, and then when he needed materials and couldn't get what he wanted, he was sour."

"You've avoided telling me who it is. Let me help you. Floyd Sanders?"

His eyes widened. "That's him. Like I say, with anyone else, he's a good guy. Look at how he lets Jack Fraser live on his land for next to nothing. That's because Jack's dad was one that really helped them out when Floyd was a boy, so now he feels he owes it to Jack."

"What happened with the two-by-fours?"

Henry nodded. "I went outside and called Gretha and told her a little about what was going on. I said that if we loaned Sanders a few boards, I'd still have enough to do me until the next shipment came in and he could give them back to us. She agreed without hesitation."

"You didn't tell her about his attitude?"

"No. Why would I?"

"Did that settle Floyd down?"

"He can be a bit of a curmudgeon, so apologies don't come easily. I think he said something like *well, that'll work* and we all went away somewhat satisfied."

"Did Sanders deliver the boards to the house when they came in?"

"Yes. He called me to find out if I'd be there and then just dropped them off on the front lawn. He never saw Gretha. As far as I know, he never even met her."

"You say he feels some kinship to Jack Fraser. Would that mean he might resent the fact that a German woman was living in Jack's house?"

"That I don't know. I see him around occasionally, but we aren't friends or anything."

"OK. I'll let you get on with your day. You've been very helpful. Thank you, Henry." Gordie laughed. "Your sister thinks you have a secret girlfriend stashed away somewhere."

Henry smiled. "My sister likes to mother people. First, it was my father and now it's me. I'm a forty-year-old man. I'm used to my privacy. I'll just keep her guessing."

Gordie chortled as he waved goodbye, thinking about his own sister's interest in his life.

\*\*\*

Calling Roxanne from the road, he took orders for lunch, so his colleagues welcomed him back to the office with enthusiasm. Rob Norris took the cardboard tray of hot drinks and Jason Ahearn took the paper bags with sandwiches and baked goods.

Roxanne stopped them from diving into the food right away. "Let's move this into the briefing room and we can do an update while we eat."

They moved everything into the briefing room and Gordie saw that a second whiteboard was in place beside the one holding all the notes on the Gretha Braun murder. He rooted around in a bag for his own bacon grilled cheese sandwich.

Jason looked longingly at Gordie's lunch as he unwrapped his own chicken and tomato panini. "I should have gotten what you got."

Gordie grinned. "No doubt the one you got is much healthier."

Jason took a bite. "Yeah. And it is good. Bacon just makes everything smell so delicious, though."

Rob had a smoked turkey sandwich waiting for him, but since it wasn't hot, he said he'd start. "Detective MacLean, let us show you how to clear up a murder case in 24 hours."

Gordie put his sandwich down. "What?"

"As we are here enjoying your very thoughtful gifts of food and drink, the suspect in our murder case is downstairs waiting for transport, after giving us a nice thorough confession."

Roxanne's mouth hung open. "Did he do ours as well?"

"No such luck. I know you were hoping for a tie-in. I was with you for a while there, thinking it might be an anti-immigrant thing, but it isn't."

She sat down and unwrapped her bagel with cream cheese. "Well, what was it, then? Not that I really care, you smug so-and-so, but you might as well tell us."

Norris nodded to Ahearn. "Go ahead. It's your first murder case, you're entitled."

"OK, here it is. The victim and his family came over as refugees.

They worked hard, bought a nice-sized house, and last year sponsored the wife's sister, husband and two children to come over. The new family lives in the basement. Unlike the victim, who was prepared to do any kind of work to make a go of it, the brother-in-law is a teacher and although he's taking English-as-a-second-language classes, he's a long way from being able to get a teaching job here. The victim, not unreasonably, wanted his man-in-the-basement to do a few hours in the restaurant to help cover some of the expenses. This apparently has been an ongoing point of contention for several months and yesterday it all came to a head. The women and children were off visiting a corn maze with some other mums and kids since there were no classes due to a teacher's professional development day. The two men got into a heated debate and the brother-in-law lost it. He stabbed the victim and then quickly hustled off to his ESL class, coming home after a couple of hours to raise the alarm when he found the body." Jason took a big bite of his panini.

Gordie had finished his sandwich and wiped his hands with a brown paper serviette. "I assume the suspect didn't take a whole lot of prodding to get him to confess?"

Norris smiled. "Sour grapes, MacLean. It took finesse to transform him from a grief-stricken family member to a guilt-ridden culprit. That, and forensics helped to point out that his shoes showed clear patterns of blood spatter that could only have occurred during the actual commission of the crime."

Roxanne balled up her serviette and stuffed it back into a bag. "So much for my theory, then."

Gordie stood up and went to the whiteboard. "Don't be too quick to dismiss it. I found something interesting today." Above Jack Fraser's name, he wrote *Floyd Sanders*.

Roxanne frowned. "I've heard that name already."

He recapped the morning's discussions, focusing on what he had heard from both Fraser and Henry Davis. He went back then and finished off by confirming that Mickey White had a gambling problem.

Norris stretched out his legs, sipping the last of his coffee. "The gambling man is a possibility, but I agree. I think this Sanders guy bears looking at. He's got no family, right?"

Gordie nodded. "No wife or kids that I know of, but we haven't done any sort of background on him yet. There's no one obvious at the farm that I've seen."

Roxanne took up the possible narrative. "He sees Jack Fraser as some sort of son. Fraser senior helped him out and now he's helping Jack. He's already got a deep-seated chip on his shoulder from having to grow up without his father. Now, this German comes into his neighbourhood and first, she takes the house that Jack keeps saying should be his, and then in his mind, she gets priority treatment, which just rubs salt in the wound."

Norris stood up. "Well, thanks for lunch, buddy. It sounds like you guys are on to something here, and meanwhile, Ahearn and I have paperwork to do."

Roxanne nodded. "I better bring Sarge up to speed."

# CHAPTER TWENTY-EIGHT

ROXANNE BROUGHT SERGEANT ARSENAULT up to speed, but she saw his mind was clearly on the successful outcome that Norris had achieved.

"Look, you've had a list of possible suspects as long as my arm. Now, this new theory about some old grudge because of World War II? I'm sure as hell not going to bring that up to Inspector Lang. Quite frankly, it sounds like you and MacLean are grasping at straws. My advice to you is to go back to basics and follow the most likely lead."

She rose, edging her way to the door of his office. "Right, Sergeant. Understood."

Gordie was at his desk, ticking into his computer. He looked up when she stopped at his desk. "Let me guess. It didn't go well with Sarge?"

Roxanne sighed. "He's not wild about this new angle. He wants us to go back to basics."

Gordie nodded. "Fair enough." He rose and gestured for her to follow him into the briefing room. "Let's go back through the list. If we've exhausted a person as a suspect, we take them off the list."

They started at the top. Roxanne pointed to Henry Davis. "What about him?"

Gordie sat on a chair in the front row. "Let's think about what someone might gain by Gretha's death. With Davis, it seems to me he'd lose a lot, and gain nothing. He had a good working relationship with the victim, as far as we can tell. Now he's out of a job. I don't see it."

Roxanne drew a line through his name and went on. "Ellie Davis?"

Gordie nodded. "That seems more complicated. They were good friends. Ellie claims there was nothing more than friendship between them, but how do we know that for certain? I don't know that Ellie had anything to gain, but we know that rage can be a motive."

"Unrequited love on one side or the other?"

"Exactly. Ellie's father just died. She's emotionally overwrought, and maybe in a moment of weakness she makes a pass at Gretha, or Gretha reads more into Ellie's need for a shoulder to cry on and makes a pass at her."

"We'll leave Ellie on the list, but God knows how we prove that." Roxanne moved down the list. "Linda Hickson, the realtor."

"Again, nothing to gain because if she was still hoping for compensation, that's at an end when Gretha died. But there's always revenge. She expected money and didn't get it. She goes over at night, knowing the victim is probably there alone. Gretha lets her in, of course, and they sit down for cake and tea. Gretha puts her foot down with something like, *I've been talking to people, and I know I don't owe you anything. So sorry, but no. I've changed my mind.'* Hickson loses it, picks up the knife and lashes out."

Roxanne frowned. "But why go back early the next morning?"

Gordie shrugged. "Alibi?"

"*Hmm.* I'm not convinced. I think she has more to lose than to gain. Definitely no hope for any money and she's putting herself at the scene by going in the next morning."

Gordie nodded. "Yeah. You're probably right. It's a stretch and unreasonable to believe she'd go back and put herself at the scene *and* get blood all over her suit. If she knew what she'd be facing, she would have been more careful."

Roxanne drew a dotted line through Linda's name. "Jack Fraser."

"Back where we started. I didn't think it back then, and I still don't think he's our guy. He wanted money from her, plain and simple. This whole charade of wanting the house is nonsense. If they handed it back to him, he'd run a mile. He lives in a trailer on someone else's land and is quite content with that."

"Jealousy? He didn't do anything with it, but now he sees what the house can be with some tender loving care?"

"Jack Fraser was never a man for showing TLC. Why do you think he isn't married or even in a relationship? He runs from responsibility. He wants whatever is the easiest thing for Jack Fraser. Nope, I firmly believe he wanted money and eventually he'd get the message and then he'd be pissed, and he'd complain to anyone who was prepared to listen, but does he feel strong enough to kill Gretha? No. I really don't see it."

"OK, you win." She drew a line through Jack Fraser's name. "Mia White?"

Gordie raised his eyebrows. "She has nothing to gain and everything to lose. Gretha was going to make Mia's life easier by buying half the business."

Roxanne tilted her head to study the name. "They got together on Sunday night over cake to discuss the finer details of the deal. Something went wrong. There had been an understanding on Mia's part and not on Gretha's part. Maybe Gretha had big plans to change the whole setup that Mia spent five years building up. She wanted to turn it into a licensed establishment to bring in more business. She wanted to enlarge it, which would essentially use up a chunk of the money Mia was getting. Whatever. They argued. Mia picks up the knife to make a point and without really intending it, the knife ends up in Gretha. Don't forget that Mia's an abused woman. She's had it with people telling her what to do and fights back." Roxanne turned to look at Gordie.

He nods. "It's possible. I hate to imagine it, but yes, I guess it's possible."

Roxanne left Mia's name and moved on. "Mickey White."

"He's still my top pick. He's a gambler who was doing well with his addiction, but even according to his wife, he's fallen off the wagon. His go-to answer, when thwarted by a woman, is violence. By his own admission, he felt Gretha was interfering in his marriage by encouraging Mia to be mouthy. He wanted, maybe he *needed,* to get his hands on money. He finds out somehow about the deal between the two women and goes to discuss it himself. *Why not buy the whole thing,* he asks. *No? OK, half will do, but you need to give me the money.* She tells him exactly what she thinks. *You're a brute. I won't give you one penny. The money goes to Mia, and I hope it gives her the means to leave you forever.* He's enraged. He doesn't do something as simple as twisting her arm. Instead, he picks up the knife. And that's that. Rage and fear that his wife might, in fact, leave him because of this woman's encouragement. Where would he be then? No. That can't be allowed to happen. Better to kill her than risk his wife leaving."

Roxanne nods. "Very compelling." She points to the line through Robert Wilson's name. "I think we've thrashed this one out already, haven't we?"

"I believe so. The painting wasn't an authentic Colville, but although Wilson was disappointed, I didn't get any sense that he was bitter about it. A guy like that? He's considering investing in the Melford Terminal project. No. I don't see him getting so bent out of shape over a painting as to murder someone to keep its authenticity a secret. Besides, if Gretha realized it wasn't a Colville, others would figure it out too."

Next to the original bullet of *A German? Money?* Roxanne added the name of Gretha's cousin, Ida Zimmerman. Roxanne turned to Gordie. "What about her?"

"Let's leave her on until we talk to the German police. We need to find out if she came to Canada. Maybe Jason can follow up on that. Hopefully, they have a way to check through a passport search or airline information."

She then pointed to the last name on the list. "What about this latecomer to the party? Floyd Sanders. Is it plausible that an elderly man, almost eighty years after his father was killed, gets so worked up that he murders a woman? A woman who wasn't even born then? When I thought it was a hate crime in general about immigration, I was in, but this? A lone farmer going after a defenceless woman? With a cake knife?"

"Let's leave him on until we get him in here to discuss it. We'll know better after that."

Roxanne nodded. "OK. Makes sense. Make the call. Get him in here tomorrow. After we talk to him, we'll regroup and see where we go next."

"We should get Mickey White in as well."

"Right. Get one in for the morning and one for the afternoon. I don't want them crossing paths if we can help it."

Gordie made the note in his book. "Good. I am working on a background for Sanders, so we'll have a better idea of the man we're dealing with."

"OK, carry on with whatever you can find in the public records. I'm going back to look at the forensics reports. Do we have any fingerprints from the scene that we can cross reference with any of these people? Let's be sure to offer both White and Sanders something to drink. I want their prints."

Gordie smiled. "You're getting sly in your old age. I like it."

\*\*\*

The first round of drinks at The Old Triangle was on Rob Norris, since they were there to celebrate the closing of his case. Roxanne had a glass of red wine on the table in front of her. They had pushed four of the small square black tables together to accommodate the ten people who had shown up to celebrate. Roxanne liked the place because away from the front where the light streamed in through large windows, the interior was dim and calming. The captain's chairs ensured no one invaded her personal space. Gordie sat about halfway down, chatting with Rob Norris, who regularly laughed loudly. Roxanne wondered if Gordie was that entertaining or if Rob had unleashed his natural desire to laugh after the success of his investigation. Roxanne didn't feel in the least like laughing.

She looked up when someone pulled out the chair next to her.

Jason Ahearn put his pint of Guinness on the table. "Mind if I sit here?"

"No problem, but shouldn't you sit with your partner to reap all the accolades for your great work?"

Jason shrugged. "Let's face it, we didn't exactly have to do a lot of digging."

Roxanne nodded and took a sip of wine. "Still, it must feel good."

"Of course, it does. At the same time, it's a bit of a letdown."

She raised her eyebrows.

"Last night I lay awake half the night, creating lists and action plans in my head. I had a dozen suspects ready to interview. Restaurant staff, disgruntled past employees, hate crime groups against Muslims, hate crimes against immigration in general, and neighbours the victim had offended somehow. You know. That was without even looking into his finances. I wondered about blackmail and loan sharks."

Roxanne laughed. "Loan sharks in Port Mulroy? Good Lord."

He laughed with her. "I wanted to be the one to break this wide open. I know I'm the new guy and people don't have a lot of faith in me." He turned and looked down the row towards Gordie.

"Don't mind MacLean. He doesn't trust many people. It's not just you. He thinks you're in cahoots with the sarge."

He nodded.

"Are you?"

Ahearn took a sip of his drink, licking the froth of stout from his top lip. "My father knows the sarge. Which means that I know him. He comes over to the house sometimes and when he's off duty, he isn't at all like he is in the office. He's just a regular guy then, but he's my Dad's buddy. Not mine."

"I have a hard time seeing him in that light. I thought I got on well with Sarge, but once he made me lead on this case, I found out how wrong I was. I imagined I'd be sitting down with him to exchange ideas on the investigation. I don't know why I thought that. I guess because Gordie used to disappear down the hall and spend time in that office and, in my head, I thought they discussed things. Every time Gordie came back to his desk, he'd be in bad humour. Now I know why. I can't wait to get away when I give my update. I always feel like a child called up to the principal's office."

Jason grinned. "Somehow, I doubt you experienced that very often."

She smiled back. "You're right. I do have a vivid imagination, though."

"I think you're doing an amazing job. I imagine you're around my age, but here you are leading a major investigation."

"Thanks, but the truth is, Gordie is still just as much in charge. I'm just there to make sure there's no appearance of bias because he lives in the area."

"And isn't that the best kind of partnership to have? Where both partners are basically equal?"

She tilted her head. "Yeah. That's true. Maybe I've been try-ing too hard to make my mark. I want people to respect and trust my judgement."

"And they do. I haven't heard one word to believe anything different."

Roxanne lifted her glass and clinked it against his. "Thanks for that."

Gordie had said his goodbyes to those sitting at the far end of the table and now came to stand by Roxanne, glancing at the wineglass in her hand. "I'm heading out. Do you want a drive home? I can pick you up again in the morning."

"No, thanks for the offer, but I'm good. I'm switching to soda after this, but I think I'll stay a big longer to enjoy the feel of success, even if it isn't my own."

He nodded to the waiters putting down plates of food. "Our turn will come. Seeing how this crew likes to celebrate, you better start saving your pennies now."

"Have a good night, Gordie. Give your favourite girl a cuddle for me."

"Are you talking about Vanessa or Taz?"

She laughed. "You decide."

Jason smiled. "That dark horse. Does he have two women on the go?"

Roxanne considered whether she should enlighten Ahearn or let him develop a whole new image of Gordie MacLean. Instead, she turned the topic. "What about you? Do you have one or more important women in your life?"

He cocked his head to acknowledge her avoidance technique. "Only my mother. What about you? Anyone special waiting for you at home?"

Roxanne was delighted to tell Ahearn about her grandmother and her golden retriever named Sheba.

# CHAPTER TWENTY-NINE

GORDIE HAD ARRANGED FOR Mickey White to come in for an interview first thing in the morning and Sanders two hours later.

When White settled himself with his hands wrapped around a proper ceramic mug of tea, MacLean started the questions. "We've been doing some digging, Mickey. You aren't very good at holding on to money, are you?"

"Who is? We live in expensive times. Just buying groceries costs an arm and a leg now."

"That's true, but we aren't talking about groceries, are we?"

"If you're talking about my business, that's even more expensive."

"Let's not play games, Mickey. We're talking about your gambling habit, as I'm sure you well know."

He flushed and took a sip of tea.

"Five years ago, you almost went bankrupt. Mia somehow pulled you out of the fire, but not before you lost your truck."

Mickey shrugged. "I quit all that."

"That's true, you did. The problem is you started again, didn't you?"

"Who told you that?"

"We have our sources. You know that in a small community, people hear things, and what we heard about you is that you've taken it up again. You're losing money. More than you can afford to lose. You know what that means?"

"Are you the gambling police now? I'm not doing anything illegal."

Gordie went on to answer his own question. "It means that you needed to get your hands on some cash, and you thought you could do that by going to Gretha Braun."

"That's crazy. She wouldn't give me any money. I know that."

"You found out, didn't you?"

Mickey frowned. "Found out what?"

Gordie glanced at Roxanne, who gave a small nod. "You found out that Gretha was going to buy half the business from Mia. The plan meant Mia would still run things. How did you feel about that?"

His eyes widened and his mouth opened in a silent 'oh'. "I don't believe you. Mia tells me all the important things."

"Like you tell her?"

He scowled. "That's different. This is a big thing."

"It is a big thing, so when you found out about it, you went to confront Gretha, didn't you?"

"I didn't know."

"We believe you did know. You went to talk to Gretha. Maybe to convince her to buy the whole business, maybe just to convince her to give you at least some of the money. You needed to sort out your gambling debts. What happened, Mickey? Did she laugh at you? Did she tell you to get out? Something sent you over the edge. This foreign woman who was already a bad influence on your wife was going to take an even bigger, more active role in things. You couldn't stomach that, could you?"

Mickey folded his arms across his chest. "Maybe if I knew about it, I probably would have said something. Maybe not. I'd have been glad of the money coming in, no matter what. But I didn't know. I swear to God, I didn't know."

Roxanne stepped in. "OK, Mickey. Let's say we believe you didn't go personally to talk to Braun. Who did you tell? Maybe you told one of your creditors that this lady had money and they should collect it from her. Is that possible?"

He shook his head. "I don't know who you think I deal with, but I didn't know. For another thing, even if I owed money to someone, and I'm not saying I do, no one is going to collect my debt from another person. That's not how things work." He shook his head in contempt at her naïve suggestion.

Gordie took over again. "You claim you were home the night of Gretha Braun's murder, but no one can verify that. Your wife went to bed early, didn't she?"

"So? She always goes to bed before me. She went to bed, and I watched the end of the movie and then I went to bed. You can't prove anything different."

"We're still following up with people who live in the area to check security camera videos. Everyone has them these days. We'll see your vehicle, won't we Mickey?"

He shook his head. "No, you won't see it because I wasn't there. I didn't like the woman, but that's even more reason why I would never go there if I wasn't just picking up Mia."

Gordie closed his notebook. "All right, Mickey. We'll stop there for now, but we may come back to you with more questions at a later date."

Mickey stood up. "Ask all the questions you want. I didn't do this."

Gordie escorted him out while Roxanne pulled out a plastic bag to secure the empty mug that now held Mickey White's fingerprints and DNA. If they ever charged him, they'd get his fingerprints officially, but this would serve to use as a comparison to prints found at the house.

***

In the afternoon, they went through it again. A fresh mug of tea in front of Floyd Sanders already had his fingerprints on it, although the man had yet to take a sip. He kept his well-worn floppy leather hat firmly in place on his head. Just below the sagging brim, Sanders' heavy eyebrows were steel grey, although the shaggy beard, mustache and sideburns were white, as were the long hairs sprouting from his large ears.

"I'm Detective Roxanne Albright, and you've spoken previously with my partner, Detective Gordie MacLean."

A short nod. "Why did I get dragged in here?"

"To help us with our inquiries, Mr. Sanders. You know that Gretha Braun was murdered almost two weeks ago. We're talking to everyone who had contact with her. You may have relevant information to share with us that will lead to an arrest. I'm sure you don't begrudge a couple of hours of your time to help us?"

"Get on with it, then."

Roxanne opened the file folder on the table and took a moment to study the contents. "Mr. Sanders, can I call you Floyd?"

"If it makes you happy."

She smiled. "Thank you. Floyd, you haven't had an easy life, have you?" She read from the file. "Your father died in World War Two, leaving your mother alone to look after you on her own. You were just a toddler at the time. That must have been terrible. Especially since, as a farmer, it wasn't like they conscripted him. He volunteered, didn't he?"

The elderly man lifted his chin. "That's the kind of man he was. His country called, and he answered."

"Yes, he did, and you are right to be proud. But it meant a lifetime of hardship for you and your mother, didn't it?"

"Like a lot of folks. What's all this got to do with anything? It was a long time ago."

Roxanne nodded. "How did you feel when a German woman bought Jack Fraser's house?"

His dark eyebrows came together in a frown. "Feel? I didn't feel anything. I don't have time to fuss over what the neighbours are up to. I'm too busy for that."

"I understand, Floyd. You still run the farm with just a couple of helpers, including Jack Fraser. Is that right?"

"Yeah. I've got 22 beef cattle, and I'm managing all right, but it's work."

"Of course. Let's go back to when you first heard that a German woman had bought Jack Fraser's old house. Even if you don't have time to stand around and gossip, this was close to home. Jack talked about it. He was angry. It made you angry too, didn't it?"

He scowled, even more deeply, his forehead a series of deep furrows. "I was angry, for Jack's sake. It wasn't a fair system. He lost his house, and I don't say he deserved it, or he didn't, but I think if someone paid more money than what was owed to the bank, Jack should get it, and he didn't. That's what makes me angry."

Roxanne sighed. "There's a process, Floyd. Jack Fraser can apply for the money. There was no need to harass the new owner. A German woman. I think you were quite prepared to think the worst of her, weren't you?"

Sanders leaned back in the chair and folded his arms across his chest. "I don't know what you're trying to say. I felt bad for Jack. I would have felt the same if it was this lady from Germany, or you or him." He jutted his chin toward Gordie.

"You're saying it made no difference that the new owner was German. The country responsible for your father's death?"

"Never crossed my mind."

Roxanne nodded and turned the pages in her file to the report Gordie had completed after meeting with Henry Davis. "Someone at the building supply place overheard you complaining about Germans. They ran out of the lumber you needed to do repairs because this particular German had already taken all the stock they had. What can you tell me about that?"

He snorted. "Someone making a mountain out of a molehill. It made me angry because I needed lumber. A lumber store should have enough in stock to meet the needs of the community. If I said some things, which I don't remember saying, they were just words said in haste. I guess now, I'm repenting at leisure."

"So, your angry words weren't specifically directed at the German woman. Is that what you're trying to tell us?"

"I directed them at the lumber manager."

"But you complained about Germans."

He shrugged. "Didn't mean anything by it and it all got sorted out, anyway."

"Because the woman you complained about agreed to let you have what you needed."

"Exactly. So, why would I hold a grudge?"

"Because it probably rubbed salt in the wound to have her in a position where she *could* sort out the problem.

"*Pfft*. Maybe that's how things work in your world, but not mine. I needed lumber. I got it. When the next shipment came in, I returned it, and I never gave another thought to the whole thing."

"I think that sounds good, Floyd, but having Jack Fraser living in your yard, complaining day in, day out, riled you up. I don't know what it was that put you over the edge, but I think you went to see her on that Sunday night. The victim invited you in because that's the sort of person she was. Gretha Braun was kind and friendly and wanted nothing more than to fit in with her new, chosen community. She let you in and you got into an argument with her. You saw the kind of arrogance you imagined caused your father's death and you lost your temper. You're a strong man. You may be older than some of us, but after working on the farm your whole life, you're stronger than many people, and that was it. You saw the knife there and stabbed her. For all the hardship you went through as a child, for all the deprivation your mother went through, you took your revenge on this German, didn't you?"

Floyd stroked his white beard for a few seconds as if to help prepare his response. "That's how much you know. Yes, in 1944, my father died in France. But the Germans *did not* kill my father. No. On the eighth of August, when the 8th U.S. Air Force mistakenly bombed the headquarters of the 3rd Canadian Infantry Division, my father died. So Detective, if I was going to hate someone for killing my father, it wouldn't be the Germans, would it?"

Albright made a note in the file as she gathered her thoughts and then she looked up. "That may have been the actual manner of his death, but the root cause was because he was over there fighting against Nazis."

Sanders shrugged one shoulder and shook his head. "It was a long time ago. You're grasping at straws, and I can tell you right now, I had nothing to do with that woman's death. I had no interest in becoming friends with her, but I sure as hell didn't have any reason to kill her. Neither did Jack Fraser. I was at home that night like I am every single night. I don't drive in the dark anymore. I've got cataracts apparently and don't see so good, so I just stay put and watch television or listen to the radio, or what usually happens, I just go to bed. I'm up early and by eight o'clock I'm tired and go to bed. And I know Jack was in his trailer as usual because I don't have drapes on my bedroom window. I'd see his headlights if he was out and came back late." The elderly man pushed himself back from the table. "Now, unless you have more questions, I need to get back. I've got a long list of chores to do."

Roxanne glanced at Gordie who shook his head. "All right, Floyd. We appreciate that you came in here today. You say that neither you nor Jack Fraser was responsible for Gretha Braun's death. Do you have any thoughts on who may have wanted her dead?"

He stood up. "I keep myself to myself. I have no idea."

Gordie rose as well. "I'll walk Floyd out."

When he returned, Roxanne still sat in the interview room, flipping through the file. She looked up at him. "I'm at my wit's end. I've sent the mugs down to the lab to check the prints, but I don't have a lot of hope."

He sat down across from her. "You don't think it was Sanders, then?"

She shrugged. "I don't see it. Do you?"

"Not really, no."

Roxanne pulled out the photo of Gretha and Ellie. "I still wonder about her." She laid the photo down. "Look at them. I'm telling you this is more than friendship." She tapped the image of Gretha. "That's love." She held up her hand as though Gordie had protested. "I'm not saying that friends don't love each other. I certainly have girlfriends that I absolutely love, but that" another tap on the image "that's something else."

Gordie picked up the photo. "I don't know. It just looks like two friends having a nice day together to me, but I'm the first to admit I'm not an expert on female behaviour. But no matter what, like you said once before, even if you're right, how do we prove it?"

"I had a thought. We only have her word that there's a missing file box. What if that's just something designed to distract us?"

"It's possible, I suppose. But to what end?"

"To throw us off. To get us chasing our tails away from her."

"But why a file box? It seems so specific. Why not invent something, I don't know, more valuable?"

"Too easy to verify. The neighbour or Mia White might question an invented valuable."

"I have a hard time imagining it."

Roxanne rubbed her temples. "I want to get Ellie Davis back in here for another conversation." Before he had a chance to say anything, she shook her head. "I'll have Jason Ahearn to sit in with me

210

on this. You've developed a friendship with this woman, and I think you're too close to be unbiased."

Gordie stared at her. "What the hell? Is this about Eddy again?"

She stood up. "It is not about Eddy. It's exactly what I said. It's obvious you've got a soft spot for Ellie, and you aren't willing to keep an open mind."

"Because I don't agree with you, you think I'm biased. Well, I think Ahearn has a crush on you and that feels good, doesn't it? You're having him in rather than me because he'll go along with whatever you say."

"How dare you? That's absolute nonsense."

Norris came in and stopped to look from one to the other. "Am I interrupting something?"

Gordie shrugged. "Not as far as I'm concerned. Detective Albright has decided that Detective Ahearn will offer a fresh perspective with an interview. I look forward to hearing all about it later."

Gordie stalked back to his desk. He heard Albright talk to Ellie and knew she was coming straight in. He sent off a note to Ida Zimmerman to ask if she had gone through Gretha's apartment yet and then spent time updating his reports, but his mind was elsewhere. *And this is why I'm better working on my own. Well, since I'm obviously not needed here, I'll just go ahead and do what I'm good at.*

He waited until Albright and Ahearn disappeared down the hall to the meeting room and then he packed up his laptop, put on his jacket and stopped long enough for a word with Norris. "If anyone wonders where I am, I'm off to Port Mulroy to follow up on a lead."

Norris raised his eyebrows. "Albright know where you're going?"

MacLean shrugged. "I don't think she's very interested. She's decided Ahearn suits her better."

*** 

Jason Ahearn was delighted to sit in on the interview at ten o'clock with Ellie Davis. "Aside from running the recording equipment, what do you want me to do? Be bad cop to your good cop?"

Roxanne frowned. "I want you to listen, take notes and ask relevant questions that will move the investigation forward. Don't jump in and interrupt me, but when there's a logical break, then ask your questions."

His eyes widened. "OK."

When Ellie arrived, Ahearn went down to escort her to the interview room. He offered her a drink, which she refused, and then Jason and Roxanne sat down across from her.

Roxanne pushed the photo of Ellie and Gretha across the table. "I want to talk a bit further about your relationship with Gretha Braun."

Ellie frowned. "You made me suddenly take time off work to ask me this? I had to get the music teacher in to take over my class and she was in a complete state over it. I've already discussed this with you. We were friends. Just friends. Good friends. I was very fond of her, but I know you're suggesting there was something sexual involved and you're bloody well wrong."

Roxanne pulled the photo back and returned it to the file. "You're very adamant about that."

Ellie slammed her hand on the table. "The whole thing is ridiculous. Even if there was more to our friendship, which again, I insist there wasn't, what does it matter? I was at home in Sydney the night Gretha died."

"Let's talk about that file box."

Ellie blinked at the change in topic. "What of it?"

"You seem to be the only person that knows anything about that file folder. Gretha must have trusted you very much to share the contents with you."

Ellie shook her head. "What makes you think she shared the contents with me? As I explained to Detective MacLean, I noticed it there beside her desk when we went up to look at something on her computer. That's it. I didn't look inside. I didn't see any private papers on her desk. She was very tidy, and her desk was clear when I was in the office with her."

Roxanne swallowed and started when Ahearn jumped in. "Did the victim talk about the files?"

Ellie folded her arms across her chest. "No. The *victim* said nothing to me about that file box or its contents. I wish to hell I hadn't said anything about it now."

Roxanne glanced at Ahearn to see if he had any further questions, but he stared at his notebook without noticing her glance. "All right. Thank you for coming in. I regret the disruption it caused, but I want to remind you that we're trying to solve a murder here and that means that sometimes people will be inconvenienced."

Ellie rose. "That's it, then? I'm free to go?"

"Yes. For now."

Ellie shook her head and slipped on her jacket. She followed Ahearn without saying goodbye to Roxanne.

*Well, that got me exactly nowhere.*

Jason Ahearn came back and took the seat that Ellie vacated across from Roxanne. "Wow. You were great."

Roxanne frowned. "What? How can you say that? I wanted to break her down to either admit she had a relationship with Braun or dig out more detailed information about that missing file box. I got nothing."

"But you were strong and in control. That's a good thing with a witness, isn't it?"

She sighed. "Did you sense anything from her? Is she holding anything back, or was she lying about her friendship?"

His handsome face puckered. "I don't know. Nothing jumped out at me."

"No. Me neither."

\*\*\*

Gordie fumed for the first forty-five minutes of the drive, and then he put Roxanne Albright out of his mind to think about where he was going. The first stop was another visit to Mickey White.

White stood with his arms folded across his chest. "You, again. I just saw you. What the hell do you want now? This is harassment."

Gordie stepped forward causing White to retreat into the house. "Mind if I come in?"

"Like I have a choice." Mickey led the way to the living room and waved in the direction of the sofa while he continued to the kitchen.

Gordie followed him and pulled out a chair for himself at the scarred pine table. "After you left, a couple of further questions came up, Mickey." He watched as the man padded around the kitchen filling the kettle and clicking it on to heat, pulling two mugs from the cabinet above the sink.

Mickey opened the box of Ty-Phoo tea sitting on the counter, pulled out a bag and dropped it into a mug. He turned to Gordie and held up another bag.

"Sure, thanks. I never tried this brand before. Any good?"

"As good as anything else. Mia likes it. Grew up with British tea, I guess. Don't know if I can tell the difference, but if it makes her happy, who am I to argue?"

He put a two-litre carton of milk and a brown and white sugar bowl on the table. When the kettle boiled, Mickey filled the two mugs and set them down, splashing water from Gordie's on the table. He turned back to tear off a few sheets of paper towel and tossed them on the table.

Gordie watched as White used the spoon from the sugar bowl to put two heaping spoons into his mug, added milk and then used the sugar spoon to lift out his teabag and drop it on a paper towel, stirred the tea and replaced the wet spoon back into the sugar bowl.

Gordie fished the bag out of his mug using his fingers, squeezing the bag before laying it on the same square of paper towel. He added milk and then compulsively took the other 2 squares of the paper towel and wiped up the spreading puddle of tea from the table before laying the teabag-laden one on top of the soggy bundle.

White seemed oblivious to MacLean's effort to tidy up. He closed his eyes for a moment and took a deep draw on the hot tea. "So, what are these questions you have? You aren't just asking me the same things over again, I hope."

"I want to know about where you go to gamble."

White's large forehead creased. "Why?"

"I have my reasons."

Mickey set down his mug and licked his lips. "You going there to throw my name around?"

"Look Mickey, there are only a few places that are likely, so I can do this the hard way and go to each of them and throw your name around, or I can do it with your help, and just go to one and I may or may not mention your name."

"Why do you want to go at all? I'll answer your questions. I've cooperated so far."

"OK, tell me about the high-stakes games."

He shook his head. "I don't know anything about that. I just play the slot machines."

"You play cards. How did you lose your truck those years ago? Not on slot machines."

"That was a long time ago. Now it's just slot machines and online games. Even that I can't do anymore because Mia took away the credit card, which I'm guessing you already know."

Gordie sipped his tea. "If you *were* interested in a high-stakes game, where would you go?"

"Maybe the Blue Lagoon. For God's sake, don't say my name there. Like I said, I only go for the slots, but I still don't want my name put about."

Despite his feelings for this man, Gordie sympathized with his fear. "I doubt if I need to mention your name."

White exhaled. "Thanks."

Gordie stood and shook his head. "A word of advice, Mickey. You've got a great wife in Mia and a nice house. Do something to deserve it."

Mickey scowled. "I'm a fisherman. I work hard."

He waved his hand at the sink stacked with dishes. "During the season, yes. But right now? How hard is it to just tidy up a bit instead of leaving everything for Mia?"

Mickey stood up as well. "You a marriage counsellor, now?"

"No. You're right. It's none of my business." MacLean walked back through the living room and outside, sucking in a lungful of fresh air.

Backing out of the driveway, he glanced at the time. *Perfect timing for a late lunch at the Blue Lagoon.*

# CHAPTER THIRTY

THE INTERIOR OF THE club was dim, and Gordie stood for a moment to let his eyes adjust. There were half a dozen pool tables lined up in the centre of the room, lights hanging over each table from the high, dark industrial-looking ceiling. Along one wall was a bar with a few high round tables within easy reach for calling out orders for drinks or food. Across the opposite wall, bright splashes of coloured lights spun and flashed where a series of video slot machines stood. Half of them had patrons sitting, silently feeding coins into the machines, faces expressionless, reflecting the pink and blue lights.

The click of pool balls and quiet exclamations of shots well or poorly played competed with country music on the sound system.

Gordie took a seat at the bar and when the petite, dark-haired girl approached, he ordered a burger and fries.

"You wanna beer with that, hon?"

"A soda water will do, thanks."

She raised an eyebrow but didn't comment. After popping into the kitchen behind the bar to place his food order, she brought him a pint glass with soda water and ice, a wedge of lime perched on the edge of the glass.

She set his drink down, a snake tattoo slithering from under her sleeve and across her hand. She folded her arms then and watched him tip the lime into the drink. "So, who are you looking for?"

Gordie took a sip of his drink and then put it back on the cardboard coaster. "Looking for? Who says I'm looking for someone?"

She snorted. "A wild guess."

"A wrong guess, then. I'm not looking for anyone. Someone told me this was a good place for lunch and an even better place at night, so I just thought I'd stop in and see for myself."

"Right. OK."

He glanced around the large room. "If I was looking for a card game, where would I find that?"

She shook her head and waved her hand. "Pool tables and slots. That's what's on offer here. Card game? You'd have to go to Sydney for that. There's a casino there, you know."

He nodded. "I don't feel like driving all the way there. I thought there might be a poker game going here."

"Sorry, hon. I don't know anything about that. I'll go check on your lunch."

She came back with his lunch and it surprised Gordie at how good it was. He enjoyed the food but noticed that the bartender made a point of staying busy at the other end of the bar, leaving him to his own thoughts.

When he finished his food, he picked up his glass and wandered around the room, stopping to watch, from a respectful distance, a man and a woman playing pool. He noticed a large bulletin board advertising a league that was looking for more players, and some pinned-up photos from past events. He stopped and peered through the dim light at the photos. He nodded and went back to the bar to pay for his lunch.

He left a ten-dollar tip for his fourteen-dollar lunch. "Thanks. The food was good. I enjoyed it."

She slipped the tip into a pocket in her apron. "Great. Come back anytime." She hesitated and then added with a nod. "It's livelier at night. You might like it better."

"I'll keep that in mind."

***

Gordie went home and set up his computer. He wrote reports about his interview with White and his visit to the club, uploaded them into the system, and then took a deep breath and called Roxanne.

It rang three times before she answered and he imagined her looking at the screen, trying to decide whether or not to answer.

"So, what mystery jaunt are you on?"

He gritted his teeth. "I went back to interview Mickey White again."

Her voice was frosty. "Why? Was there something you didn't want to ask during the formal interview?"

"Nothing earth-shattering, but after he left, I decided to pursue his gambling further. I keep getting the sense that there's more to him and the gambling than he's telling us. How did your interview with Ellie go?"

He heard her sigh and almost felt sorry for her. "Yeah. Nothing more. She's doing a good job of keeping things quiet."

"Or she has nothing more to tell us."

"Maybe. Gordie, I'm stumped. Ahern seems to think I know what I'm doing, but the truth is, I'm baffled, and I feel every day that goes by I'm getting further from the truth."

Now he felt sorry for her. "Take a step back. Go home early and we'll meet first thing in the morning and plan out our next steps. This wasn't a random killing. I'm sure of it, so we do what we always do, and figure out who has the most to gain by her death, or the most to lose by her continued life."

"OK. I'll be in for 7:30."

"You pick up the coffee and something to go with it, and I'll be there as well."

***

It was still dark when he left home, but as he neared the station, the sun blinded him as it crept above the horizon. The visor did little to help, and he drove the last ten minutes, holding up his right hand to shield his eyes from the worst of it.

Roxanne had set up in the briefing room. A box with a selection of donuts, muffins and croissants sat on the eight-foot table and a large double-double coffee awaited Gordie beside the box of pastries.

He took a blueberry muffin to start and took a seat in front of the whiteboard. Roxanne sat down beside him, also staring at the board.

"Want to tell me how it went with Ellie Davis yesterday?"

"Not particularly."

He nodded; his mouth full of food.

She sighed. "I probably just succeeded in upsetting her with no progress."

Gordie took a sip of coffee and wiped his mouth with a paper serviette. "You went with your gut. Can't fault you for that." He made sure his voice was neutral, not revealing his satisfaction.

"How did your day go?"

"Mickey White is softening. He gave me the name of the club where he goes to gamble. He still hasn't admitted to doing anything more than slots, but I know that can't be true. Slots are limited to the coins that you put in the machine. Online gambling needs a credit card. It's the games no one talks about that get dangerous. They might run some games from a backroom in the club I visited, called the Blue Lagoon, or somewhere else altogether, but people there know about it. They're involved."

"How does that move us forward? Are you thinking one of those people killed Gretha?"

He shook his head. "No, I can't see that. But it's connected. Somehow, it's connected."

Roxanne turned back to the board. "Let's do what you suggested. We'll go through our prime suspects and figure out how they would win or lose with Gretha's death."

He stood. "Ellie? Win or lose?"

She shrugged. "I thought it was love gone wrong, but if you put it in terms of win or lose then I give up. She doesn't win by Gretha's death or lose by her living."

He put a line through her name. "Mia White?"

"She wins if Gretha lives because there's a chance of the business partnership. Hey, wait. What if they already signed the papers for the business and then Gretha changed her mind?" Roxanne stood up and paced. "They signed an agreed partnership deal prior to that night, then on Sunday night they have an argument and Gretha says she wants out. With Gretha's death, Mia waits a while and then goes to a lawyer to go after the estate for the money. She has a signed contract. The estate is on the hook and who's going to argue? Not the cousin in Germany who hardly knows what's been going on. No one. Mia gets the money, or at least some compensation."

Gordie nodded. "That's good. That's possible. Is Mia capable of killing her friend, though? She really seemed broken up by Gretha's death."

"OK. Mickey White, then. Mia's upset because her friend is backing out. We know how Gretha felt about Mickey and maybe that was part of the deal. You leave him or no deal, but Mia loves Mickey, despite his failings."

Gordie took up the thread. "Mickey goes and confronts Gretha. He needs the money and in one moment he's found out he has it within grasp and then it's gone. He tells Mia, I'll sort this out. Somehow, Mia has mentioned the file box. Gretha's copy is in the file box, so better get it in case she's made a note on her copy of the contract that she's cancelling it. White goes alone, or they go together."

Roxanne nods. "Together. That makes sense. He does the deed, and she goes to find the file box." She widens her eyes. "Now we're talking premeditation, but how do we prove it?"

"We start by going back to the computer. Gretha might have drafted the contract on her computer. From there we look for the lawyer that put the official contract together. This is a legal document and there must have been a lawyer involved."

Roxanne nodded. "I'll talk to Jason. He knows the files on that computer the best."

"And I'll talk to Norris. He was going through the emails. She might have been in touch with a lawyer by email. I'm also going back to those file folders I took from the house. I don't remember seeing anything like this, but I may have missed it."

Roxanne stopped on her way out to turn back. "I wonder if the realtor knows who the lawyer might be. It's probably the same person that Gretha used for the sale of her house. I'll call her."

Gordie grabbed a donut on his way out of the room. "Don't forget to let the boys know there's food here. They work better with snacks."

"Don't we all?" Then she grinned. "I'm feeling better than I have in days. Thanks, Gordie."

"Don't get too excited. It's all just a theory right now."

"It's a step forward. That's something."

"Fingers crossed."

# CHAPTER THIRTY-ONE

ROXANNE TAPPED HER FINGER on the steering wheel in time with the music as she headed home. The afternoon had gone well when Ahearn had found the contract on Gretha's hard drive. The date was a full week before her murder, so there had been plenty of time for them both to sign it, and then for Gretha to change her mind for whatever reason. She had written it up herself. Norris didn't find any evidence that she had emailed it to a lawyer, but perhaps she had taken it in herself. Roxanne spoke with the realtor, but while Linda Hickson was happy to provide the lawyer's name, she wasn't aware of any conversations Gretha had with him beyond the real estate transactions. Roxanne left a message for the lawyer to call.

Now, as she drove, she was bursting to talk to someone. "Phone, call Eddy Tomah."

Just as she wondered if he would answer, she heard his silky voice over the sound of her tires on the road. "Roxanne. You must have been reading my mind. I was just thinking about you."

She almost laughed out loud. "Were you?"

"I was. I miss talking to you every day. It's taken all my strength not to call you, but I didn't think I'd last much longer."

"Oh, Eddy. God, I've missed talking to you, too."

"Is the case over? Is that why you're calling?"

"No, but I think we're making progress. Have you been staying away just because of my job?"

He sounded puzzled. "Of course. I thought that's what you needed and wanted from me. It felt like I was getting in your way and that's the last thing I want."

"I thought my work irritated you and that's why I didn't hear from you."

She heard him make a *tsk* sound. "No, not at all."

She couldn't help herself. "You were so annoyed about the concert tickets and then you went fishing. It felt, I don't know, like a punishment."

The road noise sounded loud again in the silence. "Eddy? You still there?"

"I'm here. I was thinking back to that weekend, and I can't believe that's what you thought. Sure, I was upset that we couldn't go to the concert, but it was the circumstances that annoyed me. Not you. I looked forward to going together and then it didn't happen. I gave the tickets away, and that was the end of it. The fishing? Why did you think that was some sort of punishment? It was a great day to go fishing. That's all. The case had you wrapped up, and I made other plans instead of putting pressure on you to make time for me."

Roxanne felt a lump in her throat. "I thought we were through. That you wanted a break from me."

"I wanted to give *you* a break from having to fit me in when you needed to prioritize your work."

She took a deep breath. "So, we're, OK?"

"Of course, we are. I'm not that fickle, Roxanne. I thought you knew that and understood how I felt. All this time, I never imagined you thought there was something wrong with us. Wow. I would have called you had I thought that."

They chatted for a few moments about his family and hers, and then she heard him yawn. "Am I keeping you from a nap?"

He laughed. "Actually, yes. I went out on a call with my brother at 3 a.m. for a single-vehicle accident. I was sleeping on my brother Denny's sofa when he got a call and since they've got a couple of guys off with the flu, he asked me to go along."

"Port Mulroy, right?"

"Yeah, but the guy was from Isle Madame."

"I wonder if Gordie knows him."

"Maybe. Last name was Davis."

She almost slammed on the brakes. "As in Henry Davis?"

"Could be. I was more concerned with cutting the door off the car than what his name was. I just heard one of the guys say Davis when they were loading him into the ambulance. Do you know him?"

"There's a Henry Davis that's connected with my case."

"Wow. Small world. Well, he's in the Port Mulroy General now."

"Eddy, I gotta go. I need to call Gordie."

She heard the smile in his voice. "Don't be a stranger. I'm leaving it for you to call me when you have time. That doesn't mean I don't want to hear from you."

"Got it. Thanks, Eddy."

Roxanne was nearly home, so she waited the extra few minutes to get to the house before making any more calls. Then she had to take a few minutes to kneel to give Sheba some cuddles while the golden retriever wriggled and pushed her nose against Roxanne's neck in excitement. After that, she took a couple more moments to say hello to her grandmother, who immediately said she'd put the kettle on while Roxanne made her calls.

Roxanne went into the spare room she used as an office and

looked up the number for the hospital. After a brief conversation, she then called Gordie, but it went straight to voicemail.

She left a message. "You're probably driving through the no-service black hole. Call me as soon as you get this. Henry Davis has been in an accident. He's in the ICU but they won't tell me anything else."

Roxanne sat staring into space until her grandmother came in and set a large cup of strong tea and a saucer with a freshly baked cranberry scone on the desk.

She smiled in thanks. "Nana, this is just what I need. Thank you."

Helen Albright stroked a wisp of hair away from Roxanne's forehead. "You look done in. Try not to fret so much."

Roxanne waited until her grandmother had left the room before sighing deeply. *I think fretting is called for right about now.*

***

Gordie was at Vanessa's house when his phone finally chirped to let him know there was a phone message waiting for him. He was so comfortable that he took his time picking it up. He sat with his stocking feet on the ottoman in front of the wood-burning stove with his own cup of tea in hand.

Vanessa had a glass of red wine and shared the sofa with Taz, who admittedly took up two-thirds of the space, while Vanessa had a small corner.

Gordie shook his head. "You spoil that dog. She has a perfectly good dog bed over in the corner."

Vanessa stroked the big white head resting on her lap. "Would you want to lie on a bed in the corner instead of the sofa?"

Gordie smiled. "Maybe I'm just jealous."

She laughed and then became serious. "How is it going with Roxanne as the lead? You haven't said much about it."

He drained his cup and set it down on the small round table beside his chair before answering. "There are days I want to strangle her, but then I remind myself that she's struggling. We're all frustrated with the lack of progress on the case, and I know she feels responsible."

"Is there something you could do to help her?"

His face clouded up. "I wouldn't sabotage the case or ignore something that might help her. If there is anything I can do, I'm doing it. It's just that there are days she thinks she needs to be all stern and in charge, and that's when I want to strangle her. Then she goes back to normal, and I take a deep breath and just get on with the job."

"Sounds frustrating."

"It has been, but I think we're all on edge by now. Sarge took Roxanne off the daily briefings, and then he cancelled the briefings. Roxanne takes it all personally. If it was me, I'd be thinking 'great, that's one less thing to worry about,' but not her. She feels he took a chance on her, and she let him down."

"Did she say that?"

"No. But I can tell. And then there's Eddy. I told you they split up, but she's miserable over it." He smiled at her. "I recognize the signs. I felt the same way last year when you and I split up for a bit."

"Do you tell her to keep the faith? It will all come good?"

"I say nothing. The new guy, Jason Ahearn, seems to have taken a great interest in her, so maybe she'll go that route instead of Eddy."

"Oh. I like Eddy. He's his own man."

Gordie knitted his brows. "What does that mean?"

"It's hard to explain. He has a sense of being comfortable in his own skin. Confidence perhaps."

His girlfriend caressed the dog. "I'll start on dinner. Shouldn't you be listening to your voicemail?"

"I suppose." He keyed in the code to pick up the message and then sat bolt upright, feet on the floor.

Vanessa stopped stroking Taz and looked at him in alarm. "What is it? Not your mum?"

He shook his head. "Work."

Vanessa slid out from under Taz's head. "That's my cue, Taz." She went to the kitchen, and the dog jumped down and padded after her while Gordie punched in Roxanne's phone number.

"Roxanne. I got your message. What's going on?"

He listened as she explained, beginning from her conversation with Eddy to her short, cryptic call with the hospital. "I don't know how he is other than he's in intensive care. They won't tell me anything because I'm not family, of course."

"No, they won't. Did Eddy say what caused the accident?"

"He didn't know. Gordie, it was a clear night. Why would he go off the road?"

"Maybe he was drunk. Maybe a deer ran out in front of him. Lots of possibilities."

"Or maybe someone ran him off the road."

"I know what you're thinking. We've been through this before. There's a feeling of déjà vu all right, but we're probably overreacting. Did you bring your computer home? Can you look at the report? Traffic must have put something in about it."

"I skimmed it, but there wasn't much there. Let me look again."

He heard her typing into the computer.

"The report from last night just showed a single-vehicle accident just outside Port Mulroy on the way to Isle Madame. They were going back out today to look closer at the scene since it was too dark last night, but there was nothing obvious, like an injured deer or whatever. It was after two in the morning. Where was he until that time of night?"

"His sister thinks he has a secret girlfriend."

Her voice lifted. "Here's something I didn't notice before. You'll never guess who called in the accident."

"Tell me."

"One Michael White."

"As in Mickey White?"

"That's him. They've got his address here."

"Well, well. I'll call Ellie Davis to see if I can get more information."

"OK. Let me know what you find out, will you?"

"Of course. Look, don't get too worked up. I know what you're thinking, but this isn't like our other case when the witness was blackmailing someone. This looks like it's just an unfortunate accident."

"I hope you're right."

Vanessa came out of the kitchen. "Sounds serious. Should I hold off on dinner?"

Gordie put his phone down. "No. Let me feed Taz, and then you go ahead with dinner. I just need to make a couple of calls. Henry Davis had a car accident last night."

Her eyes widened. "Oh, my God. How awful. Is he OK?"

"That's what I'm trying to find out. He's in the hospital. That's all I know. How long before supper is ready?"

"About fifteen minutes, but I can wait."

"No, go on." He followed her into the kitchen, where Taz was pacing back and forth. "Yes, all right, big girl. Let's get you sorted."

"I can do it." Vanessa got the can of dog food from the fridge. "You do what you need to do."

"You sure?"

"Of course. Go."

Gordie went back out to the living room and looked through his recent calls to find Ellie's number. He stood in front of the woodstove, looking into the flames as he listened to the phone ring. She answered quickly, her voice hushed. "Detective MacLean. It's not a good time."

"Ellie, I heard. Are you at the hospital?"

Her voice held tears. "Yes. I should have turned the phone off, but I'm out in the hall for a minute while the nurses do something. Oh God, Henry looks awful."

"I'm so sorry. What happened?"

"I don't even know. He went off the road and hit a tree. They have him in a medically induced coma because he has a brain injury."

"Dear God. Did the police say anything about why he went off the road?"

"No one said anything to me. I don't know, and honestly haven't really thought much about it. I just want to know he'll be all right."

"Of course. Shall I come by later and sit with you for a bit? I can drive you home. I assume you're staying at Henry's house?"

"No, a friend of mine is here with me right now and she's offered me her spare room in Port Mulroy. That seems easier."

"Of course. I understand. I'll come by in the morning. Ellie, are Henry and Mickey White friends?"

"I don't really know his friends. I used to, but now that I live in Sydney, we're not that close anymore. Why?"

"No reason. It's not important right now. Stay strong, Ellie. They know what they're doing there."

"I know. The staff has been amazing. Goodbye, Detective."

The phone disengaged before he could say goodbye.

He wandered back into the kitchen and Vanessa stopped stirring the cheese sauce she was making for a moment. "Well? What news?"

He shrugged. "He's in a coma."

She moved the saucepan off the burner and left the wooden spoon resting in it to come to him. Vanessa wrapped her arms around him. "It's good to care so much. It's one of the reasons I love you."

He returned her hug for a moment and then released her to phone Roxanne with the little information he knew. Despite what he had said to his partner, his sense of foreboding grew.

# CHAPTER THIRTY-TWO

A FTER A RESTLESS NIGHT, Gordie rose early, leaving Vanessa to sleep while he showered, dressed, and walked Taz. While Taz didn't enjoy being on a leash, tugging it this way and that, she did like all the unfamiliar scents that being in Vanessa's neighbourhood offered. The weather had turned and the vibrant colours of October had dulled as leaves joined the rain in a steady shower. Gordie wore a vintage yellow hooded waxed-cotton fisherman's raincoat that Vanessa had discovered at a yard sale, and he was glad of it. The rain pelted down on him with a noisy *pock-pock-pock* sound on his hood, and if it hadn't been for Taz tugging on him, he would have felt isolated in his yellow shroud.

"Come on, Taz. Let's go home."

The big dog gave one more pull in hopeful longing to extend her walk, but at Gordie's insistence, she turned to explore the other side of the dirt road on the way back.

The rain suited Gordie's mood. He had already felt the investigation was floundering, but now, his unease increased. Yesterday he felt they may be on to something with the theory of the Whites killing

Gretha together, but in the cold, wet reality of morning, he was less certain.

When they arrived back at the house, he smelled the welcome fragrance of brewing coffee. He shed his wet coat in the mudroom and toweled Taz down as much as he could before opening the French door into the house itself.

Vanessa stepped out of the kitchen. "Hello, you two." She gasped as Taz rubbed against her. "Oh, Taz. Get away. You're soaking wet."

As if to agree with Vanessa, the big dog shook herself, sending a fine spray against Vanessa and across the floor.

Gordie went back and grabbed the damp towel from the hook in the mudroom and hustled forward to wipe the floor. "Sorry about that."

Vanessa shook her head. "Never mind. I didn't realize it was raining that much out. How miserable. Do you have time to have a proper breakfast? What's your schedule for today?"

"I'd love breakfast, thanks. Since it's Saturday, I wasn't planning to go into the station, but I'll check in with Roxanne and see what she has in mind. I want to go past the hospital and see what the news is with Henry Davis."

"Do you think his accident has something to do with the case, or can you not say?"

He shook his head. "Honestly, I don't know. I don't see how it can connect."

She smiled. "That's good, isn't it? You just carry on with your investigation as if it didn't happen."

He nodded. "You're probably right. That's the logical thing to do. What are you up to today? Should I take Taz home?"

"I don't have anything planned, so leave her. Do you remember that it's your mum's birthday tomorrow?"

"Good Lord. I lost all track of the date. Usually, I'd go out to see her for lunch. I better call Jeanie and find out what the plan is."

"Shall I pop out and pick up a small thing for her?"

He smiled fondly. "Where would I be without you? Just some kind of food thing is the best. Chocolate, fancy cookies, something like that."

"I have the perfect idea. How about I pick up some chocolate from that Syrian chocolate maker out of Antigonish? *Peace By Chocolate* they're called. I saw that there's a shop in town that carries their products."

Gordie nodded. "You're right. That is perfect. She watched a documentary about that family. She'll love getting chocolate from them. I'll call my sister this morning and unless something blows up, we'll go to Halifax tomorrow for a visit. Are you up for that?"

"You wouldn't rather I stay home and look after Taz?"

"I'd rather you came along, and my neighbour can feed Taz. The big girl will be ready for a day of rest after spending two days with you."

"That's the plan, then."

They had their breakfast and reluctantly Gordie got set to go to the hospital.

*** 

The smell of antiseptic, blended with artificial lemon and pine cleaner odours, assaulted Gordie when he walked into the hospital. He closed his eyes for a second, feeling his full stomach gurgle in protest at the pervasive smells. When he had taken a moment to acclimatize, he went to the reception to ask where Henry Davis was. She started to ask if he was family, but when he held up his police identification, she simply tapped into the computer and came up with a room number on the third floor.

He took the elevator and when he exited on the third floor, the stench was worse as he discerned various pungent bodily fluids.

He walked down the hall, expecting to see Ellie Dawson sitting in one of the orange vinyl-covered chairs, but when he arrived at Henry's room, he saw through the window that she sat beside his bed. Henry appeared to be sleeping or unconscious. Ellie sat slumped down in a high-back visitor's chair, eyes closed, arm stretched out, holding Henry's hand.

A nurse approached Gordie. "I'm sorry, sir, but no visitors allowed other than his one contact, and that's his sister."

"I understand." Again, he pulled out his identification. "Is he still in a medically induced coma?"

She nodded. "We hope to bring him around later today, depending on what the doctor thinks."

Gordie stood looking at Henry, white and sickly looking under the fluorescent lights. The dark bruises staining his face were in stark contrast to the white bandages wrapped around his head. "He looks so bruised. I didn't expect that. I thought the airbag would have protected him more."

The nurse was silent beside him, and he turned to look at her.

She bit her lip. "I'm not sure how much I should say because of patient confidentiality, but since you're the police…"

"Yes? This man is an important witness in a murder case I'm investigating."

She widened her eyes. "Those bruises aren't from the accident. You're right. His chest is bruised as well, but that's expected from the airbag. The damage to his face and head. The broken ribs and bruised kidneys. Those are from a beating."

He lowered his voice to match hers. "A beating? The same day as the accident or before?"

"The bruises had not yet begun to heal. We believe that he incurred those injuries shortly before the accident and, in fact, they may have been the reason for the accident."

"Did you get his blood results back? Was he intoxicated?"

She blinked. "I'm just not sure what I can say." As she said the words, she gave a small shake of her head. "No. Off the record?"

"OK, off the record."

"We believe he blacked out from the beating, and that's why he went off the road."

"Thank you."

She left him standing watching through the window, but neither Ellie nor Henry moved, and Gordie left them at peace.

***

He sat in the car and called Roxanne. "I think you and I need to get together. What are you up to?"

"I'm having my third cup of tea and waiting to hear from you. What's the news?"

He told her about Henry's beating and his current state.

"There was nothing about that in the report. I looked again today, and Traffic updated it after they went out yesterday. Their conclusion was that the driver fell asleep given the time of the accident, and that there were no skids or other signs of him attempting to stop or swerve."

"Yeah. If a deer had run out, he would have swerved. It's a reasonable conclusion."

"The report also has the results of his blood alcohol level. He was at .04 so looks like he may have had a couple of beers during the evening, which is why they figured he fell asleep but wasn't technically impaired."

"The nurse gave me this off the record, so we'll leave Traffic to figure it out themselves if they want to follow up, but right now, I think you and I better get together to decide where we go with this, if at all. It might be completely unrelated, and we need to focus on the Whites."

"OK, how about we meet at Timmy's in St. Peter's in an hour?"

"Sounds good."

Gordie sat in the parking lot of the hospital and called his sister. "Jeanie? Hi. How are you?"

"Your ears must have been burning. I'm at Mum's and we're just getting ready to go to Aunt Anne's place for lunch."

"Aunt Anne?"

"You do remember Aunt Anne? Our father's sister?"

"Of course I do. I'm just surprised that you'd want to go there to listen to endless stories about our father. You do remember that alcoholic man who beat us all up regularly?"

"Oh, Gordie. For one thing, Aunt Anne doesn't spend all her time talking about Dad. For another thing, you used to love going there. She's a kind and loving woman. We were the only children she ever had, and she spoiled us whenever we visited."

"I loved visiting anywhere that wasn't at home with him." He grudgingly added, "Yes, all right. She was always good to us as kids. I just didn't realize you and Mum still had contact with her."

"You're the only one who decided to cut her out of your life. We didn't. Anne is putting on a lunch to celebrate Mum's 80th birthday. Just a couple of old friends, but it's kind of her."

Gordie heard his mother's voice in the background, telling Jean they had to go.

Jean answered her and then in a quiet voice asked Gordie if he'd be able to come to see their mother soon.

"Tomorrow. If you both are available, then Vanessa and I will come down and take you out somewhere for a meal. How about it? Do you already have plans?"

He heard the lift in her voice. "No, I was holding off until I heard from you. She'll be so happy. Will I make a reservation somewhere?"

"Perfect. One o'clock?"

"That's great. OK, must run. Looking forward to seeing you tomorrow. I'll find out where Mum wants to go."

"Nothing too cheap. This is a big birthday."

"All right. Nothing cheap. Especially since you're buying." She laughed as she hung up.

He called Vanessa to let her know what the plans were.

She listened to what he was doing for the afternoon and what he had scheduled for the next day. "Why don't I take Taz over to your place later, and then we'll leave from there tomorrow?"

"You are so sensible. I'll pick something up for supper on the way home."

He hung up and felt better able to focus his attention on the case. As he drove to the town of St. Peter's, he mulled over what next steps they could take to determine if their theory was correct. Did Mia and Mickey White kill Gretha Braun?

*** 

Roxanne had green tea and a bagel with cream cheese. "I didn't get you anything. Wasn't sure what you wanted at this time of day."

He raised his eyebrows. "Nice that I'm getting a little less predictable. Do you want a refill?"

"No, I'm good, thanks."

He got a large cup of steeped tea and a blueberry muffin. "OK, what are you thinking about for the next steps?"

She pushed the plate with half a bagel away and pulled out her notebook. "Did we check the neighbourhood around the White's house for cameras? I know *they* don't have one, but what about next door or across the road?"

"Good thinking. No. We did that around Gretha's place, but not there. We can do that today."

"I think we need to confront Mia with the contract. We can ask her to come in, or we can do it at the shop, so they don't have time to get their stories straight."

He nodded. "I agree. I thought the same thing. Let's see what she has to say. We can split up and you go to one and I'll go to the other. If we don't, we run the same risk that they'll get their stories together."

"Right. I'll go see Mia. You and Mickey have bonded, so you go talk to him again. I want to know how he happened to be in the right place at the right time to find Henry Davis as well. The first thing we need to do though, is to drive down their street. If anyone has a camera, we'll see if we can watch the footage before talking to them. It's Saturday. Hopefully, people are home."

They finished their drinks and went outside. Gordie nodded to his car. "Follow me and you can leave your car at the Mountie shop while we do the drive-by."

"Sounds good. I know where it is. I'll see you there. Let's pray for some camera footage to help us. If we see Mickey leaving around the time of the murder, we may need to do formal interviews."

Gordie nodded. "We can probably borrow an interview room and do it today at the RCMP station."

"Here's hoping."

# CHAPTER THIRTY-THREE

GORDIE DROVE SLOWLY ALONG the road on which Mickey and Mia White lived.

"There." Roxanne pointed to the house immediately to the left of the Whites. The camera wasn't on the house itself but on the boat garage. The one-and-a-half-storey building was shingled in weathered grey cedar shingles and had two small windows in a loft above the 24-foot-high garage door. On the sharp peak of the roof, a red light glowed.

Gordie nodded and pulled into the driveway. "Perfect, assuming it's real. You wouldn't believe how many people buy these fake cameras just to scare would-be thieves away."

"It's high enough that it's bound to capture Mickey White coming and going."

Gordie parked, and they walked up to the front door. There was no sign of a camera on the house. "I guess all their wealth is tied up in their fishing boat and gear."

"Yeah. It's a good place to have the camera."

After ringing the doorbell and knocking several times without a response, they had to admit defeat.

Roxanne pulled out a business card, wrote on the back, '*please call,*' and wedged it in the door.

"I'll run you back to your car and you go see Mia at the bakery and maybe by the time I come back, these folks will be home. At least it looks like Mickey's home." He nodded to the truck in the driveway next door.

After he delivered Roxanne to her car, he headed back again, but the neighbours with the camera were still out. He pulled into the White drive and went to the door to rap on it. Mickey opened it with a suddenness that made Gordie wonder if he'd been hovering near a window.

Mickey sighed, turned and allowed Gordie to follow him into the living room. He flung himself into an easy chair. "Now what?"

"Mickey, I'm going to record our conversation on my phone. Do you have any objection to that? If so, we can go into the station and make this more formal."

"I have no problem. I didn't do anything, so record away. In fact, I want a copy to have proof of what I keep telling you, so no one tries to say I confessed to something I never did. You hear of that happening all the time."

Gordie set his phone on the coffee table between them and began to record. He gave his name and asked Mickey to give his full name and date of birth.

"Michael John White. June 10th, 1975."

"Mickey, we have no interest in a false confession. We just want the truth as it pertains to the death of Gretha Braun. We now have evidence to show that Gretha Braun had completed the sales contract between herself and your wife. The document was dated a few days before her death. We have reason to believe that Gretha and your wife Mia signed the contract, but something happened, didn't it? Something that made Gretha rescind the offer."

"I have no idea. I didn't know about the deal, and if the two women signed something, I didn't hear about it."

"I think you did hear about it. Maybe not right away. Maybe you didn't even know they signed a contract, but you heard about it when Gretha backed out, didn't you? Mia was upset, and she broke down and told you about it."

"No. That's not true."

"Mickey, I think Mia told you on that Sunday night. Either she called you, and we'll be able to confirm that from phone records, or she came home and told you then. That was when you really lost your temper, wasn't it? You jumped in the truck and went to have it out with Gretha."

Mickey looked calm and kept his arms folded across his chest. "No. Mia and I were both here at home. And I know you can't just check my phone records without a warrant. Good luck getting that, but even if you do, you won't see a call between us because we were both at home."

He tried one last push. "We are about to talk to your neighbour to see the footage from the camera on his boat garage. He's got a perfect view of your driveway from the camera's vantage point."

Mickey pulled his cell phone from his top pocket. "They're out at their daughter's place in Truro for the day, but I'll give you his phone number. Knock yourself out."

"All right. Give me his number." Gordie called his bluff, but Mickey read it out without hesitation.

"One last question. Henry Davis was involved in a car accident. Do you know about that?"

Mickey squinted at Gordie. "Obviously you know I reported it, so why ask me that?"

"Just confirming my information. How did it happen that you drove past at two in the morning exactly where Davis went off the road?"

Recrossing his arms across his chest again, Mickey sighed.

"There's only one damned road from Port Mulroy to Isle Madame, as you well know. I saw an accident and like the good citizen I am, I called it in."

"Were you and Henry both at the same club last night?"

"I didn't notice."

"Come on, Mickey. Don't play games with me."

He shrugged. "I played some pool and then had a little flutter on the slots. If Davis was there, he wasn't doing either of those things, and I didn't see him."

Gordie shook his head. "Every time I turn around, your name seems to come up. Why is that?"

"Just bad luck."

"We'll leave it there for now."

Just before Gordie stopped the recording, Mickey leaned forward. "I want everybody who listens to this, to notice that I'm cooperating fully."

"We appreciate that." He pulled himself out of the spongy sofa and walked to the front door. Mickey followed close behind and just before Gordie stepped outside, White growled in a low voice "Stop coming here to my home. I know where you live too, you know. I may have to start coming around your place unannounced and see how you and that pretty girlfriend of yours like it."

Gordie spun, surprising White with the suddenness of the move. "Are you threatening me? I can arrest you for that."

Mickey sneered. "Threatening? Prove it. I've been nothing but cooperative, remember?"

MacLean leaned in close to Mickey, forcing the other man back a step. "If I even see a truck that resembles that heap you drive anywhere near my home, I'll have you picked up."

Mickey laughed as he shut the door in Gordie's face.

He was on his way back to the RCMP parking lot when Roxanne called him.

Gordie's heart still pounded in anger, and he took a deep breath before speaking. "Any joy?"

"No. She claimed she hadn't seen the final contract. She said that Gretha told her she had it drafted but wanted to run it past the lawyer first and as far as Mia knew, that appointment hadn't taken place yet. What about you?"

"I couldn't budge him. On the surface, he's all sweetness and light. He gave me the phone number of the neighbour with the camera. Tells me they're in Truro for the day. I'll call the guy to make sure that he knows we want to see that footage, but I don't think we'll see Mickey White leaving his house around the time of the murder. Either he already erased it in some mistaken gesture of loyalty, or in fact, there's nothing to see." He didn't share White's final comments. Roxanne might feel the need to make an official record of the threat, and Gordie didn't want to give the man the satisfaction.

Gordie heard Roxanne heave a deep sigh. "Let's leave it, then. Take tomorrow to recharge and we'll go back at it on Monday."

"Sounds good. Vanessa and I are going to Halifax tomorrow to celebrate my mother's 80th birthday, so I won't be around."

"No worries. Have a great day. Give your mum a hug for me, and hello to Jean."

"Will do. What will you do with your day?"

She hesitated and then he heard, "Eddy and I are having lunch together. Don't give me a hard time, OK?"

"I won't. If he's what you want, then great. For what it's worth, Vanessa is very fond of him. She says, 'he's his own man', whatever that means."

He heard the smile in her voice. "Thanks, Gordie."

They went their separate ways and committed to getting their reports transcribed and uploaded into the system that afternoon.

\*\*\*

When Vanessa arrived with Taz, Gordie went out to meet them. "My two favourite girls. Can I carry anything in?"

Vanessa stopped to watch the reunion between man and dog for a moment before handing him a bag with wrapped gifts. "If you can take that in without getting it crushed by a 110-pound dog, I'll bring in my own stuff."

They trooped inside the house and Taz nosed Gordie's hand for a treat. Once received, she flopped down with a sigh on her bed in the kitchen.

Vanessa set her overnight bag at the base of the steps and joined them in the kitchen. "I didn't think you'd be home already."

He shrugged. "Another pretty frustrating day, so we gave up and will get back to it on Monday. I'll run out to Kenny's Pizza to pick up our dinner in a bit. I've ordered it for pickup at six o'clock. That OK?"

"Absolutely. How about a cup of tea meanwhile?"

Gordie put the kettle on and pulled out a box of shortbread cookies. "I talked to Jean today to confirm lunch tomorrow."

"Excellent. Everything good with her?"

Gordie sat down at the table across from Vanessa. "I guess so. They were heading off to visit my Aunt Anne."

"That sounds nice. She's your father's sister, isn't she?"

"Yeah."

"What's wrong? You don't like your aunt?"

"I haven't seen her in several years. Jeannie reminded me I used to like her. Now I just don't think about her, I suppose."

Vanessa frowned. "Why not? Why haven't you seen her?"

"She's my father's sister. Need I say more?"

"Yes. Is she an alcoholic, too?"

"Not that I know of."

"Maybe you've been unfair to her if you've lumped her in with her brother."

"Maybe. Anyway, I imagine we'll hear all about the visit tomorrow."

Vanessa nodded. "What about Henry Davis? Did you go past the hospital?"

"I did. I didn't talk to Ellie. She was in with Henry and they both looked like they were sleeping, or at least she was. I think Henry's still in a coma."

"That poor girl. She's been through so much."

"I'll call her later to see if there's any change."

The kettle boiled and Gordie made the tea. They sat at the table, drinking tea and chatting until Gordie went to get the pizza.

Vanessa's parting words were "don't forget the donair sauce."

He grinned and called back over his shoulder. "Already ordered."

*

During the night, Taz woke Gordie and Vanessa by letting loose with a volley of barking. Gordie climbed out of bed and growled at her to be quiet. He peered out the window and saw a distant set of taillights, but nothing else.

Vanessa sat up. "What is it?"

"Nothing. Maybe she heard coyotes."

They used the shock of the late-night alarm as an excuse to sleep in on Sunday morning. After the leisurely start to the day, Gordie cooked breakfast for the three of them; grilled tomatoes, home-fries, easy-over eggs and bacon for all three of them.

The weather was cool but clear, so they decided to go for a trek along the shore to walk off breakfast.

"Darn. Look at this." Gordie pointed to a long scratch along the driver's side of his car.

"That must be what Taz barked at last night."

"Yeah. And I have a good idea who probably did it, but no way to prove it." He pictured Mickey White and his threat.

Vanessa touched his arm. "Should you make a report?"

"No, there's no point. Let's just go enjoy the day."

Gordie wore his tweed flat cap and Vanessa wore the hood up on her black and white jacket, but even still they were wind-blown and rosy-cheeked by the time they got back to the car after their walk.

Vanessa pushed her fingers through her hair as she peered in the visor mirror. "I have to spend some time getting tidied up before we head off to Halifax."

He glanced at her and grinned. "I think you look great, just as you are."

"You're a darling, but I can't visit your mom looking like this. You'll have to entertain yourself while I take some time."

"I want to check in with Ellie or the hospital anyway, so you take all the time you want."

When they arrived home, Vanessa took a mug of tea upstairs with her while Gordie settled at the kitchen table.

Ellie answered the phone on the second ring. Her voice was bright and cheerful. "Detective MacLean. How are you?"

"I'm fine, but more to the point, how is Henry?"

"You can ask him yourself in a minute. The doctors brought him out of his coma last night and you wouldn't believe how well he's doing now. Here, I'll hand the phone over to him."

He heard Ellie's voice telling her brother to take the phone, and then Henry said, "good morning."

"Good morning, Henry. You had everyone worried. How are you doing?"

"I'm itching to get out of here."

"No rush. I guess it'll be several days before they release you."

"I plan to be out of here and home again by tomorrow."

"Wow. You're tough. Is that realistic?"

"Sure. I had a knock on the head, which is now much better. I also have a couple of broken ribs, which they can't do anything about, anyway, so I might as well be comfortable at home." His voice belied his optimistic words.

"Do you remember what happened?"

"I fell asleep and went off the road. I'm glad I went off the road instead of into any on-coming traffic."

"True. That was lucky, although I'm not sure how much traffic there was so late at night."

"True. I'm handing the phone back to Ellie now. Maybe you can convince her to go home and get some rest herself instead of sitting here all day."

Ellie came back on the phone. "He's stubborn, isn't he?"

"He is indeed, but it's good to know he's on the mend. He's right, you know. You should get some rest yourself. Are you back to work tomorrow?"

"I'm taking tomorrow off at a minimum. Henry is insisting he plans to go home tomorrow, so I want to be there to help him settle in. Our lawyer is back from his African safari trip and will come out to the house so we can move on with getting my father's estate sorted out."

Gordie nodded, even though she couldn't see him. "Normal life resumes. Probably not a bad idea. I'll leave you to it, then. Glad everything's OK."

"Thank you, Detective. Have a nice day."

He called Roxanne to give her an update. "So, there you are. Henry's on the mend."

His partner's voice held the same skepticism that he felt. "Fell asleep at the wheel, did he?"

"So, he claims."

"There's more to this story than he's telling."

"I agree. Tomorrow we'll talk about how to ferret that out. Meanwhile, enjoy your lunch with Eddy, but look after yourself, Roxanne. It wasn't long ago that it seemed like he was trying to control you."

He knew by the impatience in her voice, he'd annoyed her. "I'm not a child."

"I know that. Just looking out for you."

"Says the great relationship guru."

He took a deep breath. "I'll see you bright and early Monday."

"Yup." She seemed to want to soften her tone and repeated her comment from the previous day. "Say hi to Jean and your mom from me."

"Will do."

He hung up, realizing she was right. *What do I know about relationships? Until Vanessa came along, I never lasted more than a few months with anyone, and even now I get things wrong all the time.*

He consciously decided to put his concerns about his partner and the case out of his mind for the day to enjoy a few hours of family time.

# CHAPTER THIRTY-FOUR

HIS SISTER JEAN HAD made reservations at Salty's upstairs on the waterfront. Vanessa ordered the stuffed salmon while he had the butter-poached halibut. Jean and his mother split an appetizer of pan-seared Atlantic crab cakes and then each had a salad.

Gordie nodded to his mother's plate. "How's the beet salad, Mom? I didn't know you liked beets."

"It's lovely. Oh yes, I always liked beets. When I was first married, and we had the house with a sizeable garden out back, I planted beets and pickled them every fall. Your Aunt Anne reminded me just yesterday of all the pickling I used to do. Beets, green tomato chow-chow, dill pickles. I put up jars of green and yellow beans as well. My goodness, when I think of it now. It was such a lot of work, but we enjoyed that produce all winter long. Anne did fruit. She put up pears and applesauce from her trees and we swapped, so we both had a nice variety."

Jean studied Gordie as she enjoyed a bit of her meal. "Aunt Anne asked after you."

"Did she?"

"Why don't you ever talk to her anymore, Gordie?"

He glared at his sister but didn't want to say *because she's Dad's sister* in front of his mother. "Just got out of the habit, I guess, between work and everything."

His sister wouldn't let it drop. "She's not like him. You know that."

His mother cocked her head with a puzzled frown. "What are you talking about, Jean?"

Jean dabbed her mouth with her serviette. "Aunt Anne reminds Gordie of Dad."

His mother shook her head. "Oh, Gordie. Surely you don't avoid your aunt for that reason. She couldn't be more different. For one thing, she's a teetotaler. She's always been so kind to me and was such a help over the years when I had troubles."

No one said anything specific about how the *troubles* included the way Gordie's father spent money they didn't have and how he used his fists on his family in times of alcoholic rage.

Gordie took a breath. "I'm glad you had a nice visit yesterday, Mom. One of these days, I'll give Aunt Anne a call. I promise."

His mother nodded, satisfied, and the conversation moved on to a lively discussion about the chocolate shop in Antigonish. His mother had been delighted with her gifts of chocolate and talked in detail about the show she had seen about the shop. "When I was a girl, we saw so few people from somewhere else. You were either Celtic background or French or maybe from the Deep South. Now people come from everywhere, don't they? It's so interesting. Like your case, Gordie. That woman came from Germany, didn't she?"

"She did, Mom. I wish everyone had been as welcoming to new-comers as you are." He smiled at his mother.

\*\*\*

On the drive back to Isle Madame, the topic of Gordie's Aunt Anne came up again.

Vanessa shifted in her seat to study his face. "Did your aunt do something to cause you this feeling of animosity against her?"

He frowned. "I don't feel that strongly. No, there was nothing specific. I just got busy with my life and when I did have time to connect with someone, I always preferred it be my sister or mother."

"But it sounds like you once got on with her all right. There's more to it than *too busy*." She emphasized her last words.

Gordie chewed his bottom lip for a moment. "Yeah, all right. The last time I was there, she pulled out a photo album and was going on about their childhood. Her and my father. Jean was all over it, but I realized I wasn't interested. And that was that, I guess. I stopped going."

"Aren't you interested in your family stories?"

He countered with a question of his own. "What about you? I rarely hear you talking about *your* family."

"I've told you about my family. My mother was an only child and came from a farm in Port Hope, Ontario. My father came from a mining family in Sudbury, Ontario. He left Northern Ontario to study engineering in Toronto and then got a job with Ontario Hydro. I never knew my maternal grandparents; both of whom died quite young. My mother was always convinced that the farm had contaminated soil because my grandma had a couple of miscarriages, and then both died of cancer within a couple of years of each other. I did know my paternal grandparents, and we visited Sudbury a few times when I was a kid. I'm still in contact with my cousins there."

"Sudbury? What's that like?"

"Stop changing the subject. One of the things I love about Nova Scotia is how people go back generations and they know about their families and the families of their neighbours. How come you don't?"

"I know all I need to know."

She sighed. "We live in such a transient world these days, but I think most people have a need to understand where they come from.

That's why these ancestor websites are so popular now. People want to know where they come from, and who they are."

"Maybe. Maybe like Gretha Braun, they're just as happy to make a new start. Look at all the Dutch farmers in Nova Scotia who came over in the fifties."

"True."

Gordie smiled, triumphant in his argument. "Not all of us need to spend our life looking back."

"All right, Gordie. Although I do think you're an exception."

He laughed. "I like being exceptional."

*** 

His phone pinged to let him know he had an email, but Gordie resisted the temptation to look at his phone on the way to the station the next morning. He felt relaxed after his day off and spent the drive making the feeling last as he enjoyed the view of Bras d'Or Lake on his left.

When he arrived at work, he took a moment to look at his phone just in case it was something important or from Sergeant Arsenault. He wanted to be prepared before walking in.

*Ahh. Something from the cousin with an attachment. I wonder what Ida found.*

Gordie didn't try to open the note on his phone. It would be easier to read the note and open the attachment on his computer, but he trotted into the office more quickly than he normally would.

Roxanne was already at her desk and watched Gordie unpack his laptop and turn it on before even taking his jacket off. "You're keen this morning."

"There's a note here from Gretha's cousin."

She stood up. "Oh?"

"Don't get excited. It might be nothing." He sat down to log in. "But there's an attachment, so it might be something." He shrugged off his jacket, letting it fall on the back of his chair as the computer went through the start-up processes.

Roxanne picked up her cup of tea with one hand and rolled her chair over to his desk with the other. "Please let it be something."

They sat side by side to read as he clicked on the note.

*Dear Detective MacLean,*

*I was finally able to go to Gretha's home. This was very hard for me, and I waited until my daughter, Heidi had time to come with me. Of course, my dear cousin was always very organized, and it was easy to go through her papers. The harder part will be to dispose of her things, but Heidi will help, and you don't want to know about that, I think. The one thing we found which might be helpful to you is a letter from a Privatdetektiv. Heidi translated it (her English is much better than me) and it is now attached, along with a scan of the original. He refers to other documents, but I did not find those. Perhaps Gretha took them with her. If I discover anything else helpful, I will send it on.*

*With friendly greetings,*

*Ida Zimmerman*

Roxanne leaned closer to the computer screen and tapped her finger on the note. "Open the word doc. That must be the translation."

It was very short.

*Dear Mrs. Braun,*

*I am honored to be of service to you. As we discussed, I hereby include the documents regarding the research I conducted into your family, along with my account which can be paid via etransfer.*

*If you have further questions, please feel free to contact me.*

*Cordially,*

*Patrick Kurtz, Detektei*

Roxanne leaned back and pursed her lips. "Does this help us at all? She was born in Germany, so I presume any family this guy found was in Germany, too."

Gordie nodded. "Someone didn't like her poking around and followed her here?"

Roxanne drained her cold tea. "I don't know. That seems like a lot of trouble unless there's some big castle or something she was going after from a long-lost inheritance."

"We'll have to contact this Patrick Kurtz guy. Do you want to put Jason on it?"

"Sure. OK."

She started to roll away when Gordie added something. "If she brought the documents he's referring to, they may have been in that file boxfile box. Why bring documents to Canada that dealt with a situation at home?"

She nodded. "I'll get Jason on it."

Roxanne went to brief the boss and Gordie called the White's neighbour to ask about the camera footage for the night of Gretha's murder.

He reached the wife, who told him that the husband had left for work already. Once he explained who he was and what he wanted, she responded right away. "I can look at that. I have the app on my phone. What was the date again?"

"Sunday, September 26th. Sometime after dark."

"OK. It won't be easy to see much in the dark, but we do have a streetlight right in front of the house, so that helps. Bear with me because the app always sends me a code I have to key in. Let me put you on speakerphone."

He heard a chime and then tapping as she keyed in a verification code. When she was done, he assured her she wasn't looking for details. "I just need to know if your neighbours went out that evening. You'd see that even in the dark, right?"

"Yes." Her voice was hesitant. "Strange. I'm in the history part of the app but I don't see anything for that whole day."

"Maybe nothing triggered the motion sensor, so the camera didn't record anything?"

"No, that can't be right. We went to church in the morning, so if nothing else that should be there, and I can't remember for certain, but I'm pretty sure we went out in the afternoon again to do a bit of shopping, but there's nothing there."

"Is it possible it was erased?"

"Sure. That's possible. Once in a while we go in and delete old footage, but this is too recent, and we never go in just to delete one day. It doesn't make sense."

"Is your husband good friends with Mickey White?"

"Well, we're neighbours, so occasionally they come here, or we go there. I'm not sure I'd say Ron and Mickey White are good friends, though."

"All right. Mrs. MacLellan, you've been very helpful. Thank you for your time."

He hung up and made a note in his book. *Security camera footage erased.* He was glad to have reached the wife instead of the husband. He suspected the answer to his inquiries would have sounded more like *no, not seeing Mickey White leave,* which wouldn't have been a lie, but neither would it have been the full, true story.

Gordie sat back and thought about what the true story was. *How do all these pieces fit together?*

# CHAPTER THIRTY-FIVE

ROXANNE JOINED HER PARTNER in the briefing room where he stood in front of the whiteboard, now covered in notes, crossed off names and question marks. He turned to face her when she approached.

"How's Sarge this morning? Supportive and helpful?"

She made a face. "As always."

He nodded, not asking any more questions. Instead, he told her about his conversation with the neighbour of the Whites.

Her eyes widened. "Erased? That can only mean that he or they did leave. What time?"

Gordie shrugged. "No way to tell. The whole day is gone."

"We need to bring him in. We've got him now."

"Whoa. It's damning for sure, but it's not evidence. If anything, it's a lack of evidence."

Roxanne folded her arms. "I don't agree."

Gordie's face flushed. "Roxanne, don't make the same mistake again. You jumped too soon when you got the warrant for Jack

Fraser's trailer. When we go after Mickey White, I want to make sure it sticks."

Roxanne tilted her head. "Am I missing something?"

"No. I just don't want to jump the gun. What's that saying? Slowly, slowly catchy monkey."

She clenched her teeth and gave herself a few deep breaths before speaking. "What would *you* do then?"

"Relook at the evidence we have. Did you get the fingerprints back from forensics? Maybe we have enough to get the phone records for the Whites with what we have."

"Damn." She sighed. "OK. I'll go follow up on the fingerprints." As she turned to leave, she added. "By the way, isn't it softly, softly catchy monkey?"

He shrugged. "Who knows? I just know I want to be sure we catch this particular monkey."

Roxanne left her partner updating the board while she went hunting for the results of the fingerprint comparisons between what forensics found in the house during their initial crime scene investigation and the ceramic mug Mickey White had used during their interview with him.

She was back in the briefing room before Gordie had completed his updates. He took one look at her face and knew the results. "No match, then?"

Roxanne slumped into one of the chairs. "No match for Mickey White."

"That doesn't mean he wasn't there. It just might mean he's a clever weasel and made sure not to touch things. It demonstrates premeditation."

She nodded. "But to your earlier point, how do we prove it?"

Gordie had circled one of his points on the whiteboard in red. *Mickey White reports the accident of Henry Davis.* "Let's try a different approach. What's the connection here?"

She shook her head. "I'm not sure there is one."

Gordie tossed his marker down on the ledge of the whiteboard. "I'm not sure either, but my gut tells me there is. Let's go get a cup of tea."

He drove the short distance, and she bought two cups of steeped tea with a 20-pack of Timbits. They each ate a few of the small bite-sized donut morsels and then Gordie pushed the box away. "Take these away before I eat them all. The guys will be happy to finish them off."

Roxanne took one more before closing the box. "How was the birthday lunch with your mom?"

He smiled. "Nice. Aside from everyone ganging up on me to visit my Aunt Anne."

She raised her eyebrows. "Never heard of her. Who's that?"

"My father's sister."

"Did you pick a fight with her or something?"

He frowned. "As if. No. Nothing like that. I just haven't seen her for a while."

"What's a while?"

He shrugged. "Years."

Roxanne tilted her head. "Does she live somewhere reasonably close by?"

"Dartmouth."

"So, what's holding you back? Just do your duty and go see her. Drink some tea. Admire the crocheting, and that's it. Done."

"Yeah. You're probably right. What about you? How was your get-together with Eddy? Spare me the gory details if it was all passion and romance."

She smiled. "No gory details to share, but it was nice. I admit it was good to see him again."

"You don't sound sure."

"It was something you said that has me thinking."

"Good Lord. What was that?"

"He doesn't seem interested in spending time at my place and it's not like he's not a family kind of guy. He is if it's his family."

"Did you talk to him about that? Maybe he isn't sure he's welcome at your place?"

"I haven't talked to him about it, but it's hard to believe. Nana welcomes everyone."

"That's true. Well, if that's the only thing, I'd just talk to him. It may be nothing and easily sorted."

She nodded. "My family's important to me." Roxanne laughed. "That sounds silly. I'm sure everyone's family is important." Roxanne looked at her watch. "Speaking of which, let's get back. I gave Jason all the details of that German private investigator. Maybe he's gotten through to him by now."

***

Detective Jason Ahearn must have been watching for Roxanne's return because he came to her desk before she even had her jacket off.

"I got through to him and I had my Google translate open in case I needed to speak to him in German, but his English was perfect."

Gordie stood listening. "Naturally. I think every European speaks at least three languages."

Roxanne waved at Gordie to hush him up. "Well? What did he have to say?"

Jason had a handful of papers in his hand. "He was really upset to hear that Gretha was dead. He was extremely helpful. I think it's easier if you just read his email. I have his supporting documents as well, but they're in German."

Roxanne took the one-page printed email note, and Gordie came around to read over her shoulder.

She felt her heart race. "Good God." She stood up, ready to run out the door.

Gordie put up his hand. "Wait. Have Norris get a warrant for the house and email it, so we have it when we get there."

Roxanne nodded. "Can you do that? I'll go tell Sarge what's

happening." She squeezed Jason's arm. "Great work, Jason. See if Rob Norris needs any help and email the note with all the supporting documents over to me as well."

The young detective flushed at the praise. "Will do."

Roxanne turned to her partner. "This is it. We have him, right?"

"I think so, but we'll know when we get there. I'll call the Mounties and have them back us up. I'll meet you in their parking lot."

"Don't you dare start without me."

Gordie shook his head. "It's your case."

# CHAPTER THIRTY-SIX

THE 120 KM DRIVE back to Isle Madame went faster than the morning drive into the office. When he arrived at the Royal Canadian Mounted Police station, Gordie went inside to make sure everything was ready.

The Detachment Commander knew Gordie well. "Hi, MacLean. Is this to do with the murder of that German woman?"

"It is. The warrant will be here any minute." He waved his phone in the air to show that he expected it by email.

"No problem. I called in a couple of guys from Port Mulroy to help. I've just got one here most of the time. Will they be enough? Do you expect trouble?" He nodded to the three constables sitting chatting.

"No, I don't really, but you never know. That's why I called ahead. Better safe than sorry."

"Looks like your partner's here."

Gordie nodded. "I'll go out and meet her and then we'll go ahead. You've got the address, right?"

"Yes, got it. I'll get that lot going and have them just park outside unless you want them to go in with you?"

"No, that sounds good. Once we have our guy in custody, I'll want them to secure the scene. Our forensics team is on their way and will be along shortly."

The commander buzzed Gordie back out and trotted over to Roxanne's car. "Ready?"

"Let's go. I'll drive."

Gordie didn't argue and climbed in without complaint.

During the drive, they planned out their approach. Gordie reminded her, "we don't have enough to arrest him yet. We have enough background now to justify searching the house, but it's not a slam-dunk. We can take him in for questioning, but we can't get too heavy-handed."

"I know that. So, what do you suggest?"

"We go in and say we want to talk. We offer up what we now know and see if that gets him talking. We explain we're going to search the house."

"What about her? Do we take them both in?"

He nodded. "I think we should. Helping us with our enquiries and all that." His phone chimed, and he saw that the search warrant was there.

He opened the document to have it ready to show. "We're all set."

She pulled into the driveway. It was a postcard scene with the water sparkling behind the blue house. The workshop doors were open but there were no sounds of saws or hammering today. Roxanne parked beside a black Lexus.

Gordie nodded at the car. "That's probably the lawyer. Ellie said he was coming today to discuss the father's estate."

"Convenient."

They went up the steps, and Roxanne rapped on the door.

Ellie opened the door and frowned, hesitating before inviting them to step inside. "Detectives. It isn't a convenient time. Our law-yer is here and we're about to go through my father's will."

Roxanne stepped further into the kitchen. "We're sorry for the intrusion, but we'll come inside if you don't mind. It's important."

Ellie looked as though she may make a stand to block their way, but Gordie moved up to stand beside Roxanne. "I'd like to meet your lawyer, Ellie."

She sighed, turned, and led the way into the living room. When Henry saw the detectives behind his sister, he struggled to stand. He stood silently, watching them.

Ellie introduced them to the older man sitting in an easy chair, an old-fashioned leather satchel on the floor beside him. He was darkly tanned, and Gordie recalled that the man had been away in Kenya recently. "Detectives MacLean and Albright, this is John Michaels, our family lawyer. John, I was just telling you about my murdered friend, Gretha Braun. These are the detectives working on the case. I can't imagine what they have that is so pressing it can't wait, but please, go ahead." She faced them with raised eyebrows.

The lawyer looked uncomfortable and opened his case to with-draw a black leather portfolio as if to distance himself from the scene.

Gordie looked pointedly at the lawyer. "I think Mr. Michaels may know more about Gretha than you've told him, Ellie. He piv-oted then to look at Henry. "What about you, Henry? Do you know more than Ellie?"

The white dressing around his head and the scowl on his face marred the young man's good looks. He clenched his mouth closed and didn't respond.

Ellie shook her head. "Is this some sort of game, Detective?"

John Michaels spoke then. He had opened his portfolio to reveal a will. "The detective is correct, Ellie. I think you and Henry should sit down. I have some shocking news for you, and I've been thinking about how to present it to you, but I see I have no option but just to tell you."

Ellie Davis sat down on the sofa while Henry seemed oblivious to his lawyer's words. He continued to stand in front of the glass doors, displaying the spectacular view of the water.

The lawyer took a breath. Both Gordie and Roxanne focused their attention on Henry Davis to watch his reaction to the news they knew was coming.

"Gretha Braun was your sister."

Ellie gasped and put a hand to her mouth, while Henry didn't move. Again, it seemed as though he was in a world of his own.

Ellie shook her head. "No. I don't understand."

The lawyer looked at the document and then, knowing the contents already, he leaned forward to take the young woman's hand. "You remember, of course, that your dad was in the military. Before you were born, before your folks were married, in fact, your father was posted to Lahr, Germany. He was there from 1976 to 1979. He was already dating your mother and when he came home in '79 they were married."

Now Henry spoke. "But being engaged to Mom didn't stop him, did it? When he was in Germany, he couldn't keep his pants zipped, could he?"

Michaels sighed and continued. "While he was in Germany, he had a relationship with Gretha's mother and when he left to come home, she was pregnant."

Ellie blinked. "No."

"He didn't know that, or I believe he would have stood by her. He didn't find out until just a few years ago. Gretha's mother, Liesl, wrote to him. They had a friend in common who agreed to give her his address. Liesl was worried because Gretha was determined to track down her father somehow, and Liesl wanted to warn him. She only wrote one letter and although he wrote back saying he wanted to meet his daughter, she never responded to him."

"How did Gretha find him?"

"I never spoke to her, so I can only guess that when her mother died, Gretha found your father's information amongst her papers. She came here to find him, and she also found you both."

Henry pointed to the will on Michaels' knee. "We're here to talk about my father's estate. Not his history. Let's get on with it. Cut to the chase. How much is coming to me?"

The lawyer blinked. "It's all part of the same discussion, Henry. When your father realized he had another daughter, he updated his will to include her. He divided the estate evenly between you three, and should one predecease the others, as is the case now with Gretha, the portion falls under the terms of *that* person's estate."

Henry flushed a deep red. "What? No. That can't be right. It belongs to Ellie and me. How much? How much do I get?"

The lawyer frowned. "This property is probably worth about three hundred thousand, so one-third of that."

"Aside from the house. This bloody thing is mortgaged to the hilt." Henry was angry now and speaking without thinking.

Ellie shook her head. "No, it isn't. It was paid off years ago, and since I have power of attorney for Dad's estate, I'd know if there was a mortgage."

Henry glared at his sister. "I mortgaged it, OK? I know his signature well enough." He turned back to the lawyer. "What else? There was my mother's life insurance. And his military life insurance. What about all that?"

Michaels shook his head. "Your mother's insurance is long gone. Your father's care was quite expensive. There is some life insurance, some investments, and some artwork. Your share of that will come to about fifty thousand."

Henry put his hands to his head, as though trying to think. "Not enough. Not enough."

Gordie stepped closer to Henry. "How much do you owe them, Henry?"

The young man just stared at him.

"How much, Henry? I saw your picture on the bulletin board

in the Blue Lagoon. You're a gambler and you owe loan sharks a pile of money, don't you? That's why they gave you a beating, isn't it? They're tired of waiting for their money."

Henry turned back to the glass wall and slid open the door. Before anyone realized what he was doing, Henry had stepped outside, run across the deck, down the steps and headed for the workshop.

Roxanne was quick to react and charged out after him while Gordie raced back through the kitchen and out on the sidesteps to shout at the waiting Mounties. "Over to the workshop!"

Ellie had run out after Roxanne and was a few steps in front of Gordie. When he reached the building, it took some seconds for Gordie's eyes to adjust to the dim light inside the cavernous shop. Roxanne stood several feet away from Henry, but Ellie had slipped forward to within reach of her brother. She didn't seem to see he was holding a box cutter in his right hand.

Roxanne stretched out her hand in an effort to grab Ellie. "Ellie, step back."

At the same time, Gordie also called to her. "Ellie, come back to me here while we talk to your brother."

She didn't seem to hear their cries, and she moved closer to put her hand on his chest. "Henry, what's going on? Are you upset that Gretha was our sister?"

He looked down at her, his eyes wide, but he didn't respond. Gordie and Roxane both took steps closer in a pincer movement, with Henry Davis in the middle. He blinked at the movement and reacted. In a strong, fast movement, he encircled his sister with his left arm, clasping her just below the shoulders and pinning her arms to her side. In the same movement, he raised his right hand and brought the sharp blade to a point under her jaw. He looked from Roxanne to Gordie. "Step back. I'll cut her throat. I'll do it. You know I will." He threw the last comment at MacLean, who immediately took a step back.

Gordie held up both hands in a placating gesture. "Don't do anything rash, Henry."

Meanwhile, Ellie continued to whimper and sobbed questions. "Why are you doing this? Henry, you won't hurt me. I love you. We only have each other now. Whatever the problem is, we'll sort it out together."

Rather than soothe her brother, her words seemed to anger him. "Shut up. Just shut up. It was never you and me. It was always you and Dad. Maybe when we were kids, you were there for me, but once Mom died, you only cared about Dad."

"Oh, Henry. No. That's not true."

"That's why I had to do it. I knew you'd be so disappointed in Dad." His voice was whiny now. "I just wanted to look after you, Ellie."

Gordie was aware of two of the Mounted Police behind him. He assumed the third had run to the back of the building to ensure there was no escape there. From his peripheral vision, he saw Roxanne inch forward, and he was afraid.

Ellie tried to soothe her brother. "Let me go now, Henry. You're hurting me and I know all you ever wanted to do was look after me."

Gordie nodded. "Do as Ellie asks, Henry. Let her go now. There's no way out."

Henry bit his bottom lip as though thinking about his next move.

Gordie took a step.

Henry seemed to talk to himself, his voice almost a whisper. "No way out."

Ellie screamed in the suddenness of Henry's movement. He loosened his grip on her and shoved her hard. She stumbled and fell into Roxanne's arms, and they went down together in a heap. Gordie only glanced at them for a second, but it was long enough. When he turned his focus back to Henry, the man had slashed the left side of his own neck. The box cutter fell to the floor as his hand went limp. He stood for a moment and then sank to his knees.

Gordie leapt forward and caught him during his collapse and laid him gently on the ground, shouting for Roxanne. "Roxanne! Under the workbench, there's a rag. Hurry, hurry."

He kept his hand pressed against Henry's neck, but the blood spewed between his fingers, and when Albright had scrambled under the workbench to grasp the cloth and fling it to Gordie, he balled it quickly and then pressed it hard against the wound. He heard the Mountie calling for an ambulance and then the other constable was by his side, tearing open a first aid kit, pulling out a compress field dressing and fumbling to remove it from the paper covering. She wrapped it over the cloth and as Gordie held Henry's head up, the Mountie wrapped the bandage around and around the wounded neck.

He heard Roxanne pulling Ellie away. "No, you'll only be in the way. Come out here. You can ride with him in the ambulance."

The cloth and dressing had stemmed the blood flow, but now Gordie realized he didn't hear the rattling breath anymore. He felt for a pulse on the unwounded side of Henry's neck but felt nothing, and didn't know if it was because of all the wrapped bandage or because he was gone. The Mountie grasped Henry's wrist and then laid it down. She looked at Gordie and shook her head.

MacLean stared down at the mess on the concrete floor of the workshop. Henry's face was white against the deep red pool of blood. Gordie realized as he continued to kneel there, that the rag he had used to try and check the flow of blood was a towel. Trimmed along the edge with little boats. A linen towel that matched the hand towel left in Gretha Braun's kitchen after her murder. *If only we had searched before all of this, we would have had him.*

The Mountie stood and Gordie nodded. He stood as well. He wanted to clean away some of this blood. He looked at Henry one last time and then at the Mountie who seemed to be waiting for him to move. "You're sure, right?"

She nodded. "I'm a trained paramedic. I'm sure."

They walked out into the fall sunshine, blinking in the brightness. An ambulance turned into the parking area and Ellie yelled for them to *hurry, hurry, hurry.*

They did hurry, even though Gordie knew it was obvious they realized there was no longer a need for haste.

# CHAPTER THIRTY-SEVEN

THE PAPERWORK WAS COMPLETE, and Roxanne gave the briefing to the full team. All names were erased from the board except for Henry and Ellie Davis, and Mickey White.

"Henry Davis got deeper and deeper in debt with his gambling. He didn't play the slots. He was a regular at the high-stakes card games. A couple of years ago he paid off his debt and had money left over to continue to play when he mortgaged his father's house, making sure that all paperwork came to a post office box that he rented, so Ellie, who had power of attorney over her father's estate, never knew. Eventually, he ran through that money, and he kept playing and got back into debt again. He kept his creditors at bay with the promise that his father didn't have long to live, and he was due a good inheritance."

Norris called out a question. "What does all that have to do with Gretha Braun? Did he hit her up for a loan?"

"We don't think so. We can only speculate, since both Henry and Gretha are dead. In his last moments, though, he said that he did it to protect Ellie. That's nonsense, of course, but we believe that Gretha told Henry the truth about who she was. She probably said she was going to tell Ellie too, and Henry didn't like that. He knew his sister had a kind heart, and probably felt that she would feel obliged to give part of the inheritance to her newfound sister. That didn't suit Henry, and maybe he tried to argue Gretha out of saying anything. They had tea and cake together, so there must have been a conversation of some sort, and then Henry, out of anger or desperation, stabbed her. He wanted her out of the way. He wasn't prepared to share his inheritance with her."

Gordie added. "I suspect if Henry had asked her for a loan, Gretha may even have given it to him, but for whatever reason, he wanted to be rid of her."

Roxanne nodded. "He wasn't thinking clearly anymore. The gambling had a hold of him and instead of talking to someone to try and help him, he was terrified. He took a beating the night of his accident when his creditors gave him a message, and he passed out, causing him to go off the road. On the surface, he looked like he was handling things, but in fact, he wasn't."

Ahearn pointed to Mickey White's name. "What about him? How does he fit into things?"

Roxanne nodded to Gordie who grinned. "He doesn't, really. The only connection he had was that they both gambled at The Blue Lagoon."

"But I heard that he had his neighbour erase the security cam of him leaving the night of the murder."

Gordie nodded. "Yes, the neighbour finally admitted it when the wife pressured him into calling us."

Ahearn held up his hands in question. "Why? If he was innocent?"

"I asked White that same question. Once he heard that the neighbour had given him up, he finally admitted that he's been having an affair with a woman he met at the Blue Lagoon. She's married to a long-distance driver, so when hubby's away somewhere, she calls

Mickey after the kids are in bed and he heads over there. That's what he was up to."

Ahearn shook his head. "He'd rather let you think of him as a murder suspect that a philanderer?"

Gordie shrugged. "People can be hard to explain."

Norris stood up. "So, that's it, then?"

Roxanne looked at Gordie. "We're still tying off the loose ends, but that closes the case of Gretha Braun's murder."

Norris grinned. "You're buying later, Detective Albright?"

She smiled. "I guess I am."

*** 

They didn't go to the funeral of Henry Davis. It was a quiet affair, and the priest, who was a long-time friend of Ellie's family, agreed to officiate. Everyone decided that Henry had been mentally ill, and his death was a tragedy. Roxanne and Gordie did go out to the house a couple of days after the funeral, though. They found Ellie packing boxes.

The young woman looked worn and haggard. "Shall I put the kettle on?"

Gordie nodded. "I'd love a cup of tea."

Ellie filled the kettle, dropped two tea bags into the white pot, and took out three matching mugs to set them on the kitchen table. She looked up "would you rather sit in the living room?"

Roxanne pulled out one of the ladder-back chairs and sat down. "This is perfect."

Gordie slid out another chair and they watched as Ellie fussed about putting date squares on a plate and getting two small plates out for Gordie and Roxanne.

Gordie nodded to the plates. "You not having one?"

Ellie smiled weakly. "I've had enough baked goods to last me a lifetime after three funerals in such a short span of time."

Roxanne nodded. "I can well imagine."

They were silent then until the kettle had boiled and the pot sat in the middle of the table, tea steeping.

Finally, Ellie looked at Gordie. "What brings you here, then? You can't have more bad news for me."

Gordie reached to take her hand, knowing Roxanne might view the move as unprofessional, but not caring. "This will be hard to hear, but we felt we needed to tell you everything."

She let her hand rest under Gordie's. "What is it?"

"Henry was desperate for the money from his inheritance, but based on what you had said, your father wasn't failing. If anything, it sounded like he was improving. It's why you were so shocked at his passing. Am I right?"

She nodded slowly. "That's true. Especially when Gretha came with me. I remember I left the room to talk to the administrator about some bills and when I came back, I couldn't believe how *alive* my father seemed. I joked with Gretha afterwards because even his speech was clearer." Ellie closed her eyes for a moment. "It all makes sense now. He was saying *Liebchen*. Even I understood that, and I don't know German. She told him. She must have told him who she was, and he was so happy." She gulped, trying to hold back her sob.

She pulled her hand away, rooted in her sleeve and drew out a tissue.

Gordie nodded. "You're probably right. Did you mention to your brother how well the visit went?"

Ellie blinked. "Maybe. I don't remember. I often told him that Dad was improving. The private speech therapist was costly, but so worth it. I wanted Henry to go see for himself, but he never would."

Gordie exchanged glances with Roxanne, who nodded, so he continued. "Did you know that Henry went to see your father the night before your dad died?"

Ellie leaned back in her chair. "What? No. That can't be right. He would have said."

Gordie shook his head. "I'm sorry Ellie, but it's true. I went to the facility where your father lived and spoke to the nurse who had been on duty that night. She only met Henry one other time when he came in for your father's birthday, so it surprised her to see him there that night. What really stands out in her mind was that he brought a bottle of apple juice for your father."

Ellie shook her head. "Well, that would be a silly thing to take. Dad didn't like apple juice."

"Yes, that's why she, Gloria, is her name, remembered it. She tried to tell Henry that your father wasn't fond of apple juice, and she'd be happy to get a bottle of orange juice instead if he was thirsty. Henry got upset with his father and said something like *I bring you something and even that isn't good enough for you, is it?* Then your father took the bottle and drank it almost in one go, as if to show that Henry was wrong."

Ellie kept shaking her head. "I don't understand any of this. What was the big deal about the juice? I know Henry was obstinate, but that's extreme, even for him. And he did have a feeling that Dad always thought he was a disappointment, but it isn't true. That was all Henry's imagination. This whole thing is ridiculous. I know Gloria. She's a very caring person, but she got this wrong. I'm not saying she's lying, but she must be confused with some other resident."

Roxanne spoke quietly now. "We don't think so, Ellie. When we searched this house, as well as finding Gretha's file box, we also found a wastepaper basket in Henry's bedroom. He hadn't emptied it for a while, and we found two empty bottles of eye drops. Did Henry use a lot of eye drops?"

"Not that I ever saw."

Roxanne nodded. "We checked with his doctor, and he wasn't aware of any problems with Henry's eyes, either."

Ellie held up her hands as if to say, *what's this all about?*

Gordie leaned in. "Ellie, who made the decision to cremate your father?"

"Henry was adamant. He said that Dad once spoke to him about it and that's what he wanted. I didn't agree but he was so firm. It didn't make sense to me because he should have been lying next to

Mom, but instead, when I get the ashes back, I'll just be burying them."

Gordie nodded. "I'm not surprised to hear this, Ellie. I'm very sorry, but we believe that Henry poisoned your father. He put tetrahydrozoline in the apple juice and bullied your father into drinking it. If he had chosen orange juice, Gloria wouldn't have even noticed the exchange, but as it is, when we questioned her, she remembered the incident clearly. When your father died, she was off duty and didn't hear about it until she came back on shift. Then she was so shocked and upset at the news of his passing she forgot the episode and didn't mention it to anyone."

"No, no, no." She moaned the denial, not able to accept the truth of their words.

Again, Gordie reached across the table to lay his hand on her arm. "I'm sorry, Ellie. We debated whether to even tell you this since we don't have concrete evidence but, in the end, we felt you had the right to know."

Ellie pulled away as if she couldn't bear even the lightest touch. Her voice caught; choked with tears. "He was a monster, and I didn't even know."

Roxanne shook her head. "He was sick, Ellie. He was a highly addicted gambler. He obviously felt remorse because he chose not to hurt you. I'm sure he loved you. Although I think his key motivation in killing Gretha was the inheritance, which he didn't want to share with her, I do think there was an element of truth in what he claimed when he said he didn't want you disappointed in your father."

Ellie's voice was bitter. "And what he did to Dad? How do you explain that, aside from greed?"

Roxanne bit her lip. "I think Gretha told him who she was, and Henry was angry with your father. They didn't have a good relationship to start with, and this news tipped your brother over the edge."

"Whatever way you look at it, my brother was not the person I thought he was. I was so proud of him. And I know Dad was proud of him. I don't know why he developed the chip on his shoulder, but it's been there for years. Even before Mom died. She always played peacemaker between them."

Ellie stood up. "It's too awful to take in. Is there anything you need from me?"

Gordie shook his head as he and Roxanne also rose. "No. There are some labs out there that claim they can detect poisons in the cremated remains of a person, but I wouldn't recommend you spend any money on that. We aren't pursuing it any further."

Ellie stood with her arms folded, pale-faced and trembling. "All right, then."

Roxanne stopped on the way out. "Can we call someone to be with you?"

"Like whom? I have no family left here." She sighed. "I have a friend in Port Mulroy. I'll call her in a bit. She'll come."

The two detectives left the young woman standing at the kitchen counter gazing out the window towards the workshop.

# CHAPTER THIRTY-EIGHT

GORDIE DROVE THEM BACK to his home and invited Roxanne to come in for a cup of tea. "I don't know about you, but I need a thick slice of Vanessa's banana bread, slathered in butter and a big mug of tea after that."

She smiled. "Sounds perfect."

Gordie heard Taz barking as he stepped out of the car. He opened the door to let her out, but instead, she circled him, poking at him and panting.

Roxanne stood back and watched. "Do you always get this kind of greeting?"

"No. She always knows when I'm in need of extra attention. If I'm stressed, she's stressed."

"Yeah. They know, don't they? Sheba isn't quite so sensitive, but still, she seems to sense when something's off."

When the kettle boiled, and the pot of tea was steeping under the old-fashioned, slightly stained, blue and white crocheted tea cozy, Gordie put the cutting board with banana bread on the table between them. He fetched the butter dish, two small plates and knives and put it all down on the table between them. "Help yourself."

Roxanne cut a thick slice for Gordie and then one for herself. As she buttered her piece, she nodded to the tea cozy. "Your mum make that?"

"No, actually it was my Aunt Anne."

She broke off a piece of the banana bread to nibble on. "Is that the one you aren't talking to anymore?"

He shrugged. "It's not like that. I just haven't talked to her for a long time. It isn't that I won't."

Roxanne nodded. "Right."

"What about you? I haven't heard you mention Eddy's name for a while. Are you two still talking?"

She reached for the pot and poured out her tea. "We are. We had a good talk on the weekend, and I believe we understand each other better now."

"That's encouraging."

She nodded. "I guess he just takes time before leaping into the whole family connections part of a relationship. He wants to be sure, you know?"

"Fair enough. You're good with that?"

Roxanne smiled over the rim of her mug. "He's coming to dinner tomorrow night. Nana's in a dither about what to cook."

MacLean poured out his tea. "That's nice. Families, eh? Look at Gretha Braun. She went to extraordinary lengths to find her father and then, when she did find him and discovered she had a sister and brother, she was so happy. She bought a house here. She wanted so much to be a part of their lives.

Roxanne nodded. "It's an argument for the nature versus nurture debate, isn't it? I mean, they had a completely different upbringing, but Gretha and Ellie seemed to have a connection almost from the beginning."

Gordie nodded. "You were right. There was something -- you spotted it in that picture."

"I did. I saw the bond. I just didn't understand it."

Gordie cut another slice for himself. "Did you mean what you said to Ellie?"

"About what?"

"About believing that he wanted to protect her?"

She sighed. "I don't know. It seemed like a kind thing to say."

"Yes, it was."

She drained her cup. "Thanks for the tea and banana bread. Vanessa and Nana could have a baking contest between them. It's a skill I've never mastered."

"Never too late to learn."

She nodded. "True. We should keep learning our whole lives, right?"

He frowned, sensing a message there.

She stooped to stroke Taz's big white head on her way out. "Take care of your old man, Taz. I think he can do with some comfort today. This case got to him."

Gordie walked her to the door and waved goodbye. In the kitchen, he tidied up, lifting the cozy from the pot, and pouring the dregs down the drain. He stood for a moment holding the worn tea cozy and then carried it with him to the living room, setting it on his lap as he looked up a phone number in his old address book.

He dialed the phone. "Aunt Anne? Hi. It's Gordie. I wondered what you're up to on the weekend. I'm thinking of coming down for a drive. I'd like you to meet my lady friend, as Mom calls her. That's right. Vanessa."

# EPILOGUE

VANESSA CLUTCHED THE POT with a blooming hyacinth but stopped to point out the crocuses coming up in Gordie's flowerbed. "Look, aren't they pretty? A true sign of spring."

MacLean nodded. "They are. I always thought tulips come up first."

"No. Crocuses. It won't be long though, and we'll see your tulips too."

He laughed. "They can hardly be my flowers when you did all the work."

She smiled. "You paid for them."

He looked at his watch. "We should get going. I told Ellie we'd see her around two and it's almost that now."

They drove to Roscarberry Lane and pulled into the driveway. They sat in the car for a moment to admire the new red interlocking brick walkway and the pale green front door with its huge window.

Gordie nodded. "Looks like we don't need to walk around to the kitchen door anymore."

"It looks so pretty. Gretha would have loved it all."

The front door opened, and Ellie stepped out on the front porch to wave at them.

Vanessa led the way and handed her potted flower to Ellie. "I know hyacinths have such a strong scent. I hope it's not too much for you."

Ellie turned and led them inside, inhaling the flower's fragrance. "It's beautiful. It's the smell of spring. Thank you."

There were large hooks on the wall right beside the front door on which they hung their jackets before going into the living room. A small gas fireplace burned, making the room cozy. The floor had been sanded down and stained a medium dark walnut colour, bringing out the grain of the old floors. Gordie couldn't help himself and automatically glanced at where Gretha's body had lain in her own blood. All signs of the trauma were gone, and now off-white leather furniture made the room bright and cozy.

Ellie set the pot on the old desk where Gordie had once searched through Gretha's papers. "Tea, coffee or a glass of wine? I've opened a bottle of Merlot and was just about to pour myself a glass."

Vanessa smiled. "I'll have the same."

Gordie shook his head. "Stick the kettle on for me. I'll have tea if you don't mind."

When she came back with the two glasses of wine, Ellie sat in the easy chair and lifted her glass. "Thank you for coming. The house is done now, and I want people to come and visit."

Vanessa lifted her glass in a toast. "To new beginnings."

Ellie smiled and nodded. "My father's house sold quickly, for which I'm grateful. Being here I feel Gretha around me and with me, every day and I love it. Happy memories."

Gordie heard the kettle click off in the quiet moment. "You stay. I can make the tea."

Ellie smiled and tucked her feet up under her. "Thanks, Gordie."

As he puttered in the kitchen, he heard them speaking. Vanessa admired the room, and Ellie responded. "Did Gordie tell you that

Gretha had made a will when she was here? She left most of her estate to Henry and me, which of course now means me. I feel bad for her family in Germany. There was a small portion that went to her cousin Ida, but not much."

Vanessa's voice was warm. "Gretha loved you and you loved her back, even without knowing her relationship to you. From the little that I know of her, I believe she would be very happy with the way you finished her dream here, and that you moved in."

"I hope so. I'm using some of the money to bring Ida and her daughter over here for a holiday this summer. We've become close. We email each other regularly and talk on the phone once in a while."

Gordie came back with a mug of tea. "I'm glad you and Ida have found each other. She seemed very nice. What are your plans going forward? Will you rent this out when you're not using it?"

Ellie smiled. "No. I'll be living here full-time. A teacher is retiring in Port Mulroy and I'm taking her place in the fall. It's a split grade three and four. A new challenge for me, and like you said, Vanessa, a new beginning."

The sun poured in through all the large windows. She had hung a bird feeder in front of the centre bay window of the living room.

Ellie pointed. "Look, a cardinal."

They watched in silence as the beautiful bright red male alighted and ate for a moment. When he flew away, Vanessa turned to Ellie. "Many people believe that seeing a cardinal is a message from a lost loved one."

Ellie smiled. "Yes. I've heard that."

The End

# ACKNOWLEDGEMENTS

Thanks to Mia Schlueter, who continues to be a delightful conversationalist in her nineties and gave me her favourite seasonal and event-appropriate suggestions for German baked goods. An African proverb states, 'it takes a village to raise a child,' and Mia was one of those moms who helped raise me. As the mother of my friend Marilyn, Mia continues to be an 'aunt' to me, and more than fifty years after our meeting, I'm grateful to still spend time together. While I'm here I'll mention the other moms of my 'village' who contributed to the person I am today: Mrs. Bertoia (Paola's mom), Mrs. McKay (Wendy's mom), Mrs. Ellis (mom of Linda and Diane), Mrs. Sarracini (Chris' mom) and Mrs. Bottero (Maria's mom). I'm thankful they were in my life.

Thank you to Anja Rohlfs for allowing me to use a 'before' photo of your magnificent house. Here's to eight years and counting of friendship inspired by a love of beautiful houses.

Thanks to Andrew Hickerson who continues to answer my questions promptly and thoroughly, with his perspective developed by years of policing expertise. Of course, I am so lucky to have the ongoing support of Dave Wickenden of the Sudbury Writers' Guild to edit my book and Sharron Elkouby who provides further polishing in the form of edits and proofreading. Thanks to the artistry of Robert Scozzari for another gorgeous cover. Thanks to Jimmy Carton who serves as my first reader and always gives me solid feedback and enthusiasm.

And most of all, thank you to all the readers who continue to show such support for Gordie MacLean!

Keep up-to-date on book news:

http://rennydegroot.com/newsletter-sign-up